# THERE'S N[illegible]
# LIKE *SA*[illegible]

“The book could quali[illegible]
you'll ever read.”

“A roller coaster ride [illegible] of all our deepest childhood myths. *Santa Steps Out* is a novel so refreshing and inspiring to read that it breaks down the walls of genres and sits comfortably outside of everything. A highly recommended novel. Christmas will never be the same again.”

—*Masters of Terror*

“There are scenes from this book that will haunt me forever. Reading this book made me want to bitch-slap Robert Devereaux. So icky, yet so magnificently rendered.”

—Elizabeth Engstrom, author of *Lizard Wine*

“Robert Devereaux impregnates sacred childhood figures with the irrepressible stream of his imagination and is responsible for the spectacular and unashamed rebirth of the old myths.”

—Ramsey Campbell, author of *The Last Voice They Hear*

“Prepare for a strange and stimulating ride when you hop in the sleigh with Santa.”

—Fiona Webster, *Amazon.com*

“This is strange, strange stuff and, thanks to Devereaux's splattery talents, not one bodily fluid goes undescribed. Truly disturbing.”

—Thomas Deja, *Fangoria*

“Full of magic and terror, death and miracles. *Santa Steps Out* gives us a glimpse behind the placid scenery we *thought* we knew as children . . . and what a glimpse it is! One warning should accompany this book, however: *Keep this* and all other dangerous objects *out of the reach of children!*”

—P. D. Cacek, author of *Night Prayers*

# SANTA STEPS OUT

ROBERT DEVEREAUX

LEISURE BOOKS  NEW YORK CITY

A LEISURE BOOK®

October 2000

Published by

Dorchester Publishing Co., Inc.
276 Fifth Avenue
New York, NY 10001



ISBN 0-8439-4781-0



Printed in the United States of America.

*For Caitlin and Lianna*
*beloved lovebunnies*
*whose childhoods*
*(as if their dad could possibly know)*
*must surely have been*
*perfectly normal*

# ACKNOWLEDGMENTS

Books that make their way into the wider world of readership have first found very special readers indeed, those professionals in publishing who are willing to put their time, energy, reputation, and generosity of spirit behind a writer's work. I've been exceedingly fortunate in that regard. To these good friends, I extend my thanks and appreciation:

- To David Hartwell, for taking first notice of my concupiscent elf and for being, so long and in such a recalcitrant variety of venues, *Santa's* champion.
- To Pat LoBrutto, for efforts above and beyond any conceivable call (my everlasting gratitude, Pat) and for his near-decade-long enthusiasm for this narrative.
- To Jason and Barb Bovberg, Darin and Cathy Sanders, for a meticulously crafted first incarnation in the Dark Highway Press limited edition. Long may their labors at bookmaking, of which this novel is the flagship effort, thrive.
- To Don D'Auria, my editor at Leisure Books, for offering my best-loved brainchild to a far greater readership than it has hitherto enjoyed. At long last, a mass market edition!
- To Jane Dystel, my agent, for her spirited response to this book and for a beautiful future together in the making and placing of engaging fiction.

# SANTA STEPS OUT

# *Foreword*

## *Robert Devereaux Boldly Goes. . . .*

**David G. Hartwell**

Robert Devereaux is a pleasant man, a passionate reader of contemporary fiction, involved in a decades-long affair with what we used to call "the legitimate theater," and a writer of extraordinary originality and technical accomplishment. He's also a practical man, with a job in the computer industry. What we normally like to think of as a real adult.

You might imagine then how surprised I was to find him in his late thirties a student at the infamous Clarion West writing workshop in Seattle in the summer of 1990 expressing the desire to become a Splatterpunk.

I believe I tried to discourage him, but it didn't work. He had an answer that I know would have confounded most of the members of the Splat pack at the time—he'd always really liked Jacobean drama. It stopped me cold. I have always liked Jacobean drama, which is more violent, bloody, sexy, and disturbing than ninety percent of splatter-punk fiction, but also I think of incomparably higher merit. I'd match *The Duchess of Malfi* against any work of horror of the eighties or nineties. And I'd bet Devereaux is the only writer among the genre contemporaries who knows the play.

The other thing that sets Devereaux apart is his sheer outrageousness. The image of "over the top" is outworn and useless when applied to his work. His ability is more turbulent and oceanic—the outrageousness comes in like huge Pacific rollers, wave after wave, inundating you. This is, after all, an introduction to the single most outrageous novel I have ever read: *Santa Steps Out.*

This novel reminds me of nothing so much as the centerfold Wallace Wood, the great comic artist, did for Paul Krassner's magazine, *The Realist*, in the mid-60s: "The Loss of Innocence in Disneyland." In one panoramic landscape, Wood showed every famous Disney cartoon character involved in sex acts with another or others, as Dumbo flew over and shit on them. It was the single dirtiest thing I had seen in my life to that time and a powerful work of cultural deconstruction. This novel is like that. It is so dirty it overwhelms you.

What Devereaux does in *Santa Steps Out* that is so powerful is to set up a mythic frame and an internal logic and then plug in figures of childhood sentiment and make them fuck each other and real people too. I cannot offhand think of any sexual taboo still extant in American society that this book does not violate. It wishes to offend, and thereby destroy certain normal defenses against deep involvement in art by shock and surprise. Each individual incident is raised to a fantastic and hyperbolic pitch, it assaults our sensibilities, it violates our sentimental attachments, page after page, chapter after chapter.

Of what use, or to what artistic purpose, is this done? Well, it seems to me that carrying the sentimentalities of childhood into grown-up life leads one to behave as if those around you were cartoons, not real people with problems and passions, and especially powerful sexual desires. Especially yourself. Our children's myths are emasculated, and Devereaux is giving them, and us, back our sexuality, and with it our adulthood. It's not very comfortable, nor comforting. But it is better than a pet-like existence of extended pre-adolescence. It's a very post-modern project, at least in principle.

Much of this is in my opinion absurd and very funny. Like horror, humor doesn't work consistently, and is indeed very subjective. But this book is supposed to be funny. I am sorry for any reader who does not in the least see the humor in this novel. Perhaps it might help you to think of this as a film like *Who Framed Roger Rabbit?*, except that it is about sex, not murder. I do think that some readers will be overwhelmed before they reach the end, but I don't think the effect will be lessened, except that there is a plot and one might like to know how it all turns out.

You hold in your hands one of the most interesting and unusual literary artifacts of the late 20th century in America.

—*DAVID G. HARTWELL, PLEASANTVILLE, NY*

# *Prologue*

## *Cupiditas Resurgens*

Love is not the dying moan of a distant violin—it is the triumphant twang of a bedspring.

—*S. J. Perelman*

I wonder why men can get serious at all. They have this delicate long thing hanging outside their bodies which goes up and down by its own will. . . . If I were a man, I would always be laughing at myself.

—*Yoko Ono*

Human life is mainly a process of filling in time until the arrival of death or Santa Claus.

—*Eric Berne*

# Prologue

## *Cupiditas Resurgens*

In the beginning, the Father heard rumblings from Above and cut His vacation short.

Regained His throne.

Surveyed the scene.

Flew into a towering rage.

The archangel Michael had gone berserk, his thick white wings now twitching. As he staggered before the throne, the glowering God-mask angled upon his face. Shards of Hermes jagged out of his body. The six other archangels looked on, wringing their hands. Raphael's eyes were moist with tears.

"How long has he been like this?" God asked them. Gesturing toward Michael, He expunged all evidence of the trickster-god, putting him under as He had done during the great transformation.

"Two decades and more, Father," said Gabriel, he who had been Apollo in the old times. "We couldn't stop him. As Your surrogate, he had absolute power. He wouldn't listen to reason."

The Father lifted the God-mask from Michael's face. The penitent looked pale as moonlight.

"Dear Lord, forgive me," he begged. "One of the cherubim—that one up there—whispered a suggestion in my ear. It sounded so splendid and proper at the time. But now I see it wasn't, not in the least."

God glanced upward.

As He suspected.

He flared a finger at the impish grin and plunged Eros deep inside the plump winged babe; its face became smooth and innocent once more.

"And what was the cherub's suggestion?"

Michael told Him.

God erupted. *"Omanko!"* He swore. *"Hijo de puta! Scheissdreck! Jaevla dritsekk! Oh, c'est vraiment con! Gott verdammi hure seich! Madonna damigiana con tutti i santi dentro e Dio per tappo!"*

Now the Son, once Dionysus, spoke. "Michael," He said, "you know that Santa Claus and the Tooth Fairy are never to cross paths. It's one of our Father's most solemn injunctions."

Michael hung his head. "It only happened once, for a moment, in Idaho, Christmas of 1969. They had the barest glimpse, then she vanished and it was over. Except that they began . . . doing things on their own."

"Christ!" God peered down in disbelief at the earth below. His all-seeing eye traced the effect of the lapsed cherub's suggestion, short range and long, watching it ramify over three-and-twenty years. "Oh Jesus, will you look at 1991, it's all *three* of them. They're going haywire down there!"

"Easy, Father. No need for apoplexy. I'm sure it's fixable."

And it was.

At a cost.

The twenty-fourth of December, 1970.

The Tooth Fairy, wearing nothing but a necklace of huge blood-flecked teeth, squatted on the eastern shore of her island and looked out to sea. A storm was kicking up out there, a real corker.

Good, she thought, chewing over the remains of an eagle she had dropped from the heavens with a high-flung silver dollar. Whatever resentments she harbored against the being who these days called himself God, she liked the way he made his creatures: with the tastiest part, the skeleton, on the inside.

Staring seaward, she mapped out the evening's itinerary. As always, instinct told her which dwellings to visit, which bedrooms to enter, which brats to loom over, longing to rip the teeth clean out of their skulls like moist sweet kernels of corn, but confined, alas, to the meager leavings beneath their pillows.

But this night, this Christmas Eve, the Tooth Fairy had a second agenda. Centuries of God-imposed isolation had created an itch inside as deep and omnipresent as a toothache. She sorely missed the old frolics through glen and dale, the thud of randy hoofs at her heels, the goat-breath blasting hot against her shoulderblades.

She needed a lover. Someone all-giving, warm, and cheery, whose stamina went beyond that of mere mortals.

She needed Santa Claus.

In the days before God had laid a veil of forgetting over his mind, she had enjoyed him often. A thing of danger and abandon he had been then, beautiful to behold and incredible to couple with.

She pictured him as she had seen him in Boise the year before, kneeling by the tree in the Sloane residence off Cloverdale Drive, his distressingly cherubic face radiant with philanthropy. The memory made her quim throb. Before this night was out, she vowed, she would enjoy him once more.

Until then, the ocean harbored a treasure of its own, something that would do as a stopgap.

Digestion's clink and jingle sped the masticated eagle through her system. Inside her rectum, thin disks of metallic waste stacked up neat and heavy as rolled coins. There in the sand, as the wind skimmed along the shore and blasted her full in the face, she relaxed her sphincter and shat a quick clatter of quarters.

Relieved, she rose to outface the wind.

Into the restless surf she strode. The undertow ate at the seabed on which she stood. Her palms lowered to the churning surface, straightened toward the horizon, then swept about until her thumbtips touched her navel. Again and again, as sheets of rain whipped at her cheeks, she repeated the movement, chanting words of summoning.

In an instant, the waves vanished, the wind dropped, the rain relented. It fell about her in a gentle mist, pelting the calm sea with the muted sound of hundreds of herons taking flight. Long before her drowned sailor surfaced, she saw him rise from the ship, blink his lidless eyes, look down in wonder at the tattered remnants of his body. The force of her lust had drawn his manflesh up into the crude semblance of an erection. That same lust now made what was left of his limbs thrust and kick stiffly through the sea in a mockery of swimming.

Thigh-deep in water, holding sea and sky at bay, the Tooth Fairy watched his approach, skin and bones breaking the surface not fifty yards away.

Closer, he rose to a lurch. Two things about him drew her attention. The first was the ragged column of flesh at his groin, nibbled here and there by small sharp teeth but serviceable enough, she judged, for one last tumble in surf and sand.

The second was the seductive gleam of bone. The nearer he came, the more aroused she grew at hints of the stuff peeking out coquettishly from behind curtains of flesh: a succulent patch of skull, a long curve of rib, the lower half of one femur begging for the viselock of her jaws.

Above all, the teeth.

They grinned across his skull, a full set of them, molars, bicuspids, canines, incisors, laid out in logical array like a mapped sampler of chocolates. All hers from crown to root, from enamel to pulp.

When he was six feet away, she released storm and ocean, letting them fury about her once more. Then she grabbed him, dragged him to the beach, and straddled him, filling her hungry channel with raw dead flesh. As she rode him, she prised apart his jaws and sucked seawater from his incisors.

By the time orgasm seized her, her mouth was stuffed full of dead man's teeth. Yet even in the high delirium of gustatory and clitoral ecstasy, part of her mind leaped into the night ahead and fixed on the jolly old elf in his bright red suit, remembering the generous gifts that hung beneath that shiny black belt of his, behind the large red buttons of his fly.

She knew what she wanted for Christmas.

# Part One

## Betrayal

Give me chastity and continency—but not yet.

—*Saint Augustine*

The advantage of the emotions is that they lead us astray.

—*Oscar Wilde*

A lie is an abomination unto the Lord and a very present help in trouble.

—*Adlai Stevenson*

# Chapter One

## *Seduction in Three Acts*

With Anya's kiss tingling warm upon his cheek and her grandmotherly smile of devotion dancing in his eyes, Santa Claus bounded through cheering throngs of elves and lifted the worn leather reins of his sleigh. He loved their heft, how they took to his hands like tendons stretched from his snorting stamping team straight up through the brawn of his arms to his shoulders.

As far off as his eyes could see, elfin hands lifted lanterns high and elfin voices—strong, high-pitched, and spirited—beat back the silence of the night. "Farewell, Santa!" they shouted. "God speed! God bless! *Auf Wiedersehen!*"

"Merry Christmas to you all!" boomed Santa, to which his elves cheered and sent their caps jingling skyward. The whip cracked smartly over his reindeer, whose powerful bodies responded as if to ravenous hunger. "Into the sky with you, my four-footed wonders!" came Santa's command. "Let's not keep our beloved little boys and girls waiting a moment longer!"

Random snorts and stamps assumed order and purpose. Nine antlered heads drew a bead on the stark silhouette of treetops pasted against the sky above the skating pond. Nine harnessed bodies, taut with sinew and muscle, surged forward. Like a blare of sirens, the fiery effulgence of Lucifer's antlers split the dusk in twain. Eighteen pairs of hoofs beat soundless against the night breeze, tossing up divots of wind.

They were away.

Shifting the reins, Santa raised his right hand for a final wave to his friends and loved ones. His wife beamed up at him from the porch. In her eye, a tear. In her hand, a handkerchief edged with bobbin lace. For an instant, he saw only her, felt only the love that bound them in wedded bliss.

Santa knew their holiday separation took its toll on Anya, she delighted so in his company. He missed her too, working Christmas Eve with no one but the likes of Comet and Cupid to talk to. But he loved the world's wee ones with all his heart, and he knew that Anya loved them too. For the sake of the children, then, a loss of consortium, bitter though it was for them both, had to be endured.

Behind him, his wife and fellow workers grew tinier. The stable, the workshop, the cottage itself became as miniatures folded into the night. Santa leaned forward into the jingle of bells and the busy haunches of his team, feeling the sleigh's dip and rise in his testicles.

"That's the way, pretty ones! Straight on into the night!"

A wrist-snap. The impulse traveled the length of his whip, stinging the air over a forest of antlers. Lucifer, his lead reindeer, scattered a guiding white light in all directions, and the delicious aroma of vanilla dipped and rolled along the backs of the remaining eight. Overhead, stars huddled into the depths of night like millions of impulses eager to be acted upon.

As always, and thank God for that, the winter world which opened before him kissed the hem of perfection and the children were his to bless on this most wondrous night of the year.

The first time Santa encountered the Tooth Fairy was barely six million residences into his rounds, in a modest ranch house on Elm Street in North Merrick, New York. He had just finished setting out gifts for the Draper children—Bobby, ten; Davey, eight; Anne Marie, five—and had his face pressed against their Douglas fir, hung with lights and ornaments. Santa loved the hint of forest in his nostrils.

When he rose, she was standing there where the living room spilled into a long dark hallway, wearing nothing but a pair of yellow panties, her necklace of outsized teeth, and a beguiling smile.

He drank her in, all of her carnality at once, glory enfleshed. Her necklace spoke boldly, its wide arc of glistening white teeth sweeping from shoulder to shoulder, large and canine every one. Like rough surf, they slapped cruelly at her breasts, which thrust out full and defiant. Her nipples seemed forever aroused, pointed and prominent as constellated stars, with fire to match.

Her eyes flared seduction.

Santa gave a sharp cry as a shockwave of sensuality engulfed him. He had known of course that the Tooth Fairy existed, had even on occasion cast a kind thought her way. But her sudden appearance in the flesh set off ancient echoes in his mind, brought forgotten aromas to the fore, thrilled him in shameful ways.

"Santa Claus," she whispered. Her splayed fingers framed the bright stretch of fabric that hugged her sex. More discovering than covering was that splash of yellow, so guileful the gold silk, so tight its stretch from pubis to perineum. Santa, his mouth dry as gauze, watched her arousal darken the cloth from canary to maize to mustard.

He ached to look elsewhere, anywhere but there. But something told him he was staring at the true core of his life, long forgotten, and he couldn't tear his eyes away. He felt the Clausean kindness drain from him, turning him light in the head and pendulous at the groin. *Anya is not going to like this; nosirree, not one bit.*

"What—?" His voice was thick as rope. "What are you doing here?" He sounded lost already and that stirred anger in him.

"Look at me," she commanded him.

"No. I mustn't," said Santa, but he couldn't look anywhere else. She hovered there over the carpet, beauty and terror wrapped up in one tantalizing package.

Santa's sack, which enroute from house to house grew heavy with gifts behind him in the sleigh, now hung slack and exhausted from his hand. In spite of himself, beneath the vast bulge of his belly, his manhood grew tightfisted as a skinflint.

She dipped a hand beneath the silk. Her body flexed. "Oooh, Santa, I wish this hand were yours." Her urgency gripped him like a fist of fragrance.

He shuddered. "You'd better stop that right now."

But she kept at it, burning the dark lasers of her eyes into him as her left hand joined her right, writhing this way and that with her passion.

An agonized inner voice warned him to shun the Tooth Fairy, to turn instead to the task at hand. But Santa chose not to hear it—or hearing, not to heed—fixing his ears on the immensity of her moans and gasps. Even the impatient jingle of sleighbells out on the lawn scarcely registered.

His lips moved. *Shame on you*, he thought he said, but the blood was pounding too loud in his ears to know whether he spoke at all.

Then she peaked. Above the exudacious swell of her breasts, her mouth elongated into a stretched oval and she unleashed the hell-hounds of passion from the depths of her throat. "Oh Jesus God," she gasped. They issued from her, invisible guttural mongrels nipping like flames of frost at Santa's ears. She clawed at the yellow silk, rending it, ripping it away. Her hipbones writhed into view, then the taut skin below her navel and a few stray hints of curls. The shredded cloth lemoned away like a streak of sunlight and flew across the room into Santa's face.

All sights vanished then, and all scents but one: the aroma of her arousal, fecund and fleshy, soaked into the weave of her undergarments. Santa snatched them from his face, greedy for the sight of her. But only a visual echo, fleeting as a phantom, hung in the hallway.

He starved for the sight of her, he wanted her in the woods, any woods, a copse of trees, hell a manicured backyard by moonlight would do, *Good God, what's come over me?*, he wanted her up against a tree, his hands locked around her shoulders, bark biting into his arms, his bloodpulse thrust up into her, *No I'm Santa Claus*, his muscular backlegs tense and tight as his hoofs struck sparks from exposed roots, channeling into her, feeling her thighs grip his flanks, feeling the rich spring air wash in and out of his lungs.

"No!" he screamed, more astonished than angered.

He pressed the torn cloth to his face and filled his lungs. It was a pure whiff of peace and joy, the lushness of forest and tidepool. It called out for procreation, for the rough and tumble of rutting lust, the insistent commingling of generous fluids.

Sobbing, Santa fumbled at the big red buttons of his fly. Out sprang his sex, its tip moist with pre-ejaculate. Silk tatters he fisted about it, rubbing as the bony hand of a science teacher vigorously strokes a glass rod to demonstrate the wonders of static electricity. Into the wet folds of silk the jolly old elf shot his spunk, voluminously, with great pitch and moment.

But even as orgasm overtook him, Clausean goodness came rushing back into him. His fingers twitched against the soaked and clotted panties, which bloomed into a large package wrapped in soft paper the color of lemon chiffon, topped with a large bow of a deeper yellow. Feeling low and mean, he set it down beneath the tree and fled to his sleigh, fumbling his buttons up as he went.

Outside, Lucifer's soulful eyes glinted with incriminating sparks; but Santa tossed the spent sack behind him, threw himself into the driver's seat, and with nary a word of explanation whipped the team skyward.

"Off with you!" he shouted in a voice thick with self-loathing.

On Christmas morning, John and Mary Draper awoke, to their delight, in the midst of a lovemaking most amazing. When at last they lazed down from the dizzying heights of orgasm, uncoupled, and donned robes and slippers, they found their home infused with the most delicious aroma imaginable. The kids noticed it too. They bubbled with life, more than could be accounted for by the excitement of Christmas Day alone. Even Bobby, usually the soul of fifth-grade cynicism, raced to and fro before the tree, heady with childish greed.

Little Anne Marie sniffed out its source: the pale yellow package sitting apart from the piled gifts. Its curiously quaint card read: "For John and Mary, to be opened in the privacy of your bedroom. May the coming year be new and happy in a multitude of ways. Much love, Santa." Despite the pleas of the children, Mary refused to open it but set it upon the cedar chest at the foot of her bed.

Her hands tingled as she touched it.

All through the exchange of gifts, the visits from friends and family, and the endless holiday feasting, she and John exchanged looks of suppressed excitement.

And after a day of revelry, with the kids tucked safely away for the night, they tore into the yellow enigma and brought forth sex toys galore. A profusion of them splashed across their comforter: dildos and cock-rings and ben-wa balls; frilly fuckwear for her, leather briefs with strategic zippers for him; flavored creams and gels of every variety; and condoms without number—ribbed and stippled, latex and lambskin, clear and opaque and every color of the rainbow.

Each denied the giving but delighted in the gift, as much for the sheer naughtiness these playthings suggested as for anything inherently exciting in them.

And their sex life, hitherto a dim porchlight over the dark doorway of their marriage, became thereafter a blazing hearth-fire, lending abundant light and heat to all of life's endeavors.

The second time Santa saw the Tooth Fairy, he had nearly succeeded in putting her out of his mind. For a time, he dreaded seeing her again. He couldn't shake her image, her aroma, nor his overwhelming sense of guilt. If Saint Anthony had resisted temptation of all sorts, he agonized, then why couldn't jolly old Saint Nick?

Good God in Heaven, Claus, another part of him shot back. Anthony was an ascetic, an oddball, a loner, thin as a rail and half as exciting. You're as corpulent as they come, a lover of food and drink, fond of realizing spiritual good in material form. When you saved that Lycian merchant's three daughters from whoredom by tossing a bag of gold in at each of their windows, please recall how you yielded at once to the youngest's gratitude: you followed your money through her casement, taking joy in the sweet paroxysm of her loins.

Dear Jesus, I'd forgotten that. Yes, but that was before I met and married my beloved Anya, before I vowed to cleave to her alone. If she knew about tonight, it would hurt her heart. It would wither her soul.

So keep it from her. Heavens, man, you didn't even *touch* the temptress. So unfret that brow, put your worries behind you, let's see some *jolly* light those eyes. If she presses you again, you'll be ready to resist, to play at Saint Anthony, or even Jesus in the Wilderness, if you wish.

So it went, the turmoil in Santa's mind.

But by the time he reached the Midwest, all was once more bright and calm, nothing in his mind but sleighbells and candycanes.

Humming with joy and contentment, Santa reached into his burgeoning sack and pulled forth gift after gift for the Gilberts, longtime Iowa City residents in the blue and white Victorian at 925 North Dubuque Street: Sandra, a full professor in the School of Dentistry; Paul, head dispatcher for the Coralville transit system; and their daughters—Karen, Julie, and Jane—arrayed in age from nine to five. Theirs was a lovely tree, dusted white and decorated in motifs of gold and silver. Much love filled their house. True, Paul was boffing one of his bus drivers, an earthy young woman named Debbie Travers. But his heart, Santa knew, belonged to Sandra and the girls.

This time his nose found her first.

One moment he was on his knees adjusting the ribbon around the neck of a rocking horse and breathing in the apple-cider and cinnamon-stick air of the ticking house. The next, his nostrils were ravished by the sharp thrust of the Tooth Fairy's woman-scent, alluring and arousing and monstrous all in one.

He tossed his head back in panic. There she stood at the sliding doors to the front parlor. A luminous trail of fairy dust sparkled down the dark stairway. Apparently she had already paid her visit to Julie's room upstairs, taken up her tiny tooth, and left a cache of coins behind. Now she hovered, one hand on the dark wood of the sliding door, and spoke his name.

"Santa," she said, "you know why I'm here."

Fright seized the unwary elf. He stood up in a rush, upsetting the rocking horse. A string of silver bells on the tree *ting-ting*'d in protest. "All right," he said, his voice trembling. "This has gone far enough."

"Has it?" Her body choked his eyes. Silken panties as orange as hissing bonfires hugged her hips. She cupped and caressed her dark-tipped breasts.

He faltered. "Look, I'm trying to do my job here. You're distracting me. You're spoiling the mood, the purity of the . . . of the holiday spirit. Now be a good little fairy and . . ."

Santa's mouth moved but suddenly nothing would come out. He wanted to be firm with her, abrupt as a dictator, but it refused to happen.

The Tooth Fairy tilted her head just so and hung a smile upon her lips.

Santa staggered. *Oh Jesus, I'm going to fall.* The Persian carpet's elaborate weave funneled him toward the delectable devourer.

"For the sake of the children," he moaned, "please go away. You're so beautiful—good God the word doesn't do you justice—but I can't give you what you want." Had he called her beautiful? Yes, he thought. As beautiful as an earthquake swallowing whole cities.

In a blink she wafted over to him and pressed her body against his, her breasts pushing the sharp necklace of teeth into his red-suited chest, her pantied pelvis molding and encouraging his arousal.

"You can," she insisted, "and you will."

"I have a wife," Santa protested weakly. He was losing himself in the wilds of her scent.

"Forget her," she rasped. She swirled her tonguetip inside the dips and folds of his left ear. Santa's knees buckled, taking his last vestige of resolve with them.

The steady voice of conscience, the troth he had plighted long ago, proved no match for this insistent female, whose moist lips now played upon his mouth. Her tongue licked greedily at Santa's teeth and gums, deftly probing his oral cavity.

It suddenly occurred to him that he was Santa Claus, God damn it, that three innocent children slept overhead, and that what he was now engaged in was an unforgivable violation of the sanctity of the Gilbert household. Santa seized upon the Tooth Fairy's shoulders and rudely thrust her away.

Drunken rage flared in her eyes, but she masked it and glided back against him. "So, we're playing hard to get, are we? Or maybe we're just getting hard. Is that what this is about?"

"No more, please."

"Shall we see just how hard we're getting?"

"Don't, please don't." But in the physical struggle she had begun, her playful combativeness made her body shift and arch in alluring ways and Santa felt the demon again, the not-Santa in him, surge up, robbing him of all resistance.

Now her fingers snaked down his paunch, past the shiny black belt to the bright red bulge in his trousers. His buttons must have undone themselves, for in no time, the ineffable thrill a man feels when a woman grips his loveshaft surged through him.

"No," he gasped.

Santa's hands felt numb and alien. His left splayed across her shoulderblade like a starfish on a beach. *This is not happening*. His right sculpted her neck, her hard-tipped breasts, her belly, then plunged beneath the orange silk and found the swell of her desire. *Please God, let this not be happening*.

Thus they led one another, by hand and lip—though Santa kicked and screamed inside like a caged saint—to the brink of orgasm.

With a shudder, she gripped his inserted middle finger and bellowed out a world-splitting groan. That sound was enough to tilt the balance for him as well. Santa's low taut baritone came up under her full-throated gasps, and his seed arced out of him and spattered the topmost branches of the tree, dripping downward in dribs and drabs.

*Oh Lord, I'm damned indeed*, he thought, but it didn't stop him from wanting suddenly to embrace the Tooth Fairy in all her monstrosity. His massive red arms encircled her to hold her tight. And closed on nothing. His sex hung suddenly free and unstroked and spurting, and his mouth, still atingle, gaped empty and unkissed.

Fighting back tears of humiliation, Santa gestured toward the tree and watched his semen turn to gleaming white candycanes on the branches it had befouled.

He fell to his knees. "Heavenly Father," he prayed, "give me strength. Help me withstand the temptress. Be with me in my hour of need. This I pray by all the saints in heaven and on earth. Amen." Then he gathered his things together, dematerialized through the front door, and dove into his sleigh.

Lucifer took one look at him and rolled his eyes at Prancer. But Santa's whipsmack split the air above his antlers, distressed shouts of "Up and away, damn you!" filled his ears, and before he knew it, his hoofs had left the snowy lawn and the sleigh was airborne.

The Gilberts' Christmas that year was the best any of them could recall. It wasn't so much the presents, nor the food, nor the folks who dropped by, though all of that was tinged as usual with the special clarity and goodness of Christmas Day. It seemed rather that the house itself, from attic to basement, from front porch to back, was infused with the deepest comfort and warmth.

But the girls' favorite moment was Karen's discovery of the off-white candycanes on the tree. They went wild over them, the young ones especially, licking the stiff glistening columns of white like Ponce de Leon indulging himself at the Fountain of Youth. They smuggled some of them to school to share with their closest girlfriends, and Julie pressed one upon her mother.

Sandra had never tasted anything like it. Despite a dominant strain of treacle, powerful barbs of nutrition jagged out here and there into her taste buds. There were hints of salt mingled with a sugar so pure its taste made her eyes glisten with tears of joy.

Paul Gilbert reaped his reward that night when Sandra slipped into bed beside him, peeled off his pajama bottoms with her teeth, and spent the next five hours lining her stomach with his outpourings of love. Sandra had always blanched at the very notion of oral sex, which was one reason her husband spent three lunch hours each week with Debbie Travers, a woman who loved to lick and be licked, though she refused to let him come in her mouth.

From that night, Paul swore off Debbie and stayed faithful to his wife ever after. Karen, Julie, and Jane, as well as their friends who had partaken of the special candycanes, grew to be skilled milkers of men, and even the plainest of them, once her talents became known, never lacked for dates.

The third time the Tooth Fairy crossed his path, Santa thought he was ready for her. Anya's image he kept close to his heart, catechizing in mid-flight the richness of their lives together, all the blessings they had shared. He devised devastating rebuffs for the temptress should she reappear.

But his strongest defense, he believed, was his clear-sighted assessment of the sex act itself. Devoid of love, did it amount to anything more than a poke and a squirt, the thrust of a fleshy banana into a squishy doughnut for the momentary excitation of both? Surely he could quell his sensual urges, acknowledge them yet not act on them, if the dreaded third visitation occurred.

The Townsend residence on K Street in Sacramento was a well-preserved, three-story Victorian, slate-gray with white trim. The house kept a stately watch over its occupants: Harold Townsend, a dealer in used cars, his wife Patricia, and their children Rachel and Billy.

Santa had just read Rachel's note to him and taken a crisp bite out of an Oreo.

The sudden pressure of a hand coming to rest upon his shoulder nearly made him choke.

It was her, pantied in red this time, the same fire-engine red as his suit. The savage beauty of her body was as breathtaking as before, but no lust shone in her eyes, nothing of the huntress hung about her.

That caught Santa off guard.

"It's me again," she said.

He swallowed the cookie as best he could, pretending nonchalance. "So I see."

She brought her lips to his fingers and took the last bite of Oreo out of them as if it were a communion wafer. Then she lifted the glass of milk from the table and drank it down.

The not-Santa crept back into him, peering hungrily at the long sweep of her neck and its inviting resolution in the thrust and surge of her mammaries.

*What's her game this time? And what is this thing inside me, this thing I call not-Santa?* Whatever it was, it felt disturbingly comfortable, like easing into a pair of forgotten slippers.

She set the glass down. "I haven't harvested the little girl's tooth yet," she said. "Let's take a peek, shall we?"

Santa sensed a trap. "I don't think that would be a good idea." But the Tooth Fairy insisted, poking his rotund belly and giving a maddening little laugh.

At last he consented ("But no funny business!"). She

led him down the hall to Rachel's room, passing hand in hand with him through the closed door. In her over-sized bed, the sleeping child was dwarfed by the stuffed animals that shared her dreams. It had been her gramma and grampa's bed, but they had bought a new one, and, knowing how Rachel loved it so, had given her the giant bed for her own. Now she lay on a thin sliver of mattress at the rightmost edge, one arm around the neck of a large teddy bear.

"There's the little dear," the Tooth Fairy whispered, closer to Santa's ear than she really needed to be. "Wait here. I'll only be a moment."

She glided to the bed. Rachel's head lolled toward her, her mouth open in the innocence of sleep. The Tooth Fairy ran a greedy finger over the exposed enamel of her bottom teeth. There was something menacing, something perverse, in her movements. Santa made an instinctive feint toward the child. Then the Tooth Fairy's hand slid beneath the pillow and found Rachel's tooth.

Turning to Santa, she opened her mouth and placed it, like a small white pill, provocatively on the tip of her tongue. Hunger flared in her eyes.

*Oh dear God, it begins again.*

As she chewed, the sharp crunch of bone grinding bone sang in Santa's ears.

*And it feels so undeniably good.*

Deftly she peeled off the red panties and tossed them his way. He caught and pocketed them without taking his eyes from her, fearful lest she vanish as before.

*And what is Anya?*

She squatted, legs spread wide, and shat dimes.

*Anya is but a being torn from her lifespring, denying the undeniable surge.*

Dimes dropped like tight silver turds from her anus, shiny in moonlight, ringing upon the bare wooden floor, spinning and rolling hither and yon.

*And what is the Tooth Fairy?*

With a practiced hand she retrieved them and slid them beneath the pillow.

*Pure body, pure need, pure demand. That which must be caressed and covered and filled.*

Then she lay down amongst the stuffed animals and harshly ordered Santa to make love to her.

Her skin shone flawless as a stone madonna's.

When he ran halfheartedly through his poor litany of objections, she stretched most provocatively, her body like that of a cat. And when he protested further, she merely smiled upon him, opened wide her thighs, and massaged with slow fingers the blushing wound of her love. Her breasts, mounded by the narrowing V of her downthrust arms, nippled into the night air. At the sight of them, Santa fell speechless. There were no more words in him. They had played out like line shooting madly off the spool of a fishing rod before a high-spirited bonefish that refuses to be landed.

Now there was only heat in Rachel's room. Heat that made Santa's suit a heavy obscenity, heat rising from the Tooth Fairy's splayed body, heat churning deep in Santa's groin where Santa and not-Santa conjoined most inseparably together. As quick as a nod, he unbooted and unsocked his feet, uncapped his head, unbelted, unsuited, and unred-flannel-underweared his demanding flesh.

*Feels right. Right? By God, it feels perfect!*

Massive, all-giving, and generously endowed, Santa Claus went to the Tooth Fairy and lay with her for hour after hour of magic time, sharing the delights of illicit love.

Magic time allows beings benevolent and malevolent to move unseen among humanity, distributing gifts to billions of children in one night, for example, or bartering coins for teeth. Without magic time, the pale hand that guides the planchette would become disquietingly visible. Without magic time, scoffers at superstition would sniff the vile shades that hover beneath ladders and know better than to defy the ancient wisdom. Without magic time, the limitless vistas hidden in the mirror's depths would leap into view, as would the Sandman's wizened visage and the cottontailed hindquarters of a departing Easter Bunny.

For a short while, this same magic time kept what passed between Santa and his lover from Rachel's senses. But then, as sometimes happens, there was a seepage, a commingling of their world with hers. Her brain tingling still with the numbing touch of sleep, Rachel opened wide her eyes and ears and let come to her what would, out of the tremulous darkness of her bedroom.

What came to her were two unclothed grown-ups moving against one another beyond her teddy bear, their heads pillowed on Elmer the Elephant. The glow that outlined them, as well as the numbness that held sway in her body, meant of course that she was dreaming.

Of that she was sure.

Nor was there any question who these grown-ups were. She felt blessed by their presence in her dream, looming large as gods in her bed, even though they seemed to be fighting about something or other. All their grunting and groaning seemed strange to her, hardly what one would expect from Santa Claus and the Tooth Fairy. But then it looked less like fighting than wrestling. Every so often, they would stop and take up a new position, then move and rub against one another again, just like the junior high kids in that boring wrestling match Daddy had dragged her and Billy to the week before.

She couldn't get over how wonderful Santa looked, how kind his face shone even through his sweat. She loved the vastness of him and the soft sweep of his pure white hair, playing about his face. Santa was white-haired too, she noticed, below his astounding belly. And out of that wild riot of white curls, he had grown an extra finger, long and fat and upright. Santa kept hiding it inside the Tooth Fairy, sometimes in her mouth, sometimes down where she went tinkle. The Tooth Fairy seemed to like having it hidden in her.

Rachel was awestruck by the fury of the Tooth Fairy's thrashings, how hungrily she feasted upon Santa's aura of kindness, taking in more and more yet never depleting his stock, then flinging it back into his face, her passion as tossed and distressed as a thunderstorm. She was ghastly. And yet there was something extremely beautiful about her, something that made Rachel want to kiss her.

On occasion, Santa would match the sounds his partner made deep in her throat, savage guttural noises which were transformed, by his echoing voice, into psalms of wisdom and benevolence. It thrilled Rachel's ears to hear the two of them like that. She felt she might almost explode with the joy of it. Her breath quickened but she kept as quiet as she could, lest she be noticed and denied further witness.

Hour after hour it went on, as dreams often do. She pleaded with God to let her remember every bit of it when she awoke the next morning.

Her prayers, however, went unanswered. For Rachel tumbled out of magic time and into normal sleep long before Santa uncoupled from the Tooth Fairy, grabbed his clothes, and staggered spent from her room. And though brief snatches of that night's witnessing flashed before her as she grew to womanhood, not for twenty years or more did the entire scene come rushing back full-bore into Rachel's memory.

And that would occur precisely one year before the Tooth Fairy devoured her at the North Pole.

# Chapter Two

## *Santa's First Lie*

Anya's knitting lay limp upon her lap. Resting her elbows on the curved arms of her rocker, she halted for a moment its mindless movement.

Outside her sewing room window, freshly fallen snow glinted like shattered glass where the sunlight splashed across it. At the edge of the woods, clusters of elves were at play. Some built elaborate snow creatures. Some flung themselves down and made angels. Others leaped and whirled, singly or in pairs, on the skating pond.

It was their day off. The final gift had winked from the workshop shelves, the last home had been graced with a nocturnal visit from Santa Claus, and he was winging his way home. One day each year, *this* day, his helpers got to frolic and cavort to their hearts' content. Santa would enjoy a private Christmas celebration with Anya in the morning, followed by the afternoon festivities in and around the elves' quarters. Then it was back to the industrious joy of creating playthings for the world's children.

Anya winced. Pain took a bite out of her left thigh. "Damned sciatica," she muttered, shifting in the rocker and readjusting her skirts.

A face popped up at the window.

Anya started, then she relaxed into a smile.

It was Fritz, her favorite elf: red-haired, gap-toothed, and ageless. Just yesterday he had run up to her, panicked, cradling a squirrel with a broken and bloody leg. It lay still in her hands as she healed its hurts with her tongue. Then it licked her cheek once in gratitude, leaped out of her grasp, and bounded off good as new into the woods. Now Fritz, rapping sharply on the glass, shouted something incomprehensible and beckoned to her. Shaking her head in a play of sadness, she held up her half-finished sweater. Fritz gave her a little-boy grimace and dashed off to join the rest, his cap jouncing this way and that like a buffeted leaf.

Such exuberance, such energy these little men showed. One would hardly guess that they were centuries old. Anya sighed.

Kindhearted though she was, she resented it sometimes that God had waited to grant her immortality until she had grown white-haired, bespectacled, and well past sixty. On those rare occasions when she opened herself to bitterness and regret, it struck Anya as grossly unfair that no rollback clause had been written into the bargain—no divine afflatus that would pull the skin tight over her bones, blow away her aches and pains, and breathe the buoyant winds of rejuvenation through her limbs.

It didn't help matters, she thought, to live with a man whose energies never flagged, who sacrificed sleep for toymaking, often disappearing for days into his workshop and emerging brimful of vitality, a sly hint of marital urgency lighting his eye.

It pained her to remove, night after night, Santa's speculative hand from her flannel thigh. But menopause had claimed Anya way back in the fourth century when they dwelt in Myra and had not yet become immortal. Since then, her carnal urges, never very strong even at their zenith, had dwindled to nearly nothing. It was a banner year if they made love a handful of times between one Christmas and the next.

He was a good man, Claus; the best of men. Sometimes it was a trial being married to him, feeling the need to prove herself worthy of his goodness. Among his many fine qualities, she counted his saint's measure of patience with her; the way he treated his helpers, paternal yet not patronizing; his wholehearted dedication to the children.

In the distance, a silent ruckus began. Flurries of snowballs flew in wide white arcs between two impromptu armies.

"Land sakes, where do they get all that energy?" With a shake of her head and a cluck of her tongue, she resumed her knitting and lost herself once more in the rhythm of the rocking and the clicking of the needles.

Fritz dashed across the commons toward the skating pond, kicking up powdered snow as he went. He wished, just once, that Mrs. Claus would leave the cozy confines of her cottage and join in the festivities.

"Fritz! Look out!"

Knecht Rupert's high-pitched shout rang out too late. The *whoosh* of a snowball—the smack of it against his forehead like the blow of a frost giant's fist—came out of nowhere. Down he tumbled, backward into the snow, and the gleeful taunts of the others washed over him.

He felt his face redden. Johann the Elder and Gustav, Rupert's perennial sidekicks, gave Fritz resounding backslaps of encouragement and bent to the business of turning the gifts of nature into weapons. Then Rupert's strong arms helped him up and the battle was joined.

His allies loped about him, scooping up handfuls of snow and packing them tight, then letting fly toward the porcelain doll contingent which swooped in on the right. So many years had the dollmakers worked together at their specialty that they were almost identical sextuplets. Though their faces were blunt as bulls and they sported long black beards, their lips were bowed like the painted lips of the dolls they made and their voices strained high and tight in their throats.

Everyone called them Heinrich. It was the name they all answered to, and none of them had ever tried in any way to distinguish himself from the others.

Heinrich, then, a twelve-armed wonder, lobbed his battery of snowballs into Fritz's beleaguered group, downing Gustav and smacking Fritz on the ear. Fritz raised his fists to the skies, howling. He stooped and threw like a madman, shaming the restraint of Knecht

Rupert and his companions. After an initial flurry of misses, Fritz's canny arm remembered trajectory, adjusting for wind speed, anticipating moving targets. The ensuing barrage turned Heinrich's unstoppable onslaught into first a standoff and then a rout.

"After them!" shouted Fritz, heading for the woods. But as he and his comrades-in-arms pounded closer to the snow-laden firs, reinforcements for Heinrich popped up from behind a great outcropping of rock. Fritz identified the two instigators of this new assault as his bunkmates: Karlheinz, he of the rolling-thunder snore, and Max, whose occasional bedwetting had consigned him, by a two-to-one vote, to the lower bunk. These turncoats descended upon him, flanked by elves from the rocking horse contingent, tubby little men with arms that flailed as they ran and wide eyes that flashed fire.

Now it was Fritz's turn to feel the brunt of attack everywhere on his body. First on face, chest, and arms. Then, as he fled, against his shoulders, hard upon his back, and dripping slow and cold down his neck. Elves swooped in from all directions to gang up on him and his cohorts.

At his heels, Gustav shouted, "For the love of God, Fritz, can't you run any faster?"

No time to answer. The attackers drew closer, their volley of snowballs filling the air like some giant ski shushing to a stop.

Ahead, Mrs. Claus bent to her knitting, framed by the wide rectangle of her sewing room window. How lovely she was. So kind and gentle a woman. The sort Fritz would be glad to spend his life with in holy matrimony, if God had intended elves to marry or entertain thoughts of intimacy.

It occurred to him, as his legs carried him toward Santa's cottage, that many centuries past there had been wild times indeed, intimacies as commonplace as they were scandalous. But memories of those days—before God had conjured them out of nothing to work with Santa—were so hard to dredge up, and so evanescent when you succeeded, that it was scarcely worth the effort.

Another volley of blows hammered against his back. Snowballs whistling overhead fell just short of Santa's cottage. The huge one that finally hit swept rudely past his right ear and boomed against the sewing room window, blotting out Mrs. Claus's matronly bosom.

It came straight out of the blue. One moment, the rhythmic ticking of cuckoo clocks above the low, steady swing of their grandfather clock's gold pendulum; the next, a sudden whump, the heart-clenching report of balled snow smacking glass. Anya rose sharply, threw her knitting into the rocking chair, and glared out at the halted hordes of helpers.

Dear God, how many times must she warn them not to play so close to the cottage? At least once more, that was clear. She made her way out of the sewing room to the front door, muttering all the way.

Outside, two score elves stood chastened in the

snow, eyes downcast, shoulders slumped. Some held their caps over their crotches or let them hang listlessly from their hands. Bald pates glistened in the sun. Karl-heinz moped forward and made a shamefaced confession.

In her kindest voice, Anya said, "It hardly matters who threw the snowball, does it?"

They shook their heads.

"I'm old. My system doesn't take kindly to shocks. It's fine to let loose on your day off. But please. Not so close to the cottage. You've got that whole expanse out there to play in." She pulled her shawl about her shoulders and gestured to the commons and beyond. Her hand, she noticed, was frail and arthritic, its dexterity lost in the passage of years.

It was cold out here. Her cheeks tingled. Her ears rang with the faint whine of fresh snow in still air.

But no. The sounds she heard came and went. Not the steady throb of winter but high discrete pulses, like the tremolo of distant violins, like zephyrs wafting over harpstrings.

Like sleighbells.

She lifted her eyes. Out past the skating pond, out beyond the elves' quarters, above the tops of the tallest trees that tickled the sky's underbelly, a black dot hung in the distance, growing imperceptibly larger.

Love swelled warm within her.

As effortlessly as a morning glory opens to the sun, Anya smiled.

* * *

Fritz raised his eyes to Mrs. Claus. Her left hand gripped the porch railing. Her right froze in mid-gesture as she gazed into the sky.

He was the first to notice her radiance, the first to divine the reason for it. But the others quickly caught fire. Bright green caps, buoyed by whoops and shouts, pancaked into the air. Fritz endured with good humor the sixfold embrace of Heinrich the dollmaker. On all sides, his bearded brethren leaped and hopped about or attempted cartwheels in the snow. Mostly, they jumped for joy, pointing ecstatically to the heavens and rolling out shouts of welcome for their returning master.

Fritz turned about and looked up at the long brown insect struggling through the sky. Santa's whip was an eyelash, his team the third part of a centipede, himself not much larger than a ladybug rearing on her hind legs.

The elf's eyes brimmed with joy.

Santa felt soiled.

And cleansed.

Coursing across the arctic sky, brutal winds above, frozen tundra below, he marveled how these two feelings, so violently opposed, could take root and thrive in his breast, entwined like old friends. Not-Santa had butted his way in, and the Santa Claus he had been before—pure goodness, all giving—stood there in shock, incapable of tossing the intruder out.

He felt deep shame.

Shame for betraying his wife, for reveling in the

flesh of another woman. Shame for having befouled the bed of little Rachel Townsend while the darling girl dozed innocently beside them. Shame for the desecration he had visited upon one dwelling after another thereafter, his mind fixated on copulations past and to come, while it ought to have been fully on the task at hand.

But he also felt delight.

More precisely, the not-Santa, that vile intruder lured out of his depths by the Tooth Fairy—*this* creature felt delight. Delight in the hot savagery of his lover's supple body, in the way she opened herself to his hunger. Santa was shocked to realize that the perverse divinity of their coupling inspired in this not-Santa a feeling that could only be called reverence.

Ahead, a glow on the horizon.

The mild bubble of winter God had given him and his little community so many centuries before.

Home.

"Almost there, my lovelies," Santa bellowed into the deafening wind. "Straight on between Lucifer's antlers. There await warm elfin hands to rub you down, young aspen shoots and willow buds and berries in abundance to satisfy your hunger, and a cozy stall to rest yourselves in."

Santa grimaced. *There await the purest beings God had the good grace to set upon this gentle earth, and the purest of them all—my dear sweet wife Anya.*

He longed to be with Anya.

Yet, God help him, he dreaded it.

Would she sense the change in him? Would she catch the musky aroma of the Tooth Fairy on his clothes, in his whiskers, hanging thick about his sex?

The bubble arched up bit by bit, stretching wider along the horizon and taking on a thin bristle of trees.

He shifted in his seat, eager to entrust the sleigh to Gregor and his brothers for a wax and polish, a new paint job, careful storage until next year. What a relief it would be to roam the woods again after being gone so long, to cast a benign eye upon his elves' labors, to sit by the fire, of an evening, puffing on his pipe and watching Anya knit and rock, rock and knit.

God grant it be so.

Now the tree stubble took on stature, rising majestic from the snow-clad wilds ahead. The sub-zero temperatures of the polar icecap abruptly yielded to the milder weather within. Ahead, like miniatures in a model train set, he saw the tiny workshop and stables, the mica shine of the skating pond, and dead on, his and Anya's cottage, green with touches of red and white. He wept to see their home, floating upon a sea of snow, smoke skirling up from its chimneytop.

And waiting on the porch, his darling Anya.

But fear tainted his joy. Fear that she would slip away, turn her back on his betrayal and vanish forever.

One thing was clear. His unwelcome guest must be locked away, given no chance to show himself before the polar community.

As he began the slow descent, Santa did his best to put on his prelapsarian face.

* * *

He was beautiful up there, her man. If anything could rekindle the fires of her infrequent passion, it was watching him sail in over the treetops, cherry-red and rotund, a radiant smile playing upon his lips. The sight always made her stand taller, breathe deeper, go as moist as a lusty young bride.

He urged his team onward, sweeping in ever narrowing circles overhead. The insistent jingle of sleighbells slapping at the haunches of the reindeer made her feel all saucy inside. Part of her wanted him right then in mid-descent with all the elves watching. But the rest of her was more than content to prolong the wait, to savor every moment that stretched from right now to the delicious suspension of time beneath their blankets after the day's festivities were done.

She couldn't be sure, afterward, when she had first begun to feel unsettled. Without question, the feeling was heavy in her by the time hoof and runner touched snow. Before that, its stages were impossible to define. It seemed much more an accretion of small noticings: the way he held back his descent, the angle at which he cocked his head, a hint of tension in his upraised arm, an unsettling disharmony in the team, the unmistakable impression that he was at once avoiding her eyes and forcing himself to smile in her direction.

The elves appeared to notice nothing. They swarmed over him as always, lifted him high on their shoulders, carried him (according to tradition) once, twice, thrice around the sleigh, then wrestled him to the snow and fell to tickling him and mauling him until, through the boom and roll of his laughter, he begged for mercy. When at last they calmed down, the elves set Santa back on his feet, brushed him off, and led him up to the porch where his wife stood waiting.

Without knowing why, Anya felt sick inside.

No, that wasn't true. She knew this feeling well. She understood precisely what was going on. A name flashed inside her head. *Pitys*. Spoken in a voice that belonged and did not belong to Santa, thick with crushed grape and guile and eternal boyishness. Then the voice and the name it had spoken were gone, and all that remained were a hard knot in her stomach and a wife's unerring instinct for betrayal.

Shiny black boots crunched the snow on the steps to the porch. An alien face loomed over her. A chill white beard brushed soft and swirly against her cheek. Around her body, bearish arms wrapped an embrace.

She watched herself return a kiss, heard the roar of the elves, felt the fire's warmth reaching out to claim her as they stepped inside and closed the door.

As Santa stood beside Anya at the fireplace, the crackling flames seemed neither as bright nor as warm as memory claimed they should be. Home didn't feel like home. It felt like some painted replica, a stage set waiting to be struck at the ringing down of some final curtain.

*(That's cuz we don't belong here, Santa old buddy.*

*This place is too perfect, not enough blemish, no room for passion, you catch my drift?)*

Oh fine, thought Santa. Now his intruder had found a voice. Raspy as a hacksaw, biting as a freshly opened can of shellac, as dark as three coats of walnut stain.

"I must have snow in my ears, Anya dear," he joked. "Couldn't quite hear what you said."

She grimaced. "I said it's good to have you home." Tension lined her face.

*(Sexless bitch is on to us. Best we should—)*

*I won't have her talked about that way.*

"Is . . . is something wrong?" Santa gasped out. His scalp beaded with sweat. A fist clenched deep in his gut, down where truths hide unspoken. Her unwavering gaze unnerved him, and unworthy thoughts—seeds of resentment toward his wife—came upon him. Looking away, he fished for his pipe, his pouch, busying himself with them.

*(That's it, chum. Evasive action's always good. And we've got lots of evading to do, all that fine humping—)*

She took his face in her hands, searched his eyes for oddity. "Something happened to you out there, didn't it? Something you're keeping from me."

*(Oooh doggies, we're in for it now, fat boy!)*

Santa froze. How could he just blurt out the truth? It felt so bitter on his tongue, this blunt admission of adultery. Yet even if he were successful in putting her off with vague denials, his unspoken misdeed would stand there solid but invisible between them. Better to lay it before her, he thought, come what may.

*(Hold it right there, chubbynums. This situation calls for a bit of good old husbandly deception. I—)*

*That's enough. I'm telling her.*

*(Heh-heh-heh. Guess some folks gotta learn the hard way. It's your funeral, bub.)*

Santa sat beside Anya on the couch by the fire, looking down at the plush throw rug and holding her hands. And as the grandfather clock's great pendulum knocked aside every other second, he began to tell her what had happened, leaving nothing out.

Fritz loved the reindeer so. While Gregor and his brothers led them to the stables, Fritz walked beside his beloved Cupid, smoothing his chestnut pelt and fondling the intricate branchwork of his antlers. But as Gregor decoupled team and sleigh, Fritz's enthusiasm made him more hindrance than help. After two unheeded warnings Gregor dismissed him, telling him to come back the next morning when Cupid and the others were rested.

On his way across the commons, heading for the elves' quarters, Fritz heard voices raised and the slamming of doors inside Santa's cottage.

He froze.

His pale blue shadow stretched across the drifts as he strained to distinguish words. Elusive shapes moved from room to room. The muffle of window and wallboard stripped away all consonants, leaving only naked vowels that traced the unfamiliar sounds of marital strife.

A chill slipped into Fritz's bones and held. He raised his hands against the sights and sounds. When he put a finger to his lips, they were dry, hard, tight, the painted lips of a ventriloquist's dummy. He faced about then and ran, kicking up snowy waves of panic and denial as he closed the distance between himself and the dormitory.

Midway through Santa's narrative, Anya startled him with a mangled cry. Santa looked at her for the first time since he had begun. Her rage hit him before he could piece together the face it flared from. She slapped him, hard and stinging. Then she bolted from the couch.

"Anya, wait!" he shouted, his jaw awkward and gangly from being struck. He took off after her, deflecting doors slammed at his nose, begging her to be reasonable, to hear him out. At last he found himself kneeling beside their bed. Her steamed spectacles she protected by propping herself up on her elbows and bending her forehead to the pillow.

"Bastard!" she hissed. Tears curved along her lenses and hit the pillowcase. "Didn't you for one moment stop to think how I'd feel?"

"Anya, she seduced me," protested Santa. "She came up to me and started rubbing against me. Not that it's her fault, that's not what I mean. You don't know what that does to a man, to have a beautiful barely-clad woman drool all over him. I know, I know. I'm as much to blame as she is."

She fisted the pillow and glared up at him. "How dare you make excuses for that fairy slut. Just look at yourself. Big saintly man, brimful of love and presents for the little ones. Ah but put down the pack, strip off the red suit? You're nothing but a rutting animal, just another overweight hog with a twinkle in his eye, sniffing at the hindquarters of any sow that trots across his path."

"Anya—"

"Don't you touch me!" she screamed. "You touched *her* with those hands, didn't you? I know your way. Get a woman all fired up under those incredible hands of yours. Dear God, I'm going to—"

She bolted for the bathroom and slammed the door. Santa heard the sharp report of the toilet lid striking the tank, then the sudden uprush of vomit and a splash as of diarrhea into the bowl.

He went to the door and called her name.

"Don't you come in here!" she threatened. He heard her spit into the water, wad up lengths of toilet paper, flush them away. The water ran as she rinsed her mouth.

Then, eyes watery, white strands of hair gone astray, Anya walked past him and collapsed on the bed, staring up at the ceiling. She had left her glasses in the bathroom. Without them she looked older.

Santa, weak-willed as a dreamer, felt the mattress yield to his weight as he sat upon the edge of the bed, careful to avoid all contact with his wife. Words came into his mouth, words not of his own choosing, the wily intruder's words. Powerless to stop them, not even sure he'd want to if he could, he heard them fall from his lips.

"Dearest Anya," they began, "I never wanted to hurt you. Far better to sink into the earth than hurt you, my perfect mate, my beloved friend. As much love as God has given me for the boys and girls of this world, never have I loved any of them with one scintilla of the love I hold in my heart for you."

It sounded so stilted to him, this speech. It amazed and appalled him. The sentiments were undeniably true, but the words felt absolutely false in the speaking—as they must, he thought, in the hearing.

"You're the only woman for me, Anya," he assured her, blinking back tears, fighting against the raw hurt in his throat. "That's the way it's always been. That's the way it will always be."

Santa dug into his pockets for a handkerchief. Just as his right hand found one, the fingers of his left hand closed on silk. Red silk.

*(Ah, that's it, now you've laid hold of a piece of reality, the good stuff, a sweet reminder of the breached gates of heaven.)*

*Enough. No more. Leave me alone.*

Clutching the panties, he felt the tingle of flesh-memory woven into them and became aware of his manhood's demand for stiffening blood. Later, he thought, he would discard them, toss them into the fire while Anya slept.

*(Oooh, don't even* joke *about such a thing. Lord o' mercy, you gonna make me keel over and die with talk like that. You keep those babies around, hear me, Santa?)*

*Yes . . . yes I think I must.* It made him ill to picture the red silk falling upon the fire, catching slowly at first, then quicker, seething into oblivion. They were too precious for that; an icon, a totem. He could never bring himself to destroy them.

"Please believe me, my beloved," Santa's false voice continued, "the Tooth Fairy means nothing to me, nothing at all. It was a mistake, a terrible mistake. I'm sorry for the pain I've caused you. If you could see your way clear to trust me, I give you my word it will never happen again."

He was sobbing now, but only partially in repentance. The rest were tears of rage, tears shed for what he seemed to have become. For he knew, even as the words reeled out and honestly begged Anya's forgiveness, that any promise he made to stay away from the luscious body of the Tooth Fairy was an empty one.

The lies lay like spoiled meat in his mouth.

And yet (heaven help him, was he going mad?) he felt good about lying to Anya, liberated somehow, reveling in hidden guile, tasting the fruits of a newfound freedom. Or was it new? At the fringes of his memory, forgotten images, tantalizing and elusive, teased his senses—forest smells, the thick richness of moss beneath his back, the feel of nymph tongue on genital.

"If she appears again next Christmas, I swear to God I'll stand strong against her wiles. I'll send her packing." Anya lay there looking at the ceiling, but her breathing had slowed. "I know that the memory of this terrible time will never fade entirely, not for either of us." The tingle of silk made visions of nudity dance in Santa's head. "But I want to try to get through this with you in a way that, hard as it may seem now, strengthens our love for each other."

Anya had calmed considerably. She looked at him. "All right, Claus. Let's see how things go. I believe we're strong enough to weather this. But don't expect me to want to . . . to engage in intimacies any time soon. It's going to take some time, some adjustment."

Santa nodded. "Take all the time you need."

"I don't know about you," said Anya, attempting a half-smile, "but I'm exhausted." She touched a hand to his knee. "The elves are probably wondering what's keeping us. Go take your shower and let's do what we can to survive the rest of today. We'll start fresh in the morning."

Thank God, he thought, I haven't destroyed it. Not yet.

But in the depths of his coat pocket, Santa's left hand luxuriated in lust.

# Chapter Three

## Twenty Years of Secrecy

Throughout much of the following year, caught up in the invention of a softer teddy bear, a whizzier gyroscope, a more meticulously detailed dollhouse, Santa was certain he had conquered his lust completely. The intruder's voice had fallen away. Santa hoped he was gone for good.

But alas, in elf as in mortal man, concupiscence is not so easily quelled. Despite his honorable intentions, despite the ardency with which he nightly knelt and prayed beside his bed, despite the endless stream of cold showers he shivered under as Christmas Eve approached, Santa fell and fell hard for the Tooth Fairy. The mere sight of her naked flesh—lying open for him the following Christmas beneath the frosted spruce of George and Bertha Watkins of Augusta, Maine—swept aside all resolve and brought his alter ego fully awake and panting. Into the wanton profusion of her limbs he plunged with all the abandon of some parched wayfarer, desert bound and nigh unto death, who, stumbling upon an oasis, tumbles headlong laughing into its lake of living water.

That Christmas she seduced him once in each of the

fifty states, letting him anticipate her presence in every dwelling he gifted, then looming up under his nose when he least expected it and drawing him down into a maelstrom of desire. She had him in hovels, in palatial mansions, on worn runners in dark apartment buildings. She had him in dens, in basement playrooms, in cramped attics thick with time where their oozings left heart-shaped stains in the dust. She lured him into hall closets, where, as she knelt among snowboots, Santa clung to the thick dowelling overhead. And there, his face flushed among the hangers, his breath tightening, urgent love leapt out of him like a surge of panthers into the darkness below.

After their fifth such encounter, Santa, feeling soiled by his infidelity, resolved to call a halt, to plead with the Tooth Fairy to save him from himself.

Sweeping down Broadway in the midst of a blizzard, past Columbia University on his left, Santa banked over Barnard until his team pounded against flurries of snow above West End Avenue. They touched down at last on the tarred roof of a four-story brownstone on West 91st, its black surface aswirl with driving snow. Drifts washed off like capped waves in all directions, their shifting crests blue in the moonlight. And there she lay, upon a soft mound of white near the roof edge—the Tooth Fairy, sleek, round, and ready, her breasts stiff-nippled and flecked with flakes.

She twisted toward him as he stepped down from the sleigh, the wind fanning his beard out around his face. Her arms reached up. "Take me," she whispered, more to groin than ear. Although her voice was low, Santa could hear what she said as plainly as if the boom and moan of the blizzard were no more than a deaf man's dream.

*(You heard the lady, bunkie. Have at her.)*

*That's enough. It's time to call it quits.*

*(It's never enough, fat boy, never. You know that. We both know that.)*

Santa stroked Dancer's flank and lifted his eyes to his team, whose heads were turned every one to take in the naked fairy banked in snow. Lucifer's antlers pulsed in what Santa took to be disapproval but which was really arousal. Santa gave them a comradely shrug, as if to say, "What's a fellow to do?"

Beneath his boots, packed snow squeaked and crunched. Santa crouched beside her. "Listen," he shouted into the storm. "We can't go on like this."

Her only answer? A mock pout. She traced with thumb and forefinger the long fat arc of his erection. Then she unbuckled his wide black belt. In the fury of the wind, her crimson hair blew all about, trapping snowflakes like stubborn gems.

Feeling his saintly goodness crumble once more—far too easily, he thought, for one who had been selfless for centuries—Santa closed his eyes momentarily against the force of her charms. Then, in a last grasp at purity, he snapped them open and grabbed her wrists in a tight grip.

"Don't you hear me, woman?" he pleaded. "I've got a wife. I love her. I've vowed by all that's holy to be faithful to her."

*(Don't be a chump, fat boy. Take her.)*

*You've had your say. Now shut up, whoever you are.*

The Tooth Fairy smiled and stretched. Her thighs parted. Santa saw, with sinking heart and rising petard, the hot fluid of her lust pooling there, demanding intimacy. She drew her mouth up past his cheek and gasped, "Fuck fidelity, you fucking stud! Fuck *me*!"

The feel of her lips against his ear, her hot breath, the carnality of her fricatives were too overwhelming to be denied. Sobbing against his fate, Santa fumbled at his suit—*(That's the ticket, Nick old buddy; you and me, we're halfway home, oh yes indeedy, and what an inviting little dwelling place it is.)*—stripping himself bare against the blizzard.

And there, with his faithful team looking on, blowing and snorting impatience and arousal, Santa dug his toes into frozen slush and brought them both to the heights of ecstasy, he feeling the chill winds of winter blasting along his spine and freezing his buttocks, she opening her lips wide to orgasm and choking with delight upon the deluge of snowflakes that swirled down into the depths of her throat.

That night, after Manhattan, Santa found it less and less difficult to give in to lust. His pleas to God to steel his will, his regrets that at his creation there had not been included some small inoculative mix of baseness, if only to remove the element of surprise which befuddled him now—these diminished as his prayers for a stronger back and finer taste buds increased.

And beyond that night, other Christmases saw the two of them scheming to cross paths with increasing frequency. Santa's first stop, and his last, became always his fairy lover's wind-whipped island. There upon the rocky shore, beneath the blasted cypress—its twisted limbs decked in shells and seaweed, a dead starfish nailed aloft—the two of them humped and plotted, plotted and humped, bringing into precise and satisfying conjunction their bodies and their evening's itineraries.

Santa preferred things that way. Once he knew where she'd be when, he could give his giftgiving the attention it deserved. The blessed children, after all, had first claim always on his love. Lifting aloft drained and happy from her island, Santa pictured the uncountable millions of sleepy wee ones, nightie'd and pajama'd. The special dreams of Christmas wrapped them round snug and warm. But it was his visitation, the nocturnal touch of Santa Claus, which brought the magic of selfless giving into their homes.

And if, at times, he turned away from the holly and the ivy, set aside his pack, and pressed the lurch and lunge of his gotta-have-it desire up against that of the fairy with the ravenous eyes and the necklace of teeth, where was the harm in that? There was enough of him, by heaven, to go around. He could be Anya's loving mate; he could be the Tooth Fairy's hump-and-grunt of a fuckfriend; and he could be Santa Claus, jovial, roly-poly bestower of gifts and goodies upon children young and old.

Only in the minds of the pinched and narrow, he assured himself, did these roles conflict.

Santa's elves are sturdy creatures. Never growing older, always in the best of health, they laugh and toil year in, year out, free from the vicissitudes of change.

However.

Sometimes, whether it be in the gruff and grumble of a snowball fight, or in the misjuggle of a fistful of ball peen hammers, or in some other such hapless circumstance, sometimes an elf loses a tooth.

In the fifth year of Santa's affair with the Tooth Fairy, Friedrich the globemaker, whose head was as oblate as the earth he modeled, lost his right lateral incisor to a doorframe that didn't look where it was going.

He placed it beneath his pillow.

And the Tooth Fairy, welcomed thus to Santa's domain, ate the elf's tooth, replaced it with one thousand newly-shat shiny copper pfennigs, drifted across the commons, passed through the door of Santa's cottage, hovered over her lover's bed, glared at the dozing Anya, kissed Santa out of slumber and into magic time, lured him across the snow to his workshop, and fucked out his lights amid pinwheels and piccolos, race cars and rockets, gizmos and gadgets galore. The glazed eyes of countless stuffed dolls and animals looked down upon their maker as he brought adultery most foul to the North Pole.

Truth be told, Santa grew uneasy there in the near-darkness with all those unblinking eyes staring at him. But where else could they go? Up here, in this tight little community, no ideal place existed for them to have at each other with complete abandon.

So when the Tooth Fairy drank him spermless one last time and slipped away, Santa remained in magic time and built them a cozy hut way off in the woods where no one had ventured before.

It was the perfect locus for love. Concealed in a copse of ash trees, its stones rose from snow, solid and inviting. Inside, a great stone fireplace roared its paean to love. Blazing Yule logs splashed into every crevice and corner waves of liquid light. Down across surfaces of fur and quilting they went and up over a huge four-poster built of ashwood, its large mattress awash with pillows and stuffed with swan's down. At each side of the bed, wide windows looked out on moonlit snow-drifts and the silhouettes of trees.

Despite his pride in its workmanship, Santa knew that this hut represented a sharp departure from his old ways. Pure selfishness. An absolute concealment from those he had always been open with. Yet the trees themselves seemed to conspire with him, to remind him of some former life he had forgotten utterly, a life his sly intruder had played a leading role in. Names came to him from their swaying limbs: Syce, Crania; Ptelea, Morea, Carya; Ampelus, Balanus, Aeiginus; and repeatedly and with peculiar urgency, Pitys. Names meaningless to him, yet freighted with meaning.

The next night Santa couldn't sleep. He lay awake

beside Anya, staring into the darkness, imagining the Tooth Fairy's return, how he would take her to their new-minted hideaway and have her there.

But she didn't come that night.

Nor the following night.

The third night, Santa got smart. First he went to the stables and, one by one, woke the reindeer. No, each of them shook his antlered head, blearing up at him. None of my teeth are loose, none need pulling. Nine times he asked the question. Nine times he took denial, kissed the soft tufted fur between the reindeer's eyes, and let him lapse into sleep.

Next, cloaked in magic time, he visited each of his multitude of dozing elves. His fingers probed their tiny mouths, testing the seating of every molar, every cuspid and bicuspid, every incisor both central and lateral. For hour upon hour, he searched in vain for that one loose tooth which, wrenched free and placed twixt sheet and pillow, would summon his paramour to his side.

Then the lightbulb went on.

To his workshop he went, cursing himself for a fool all the way. Feverishly he snapped on his worklights, gathered materials and tools. His seasoned hands flew among them. Out of the chaos scattered across his workbench, he whipped together a child's bed. Simple, functional, inviting. The sort of bed an eight-year-old would dream wonders in after a trying day battling giants and ogres at school.

Another swatch of chaos, another miracle: a doll so

lifelike that in the dimness of a room lit by fire, one would swear she was a real little girl, eyes gently closed, lips parted in sleep. Inside the lips? Teeth. Just a few, made of soft wood with a thick coating of ivory from a store of cast-off piano keys. Teeth that snapped firmly into place in the girl's plastic gums, teeth that snapped out just as easily.

Santa prayed it would do.

To the hut he carried her, bed balanced on his back. He brought the fire to a fine blaze, then turned away to decide where to position the little girl, whom he had begun to call Thea. He settled on one corner of the room, just past the window on the far left side. Thea's bed fit to perfection there. She looked as if she'd been sleeping for eons. Santa bent, like a protective parent, to kiss her forehead. With fingers that shook, he brushed past Thea's lips, took hold of one of her two front teeth just at the gumline, and drew it from her mouth. Scarcely had he slipped it beneath Thea's pillow when two fairy arms enwrapped him from behind and the Tooth Fairy's hot breath thrilled his ear.

"What a lovely gesture," she said, turning him about and tugging his workshirt out of his pants. "And what a lovely little love-nest."

"You like it?"

"I do." Her eyes took the place in as she caressed his clothed erection. "Such industriousness deserves its reward."

Santa's heart pounded. As why should it not? The old ticker had a lot of work to do over the ensuing hours, keeping up with his lover's demands. Just as a tomcat, settling into new surroundings, sprays urine here, there, and everywhere to establish his territorial rights, so the Tooth Fairy, delighting in the romantic rusticity of the woodland hut, brought herself and her fat lover to a boil anywhichwhere she could. Upon every couch and quilt, sprawled over pelt and pillow, pressed to every square inch of Santa's deft handiwork, they oozed love.

Once, she caught him off-balance and they tumbled straight into the fireplace. "What are you—?" he said. Then the flames engulfed them.

She lay upon the logs, burning.

Santa's flesh was afire too. But instead of searing torment, he felt the gentle brush of sunlight on skin. Though his eyes were goggled in flame, he could look down upon her, watch her hair crimp and crinkle yet defy the fire's insatiable hunger. For as fast as it entwined among her flowing tresses, consuming them, so fast did those tresses grow out. Flames licked at her nipples like the tongues of greedy lovers.

Below, her juices stewed.

Santa's manhood flamed from testicles to tip. Everywhere, his hair crisped and tickled like seething centipedes. Closed round by a wall of restless flame, Santa pressed his burning flesh to hers, breathed fire, giggled sparks and cinders. Like a smith's beaten iron plunged hissing into water, Santa drove his fiery rod into his lover's boiling stewpit, so that their flesh seethed and sizzled there.

That night, in the matter of consuming passion, the god of fire took lessons from them.

One morning, in the third year of his affair, Santa fished his master weaver Ludwig out from under a riotous sea of patterned bolts and took him aside. "Ludwig," he said, "we've known one another a long time, haven't we? We respect each other. I'm sure we've gone beyond having to sugarcoat a bitter pill when it's time to take our medicine."

"Medicine, Santa?" Recumbent question marks curled above the elf's puffy eyelids.

"Tell me, my friend. And please be candid." Santa draped an arm round his helper's shoulders. "Has my work been up to snuff lately?"

Ludwig wheezed out a long, slow, painful breath. His fingers worked the corners of his mouth. He cocked his head. "Truthfully?" he asked.

Santa nodded.

Ludwig looked with great deliberation into Santa's beard, pursed his lips, and squinted up into Santa's eyes. "I'd have to say, without the slightest hesitation, that your work is—as it has always been and shall, no doubt, ever remain—exemplary, superlative, without peer, if I may be so bold, among elfhood and humankind alike." The color drained from him as he spoke, and his voice dwindled in firmness from strong coffee to weak tea.

"Thank you, Ludwig," said Santa, shaken to the

core. "I prize your good opinion, more than I . . ." Santa's throat tightened.

Ludwig gave a curt smile and a nod, then ambled off as one scattered in his wits.

Santa watched him go. He felt a tangle of emotions. Deep sadness. Amusement over the elf's eccentricities. A feeling of superiority, which disturbed him greatly. And a fear that he had betrayed the love of the young people of this world.

But beneath all of those feelings throbbed the steady hum of desire. Santa marveled at it. He wondered if he had been this way as a mortal in Myra long ago. Perhaps the Heavenly Father had sanitized his memories, washing the worst of his urges out of him. Now, spurred on by a chance encounter with the Tooth Fairy, they were flooding back full force.

Which was as it should be.

Far better, he thought, to embrace his every side, damned and blessed alike, than to live on in ignorance.

Reaching into the depths of his left pocket, he fingered the cool silk of the Tooth Fairy's red panties. Pictures danced in his head, pictures of scenes lived, scenes imagined, scenes hoped for.

Yes, he thought. Far far better.

Santa dwelt much upon Anya, whom he dearly loved yet could no longer fully confide in. More was the pity. As with his toymaking, so with his marriage: The indefinable something at its core had turned strange or melted away over the years.

Yet she seemed not to notice. She appeared, trusting soul, to have taken him at his word. The day after her blowup that first Christmas morn, she had gone about her affairs as before. A homebody always, Anya strayed rarely from the bright confines of the cottage. Her days she spent in the kitchen or at her crafts, her evenings in the ebony rocker beside the hearth, sharing his delight in the letters he slit open at his writing desk and rushed out of his study to read to her. And when she lay beside him in bed and signaled, by backing up against him, that she was that night receptive, Anya was as earth-moist as the richest silt, chthonic and cavernous as a queen's tomb.

But, God forgive him, her subdued drives maddened him. Months would go by. There she would lie, nightgowned in the fire-toasty bedroom, a book propped open on her breasts—reading, page after page, while he tentatively touched her thigh and fantasized himself erect or fell asleep in the solitary envelope of his unmet needs.

It spawned dark thoughts about her. It made him want to hurt her, to shake the complacency out of her bones, to wrench open the sexless creature she had become and pull out the hidden body of the lusty wench she had once been.

Instead he resorted more and more to the hut.

"I'll tell you what it is," he confided to the head of a marionette one day after painting the tan curves of its ears and its bright blue saucer eyes. "The Good Lord never intended man to be monogamous." A question swam up from the paint drying on the wooden face. "Sure I'm an elf. But before that I was a man. I know what it's like."

He dipped a fresh horsehair brush into a jar of crimson and swept a smile across the shiny sphere cradled in his hand. "Grin all you like, little one. Your body, when I get to it, will be all wood and joints. No sex added because none needed. But the bodies of men are thrown on God's wheel, slapped together from blood and bone, flesh and fire, gristle and gland, then glazed with liquid lust and baked to a frenzy in the kiln of desire. A man's member hangs there between his legs like a dark talisman, directing his life, driving him hither and yon, distracting him from the uninterrupted enjoyment of other than sensual delights."

Santa turned the head this way and that, trying to read its enigmatic expression. He loved crafting dolls, puppets, figurines of every kind. Especially the faces. Their prevailing emotion—joy, anger, sorrow, grief—was usually bold and transparent. But this face, emerging now from the wet womb of his imagination, troubled him with its uncertain mix of emotions. It grinned stupidly up at him. He wished it could talk. Then he quickly changed his mind about that, chuckled wryly, and set it upon a heap of rags to dry.

The Tooth Fairy's island looked, from the stormclouds above, like a gray-green gash knifed into the wet flesh of the sea. Where the waves washed against it, jutting rock alternated with stretches of strand. The sand was finest, the tough dune vegetation least choked together, at the gash's two jagged extremities. From the sparse beaches and ocean-dashed rocks, the island rose abruptly into steep wooded slopes, as though God had placed His hands to either side of a flatland forest and bunched the earth together between them. Save for the blasted cedar at the north tip of the island, the trees were exclusively ash.

When she was in residence, the mistress of the island preferred either to squat upon the shore near the cedar, brooding into the ceaseless storm, or to take refuge up among the ash trees in a grim cavern punched into the mountainside and decked out with bone-furniture. She sat now at the cave entrance on a bleached-white armchair, munching on a bowl of molars and staring past the wind-tossed treetops. Incessant rain beat at her breasts and belly. But her mind was fixed on the fat fellow with the generous cock and the sensitive hands.

These days he called himself Santa Claus. But she knew who he really was, who he had been before the Christers had wrested control from their pagan predecessors.

A rough wind set the tops of the trees to rioting. Vacant now, every one of them, despite their animation. She could still hear, as if it were yesterday, the shriek and moan of her sister nymphs as they perished. She could feel the jaws of death close over her. She recalled how the rescuing hand of Almighty Zeus—in the midst of his own self-transformation—sealed a pact with her and infused her with life.

Bitter pact. Grim life. Sundered from the ecstatic community of nymphs and satyrs—constant byplay, constant sensual delight, life lived to the full. Set down alone on this island, given a craving for bone which could never match, marvelous though it was, her old cravings for wine and fruit and the frenzies of the flesh.

Their god, the One-and-Only-God, he who sometimes glared at her in patriarchal admonishment through swirls of stormclouds, had obliterated Santa's memories of those days, slipping more convenient myths into his head. But whenever she tried to speak of these things, her words would not come.

"You really don't remember," she'd say.

"Remember what?" he would ask.

"The time before you were . . . the time he who calls himself God was . . . back before you were . . ." The hut walls shook with her frustration.

"There, there, don't trouble yourself over it."

But she did trouble herself, and greatly. She wanted Santa to know. Together, they would conspire against the big blowhard in the sky; they'd topple the turncoat whose betrayal had led, in spite of his rescue of her, to the slaughter of her sisters and their goatish lovers.

At times, it was hard to see the old satyr in Santa. From time to time she caught hints, a special stance, a casual scratch behind an ear. But he looked so different. The hornless forehead, the kind eye, the impossibly white curls. They thrilled and disgusted her.

Desolation blew through the dripping forest before her now. A curious feeling harried her heart these days when she thought of Santa. In the beginning her lust had been pure, her desires wholly selfish. She had wanted the jolly fat man because he, of all beings, could best cater to her insatiate whims, could give give give until there was no giving left—and then give some more.

But of late, his selfless giving had seeded her gut, had sent out runners from her viscera to her every soul and limb. More often than not, to her astonishment, she found herself mouthing her lover for the sheer pleasure of hearing him moan, without a thought to the payback to come when he turned her about, as he invariably did, to feast on her fairyhood.

She wondered—perverse thought—if it could be love she felt. "Love. Love for the fat man. Love for Santa," she said. She liked the way that sounded. It made her skin shiver, that word. Seeing him turned her ravenous; she wanted desperately to devour him. But then, fighting that urge had always been the most harrowing part of the copulations of nymphs and satyrs. She recalled the old community, roused by the smell of blood, circling about and egging on a thrusting couple who had lapsed into total anarchy and died feasting on one another's innards, the green moss beneath them drenched red.

She sighed. Tears of rain, rolling down her cheeks, depended from her nipples. She knew, because he'd told her so often enough, that Santa Claus did not love her, not in that way. No, it was lust alone, he assured her, full-throttle lust and nothing more, that tore him from the side of his wife. More rhizome than root, his feelings for her.

A chill rippled through her.

Her eyes clamped down upon a glare.

There had to be a way, she thought. A way to unseat Mrs. Claus, to swivel Santa's head forever away from her, from his elves and reindeer and his blasted beloved brats.

A way to claim him exclusively for herself.

Good Friday, 1990. St. Mary's Cemetery and Mausoleum on 21st Street in Sacramento. A young woman in black held her daughter's hand and watched her husband's coffin sink into the earth.

Time had not stood still for Rachel Townsend. Now nearly thirty, she had lived a full mortal life, joyous and painful, zesty and bland by turns. Of that special night twenty years past, when Santa Claus and the Tooth Fairy tussled naked upon her bed, she remembered nothing.

"Mommy?" Wendy looked sadly up at her. "My legs are getting tired."

Rachel stroked her daughter's braided hair. An image came and went of Frank holding a baby spoon in his hand, bending intently toward the high chair, his eyes smiling in disbelief at his daughter's loveliness. That loving look stayed with him through the years since, and Wendy had loved her father as fiercely. It was a shame Easter had been spoiled for her this year.

So few years, so quickly lived.

"Be patient," Rachel told her. "It won't be much longer."

"Can you lift me up?"

"Later," she assured. Rachel rested her hands on Wendy's shoulders and listened to Father Doyle intone the words of the burial service.

She liked Father Doyle, though she felt nothing but indifference for his Church. But Frank—or Francis Xavier McGinnis, as the reverend father now referred to him—had been raised a Catholic and had remained devout to the end. Frank would have wanted Father Doyle to give him the complete Catholic sendoff.

A light breeze stirred the treetops. Her husband had been a huge man, with a love of life and a sense of humor as expansive as his girth. He'd brought joy to everyone he touched in his fifty-seven years. Little wonder, then, that the funeral party numbered nearly three hundred, and that its mood was not so much funereal as celebratory—of Frank himself, of his caring heart, of the privilege they had shared in knowing him.

Rachel expected that Frank's friends would drop away. The lecherous ones—George Seacrest of the wayward wife, and Harold Stamm who sported a gold tooth—would hit on her once or twice, then take the hint and be gone. The others might hang on a bit longer but she'd be glad to see them go. It was time for her to think about a new life, and that was easier to do without the flotsam of the old floating past.

The sole exception was Mrs. Fredericks from next door, dear old Ellie Fredericks, eighty years young and still full of fire. She couldn't imagine that feisty old woman ever giving up the ghost, let alone abandoning her "little Rachel." She'd been Rachel's pretend granny for as long as Rachel could recall, and now she was Wendy's as well.

She glanced down at her daughter. It had been a rough year for both of them, a year full of death. First Frank's parents. Then Rachel's, a boating accident out on Folsom Lake that also claimed her brother Billy and his wife. Frank had questioned the wisdom of moving into her parents' house on K Street, but they'd been looking for an old house anyway and Rachel's girlhood had been a time of magic, rich memories woven into every room. Rachel hadn't regretted the move for a moment, and Frank and Wendy quickly fell in love with the place.

Now she and her daughter would be alone there. Her husband of seven years—that rarest of all breeds, a truly compassionate underwriter of life and health—had cared more for his clients' well-being than his own. High blood pressure, ignored to the point of disdain, had felled him while Rachel retrieved Wendy from school and stopped at Corti Brothers for groceries. Wendy cried for days. So did Rachel.

She bent over and kissed her daughter on the top of the head, pausing long enough to breathe the sweet scent of Wendy's scalp. Wendy gave her a look of disapproval that was pure Frank.

Funny how they'd met. At nineteen, she had come home from Chico for the holidays, happy to divert her thoughts for a few weeks from the study of bits and bytes, pixels and Pascal, semaphores and CPUs. Her intense flirtation with lesbian love was a year behind her, she was a junior now, between boyfriends, and happy to be home for the holidays. She had gone to Macy's on the corner of 5th and K to hunt for Christmas gifts.

Rachel usually avoided large department stores. She much preferred out-of-the-way places: bookstores, toystores, stores filled with exotic foods or given over entirely to puzzles and games. But Macy's was different. Macy's laid claim to Santa Claus in a way no other store could match. She had seen *Miracle on 34th Street* many times on TV. Once she had even seen it downtown at the Crest Theatre.

Though she'd stopped believing in him around age ten, the figure of Santa Claus held an eerie fascination for her. That year, she lingered at Santa's Workshop, watching him dandle kids on his knee, pose for Polaroids with them, hand them candycanes. In that lingering, the man wearing the red suit captured her heart. She stood transfixed; he noticed her; when closing time came, he changed clothes, met her at the doors, and took her to dinner at his favorite restaurant, Fat City in Old Sacramento.

Six months later, she and Frank were wed. He urged her to complete her degree, then look for work in the Sacramento area. Every few weeks, he'd drive up to spend time with her, inner-tubing down the river (quite a sight, Frank at fifty, floating among the youngsters), or taking long walks through Bidwell Park (where Errol Flynn had once played Robin Hood), or indulging in an endless night of marital bliss locked away in her apartment off the Esplanade six blocks north of campus. Her pregnancy ran neck and neck with her studies that year. She graduated in mid-May of 1984, gave birth to Wendy the following week, and began work three months later as a software engineer for HP in Roseville, some thirty miles east of Sacramento.

"Mommy?"

"We'll be going home soon, honey."

"Where did you say the Easter Bunny lives?"

"Underground in a big burrow. Just show a little more patience, Wendy. You've been very good."

Graveyard grass swayed long and green in the breeze. Father Doyle's lilting voice caressed the words he held in his hands. Opposite Rachel and Wendy, old Mrs. Fredericks coughed into her hand and shifted her feet. Tears welled in her eyes.

"Mommy?" Wendy whispered.

"Not now, dear."

"Is Daddy going down there to be friends with the Easter Bunny?"

# *Part Two*

## *Discovery*

The rabbit has a charming face;
Its private life is a disgrace.
I really dare not name to you
The awful things that rabbits do.

—*Anonymous*

Adultery is a meanness and a stealing, a taking away from someone what should be theirs, a great selfishness, and surrounded and guarded by lies lest it should be found out. And out of the meanness and selfishness and lying flow love and joy and peace beyond anything that can be imagined.

—*Dame Rose Macauley*

# Chapter Four

## What the Easter Bunny Saw

Up from the perpetual ice and snow of the North Pole his hind legs rose, invisible as the body they supported. His front paws rested on the sash of the bedroom window, his nose twitched, his eyes sizzled into the writhing pair of lovers upon Santa's bed. He had chanced, the Easter Bunny had, upon far better entertainment than befriending corpses.

'Twas the night, you see, before Easter. And in this cottage, at the tail end of his rounds, two creatures were stirring it up quite nicely. Beside them, a white-haired woman, beautiful beyond describing, slept the sleep of the dead. The Easter Bunny's eyes darted betwixt her and the humping couple. The contrast between their carnal frenzy and her innocent oblivion excited him to no end. His heart pounded lubba-di-lubba-di-lub in an odd mix of envy, love, and outrage. Like erratic brushes riding a cymbal, his whiskers skritched against the glass.

How he adored peering in upon nocturnal copulations. Petunia'd once asked him why. She'd stared at him out of those vacuous, shit-brown eyes of hers as he lay spent on the burrow floor, peering up through the dimness. *Why do you peep?* he heard her say.

He shrugged. "Forgive me, dear Petunia, but I like seeing love happen. I like to pretend I'm the man who's making the happy lady even happier. Even though I feel quite sad, suicidal even, right after my genitalia spurt, when the bubble of my fantasy pops and I'm not that man, it's worth it to feel like I'm giving someone my love—someone alive and responsive—even for a few seconds."

She didn't speak to him for days after that. Just sat in her room and sulked.

Usually he had to slip out of magic time to animate the lovers he caught. No problem, most nights. But on Easter Eve, that was an extravagance he could ill afford. He simply had to get on with the business of distributing baskets and hiding brightly colored eggs in grass. There was his schedule to contend with, not to mention the Father's stern face glaring out of the night if he dared dawdle. Whenever he chanced upon pudendal play, he was forced to limit himself to witnessing two seconds, tops.

But these lovers were different.

These lovers were themselves wrapped in magic time, though their beautiful companion languished in the real time of an open-mouthed snore. That meant he could stay and watch for as long as he liked, particularly since his invisibility, God bless it, hid him from immortals as well as mortals. He grew hot with desire at what he witnessed. Hot too with envy. Love for the adorable white-haired woman thumped in his heart; and in his head, a righteous anger at Santa's adultery mixed with strange new thoughts indeed—disquieting thoughts that whispered around the corners of an obliterated past, whispered of powers lost and of divine betrayal.

Nonsense, he thought, shaking such notions out of his head and concentrating on the scene within. His scent glands drooled exudate down his chin and into the snow. His claws unsheathed against the sash. His penis poked out, red and hard, into the chill arctic air.

At the window, soundlessly, he chittered.

Earlier that evening, the elves' quarters had been unusually noisy, what with the anticipation of Easter candy on the morrow. They jostled one another at the sinks, each elf jamming his face close to the mirror, holding his beard free of the water with one hand and working his toothbrush with the other. Hans and Dieter had an argument over whose nightshirt was whose. Pillow fights broke out spontaneously at the east and west ends of the vast dormitory, spreading like two waves toward the middle until a great surge of shouts and feathers whitened the air with happy violence. When at last the ruckus died down, general exhaustion settled upon them like a comforter and they tucked themselves in for the night.

Each elf had his own bed except for Heinrich, the six dollmaking elves who went by one name. In the forgotten reaches of time, they had made one large bed for themselves. Therein they slept, tightly packed, their stubby arms and longish black beards sticking out over the covers.

That night, soon after falling asleep, Heinrich had a dream. In Heinrich's dream, only five Easter baskets lay waiting by his bedside the next morning. One mouth, the dreamer's, went without; one pair of fists, the dreamer's, pummeled five grinning mouths that munched smugly on jelly beans. Heinrich opened his twelve sleeping eyes to find himself embroiled in a bloody brawl, fists flying, sheets and pillows tossed hither and yon. When things wound down, the six sat there bewildered, looking out at a moonlit sea of snoozing elves and consoling each other.

In cleaning up, one of them spat a tooth into the sink. Should Santa be told? Should Knecht Rupert? No. Both were asleep. They positioned their injured brother at the east edge of the bed, placed the tooth beneath his pillow, soothed him, and eased back into sleep.

Hovering voluptuous over Heinrich, the Tooth Fairy smiled to see where she was. She drew her toothsome treat from beneath the pillow, bit into it, savored its elfin sweetness, and replaced it with coins from her anus.

Gold doubloons, six of them.

"One for each of you," she said, planting a kiss on

Heinrich's foreheads, hungering for the thick flat bone beneath. She ran greedy fingers in and out of his mouths, reading the raised runes of ancient molars.

As swift as thought, she drifted the familiar path to Santa's bed. The blanket bulked huge as a bear over his rotundity. Behind him, Anya's blip of blanket seemed an annoying afterthought. With a gesture, she paid out her invisible net of magic time until it compassed round both herself and her dozing lover.

For a moment, she watched his untroubled breathing and felt again that odd love she had felt on her island. How giving he seemed, even in sleep. His great mane of white hair spilled like a gift of blizzards from beneath his red stocking cap onto his pillow. His face, bearded and wise with age, was yet the face of a cherub.

His mouth stopped her heart.

She pictured those lips nursing on her, bringing her nipples up high and hard. She was tantalized by a nearly overpowering urge to dig her teeth into his ruddy cheeks and rip them free. She shuddered and shut her eyes. Down below, there came the swell and flush of arousal. Dipping a finger inside, she eased her eyes open and anointed the rims of her lover's large nostrils with divine fluid.

"Santa," she murmured.

A sharp intake of breath, a noisy yawn, the rubbing of hands at eyes, and he was awake. He looked about the room in confusion. Then he brought her into focus. "What in heaven's name are you—?"

"Call it a surprise. For both of us. One of your elves offered up a tooth. I took it and paid him off."

Santa chuckled. He glanced at Anya, then made as if to rise. "Let me put some clothes on and we'll be on our—"

She restrained him, firm hand on shoulder. "No need to go anywhere. I want you here. Right now."

"But Anya—"

"She can't see or hear us. She won't know what's going on."

Santa shook his head. "I will not make love to you lying beside Anya and that's final."

She tried coaxing. "Come on, Santa, it turns me on so, the thought of sucking you off while your frumpy old wife just lies there." She nuzzled his neck. "Don't you want to see what it's like, just once, to rock your dull Anya in the rhythms of our lovemaking?"

Again he refused.

The Tooth Fairy exploded with rage. She tore back Santa's sheets and blankets, exposing him and Anya in their nightclothes. She stood over Santa, straddling him. "Foolish elf, look at my body. Take it all in. Think about the taste of my breasts, how you love to cradle your head here and finger the sweetness between my legs."

Santa was, for the moment, stunned.

"Now look at your wife." Her hands swirled over the sleeping woman, as smart and sharp as fans snapping open. Anya's nightgown went transparent. "Look at this wretched excuse for a woman. Her face a map of wrinkles; two tired old dugs as ugly as they are flaccid; nipples that would shame a sow; a flabby belly that looks more like cottage cheese than flesh; a few spare wisps of crotch hair, dull as flax; an old crone's cunt, as tired and sexless as the lady herself; legs veined and thick; feet grown old and idiosyncratic from years of pointless ambling. Good God, what do you see in her?"

Santa's face burned red during this outrage. Now he grabbed her wrists, pulled her atop him, and drilled into her face with his eyes. "Cover my wife."

"Just tell me—"

He shook her hard. "Do as I say."

Her necklace rattled above him, her breasts swaying with the force of his ire. She glared at him, then shot a scornful glance at Anya, whose nightgown regained its bulk, pattern, and opacity. She snapped back into Santa's anger, writhing upon him. "I've been naughty, haven't I? Maybe you'd like to punish me. Slap me around some. Give me a good spanking."

When Santa opened his mouth to speak, the Tooth Fairy spat into it. His lips flecked white with spittle. She darted forward and pressed her mouth to his, tonguing deep as though to retrieve her saliva. Through the nightshirt, her labia found his rod and rocked upon it like a hen upon an egg. By Zeus, she'd fuck the bastard into loving her if she had to.

He clamped his huge hands tight around her head and pushed her lips away. "Not next to my wife!" he shouted. "Not here!" Her skull strained toward buckling under his grip.

Still she rocked upon his hard-on, crying out at the bone-bending pressure of his hands, laughing her defiance. Her hands yanked at his nightshirt, pulling it above his waist. She straddled him then and her flesh closed about him.

Throwing aside all consequence, he gave off hurting his mistress and hugged her as tight as he could, raining kisses on her face and arching up to meet her as she rode him. And ride him she did, skillfully, as a moth flits and flirts for hours near a flame, swooping near, tempting the heat, singeing a wing, until at last it dips and plunges to a perfect death.

After six hours of bug-eyed voyeurism, the Easter Bunny lost track of how many penile anointings he had graced Santa's cottage with. Enough anyway to turn the snow at his feet to slush.

No matter.

Satiety had come at last. He had wearied of watching these two inexhaustible fornicators and the lovely woman caught in mid-snore beside them. Tired too he became of fending off recurring notions of some long-forgotten role in the world's creation. Whatever he might have been in the past, he was the Easter Bunny now. Time to get in there, do his job, and move on.

He hopped away from the cottage in a zigzag through the snow. Then he sprang up, twisted about so that he once again faced the window, and bounded toward it with the full thrust of his back legs.

Silent as moonlight, the Easter Bunny tumbled through the glass onto the bare wood floor at the foot of Santa's bed. Warm air wrapped him round. The sounds of sucking, no longer muffled by glass, filled his ears. Soundlessly, he padded toward the naked lovers, nearly indifferent in the face of their umpteenth variation on mutual orality. Yet he felt compelled to move in for closer inspection.

It was the glow about them that drew him now. That and the rich aroma of lust fulfilled. He was stunned by the tightly packed beauty of the Tooth Fairy, her hands leaning upon the fat inner thighs of her lover, her lips moving up and down in slow undulation. This close to her, he felt an abrupt rush of danger, a violence in his groin that made him shy off, avert his eyes from her, and fix them on her lover.

God damn your jolly old soul, Santa Claus, he thought, surprised at the depth of his anger. Not only do kids love you more, but your penis is lots bigger, easily twice the size of mine. You enjoy such wonderful repute, yet now I find you're nothing but an adulterer, betraying your adorable mate by allowing this fairy slut to . . . to . . .

A chill coursed up his spine. Would anyone, he wonder, ever do that amazing thing to him? Or was he forever confined to merely imagining its delights, a furtive witness to the fellating of others?

At the pillow, Santa *mmmm*'d into the Tooth Fairy's vulva. The Easter Bunny's troubled eyes sought the elf's face above his matted beard. Fancy house, fine wife, a voracious lover, the untainted adoration of human beings of every stripe and color, a huge longlasting loveshaft. To top it off, a sickening excess of generosity oozed from every pore. It made him burn with envy, this Clausean outpouring of good will and gratitude, gift after gift after gift.

His eyes narrowed. He reached a paw into the void and pulled out the most pitiful Easter basket he could find. A wretched affair it was, with a handle on the verge of breaking, one tired clump of grass, a chocolate bunny staved in on one side and tan-crumbled with age, and nothing but red jelly beans.

Santa, he knew, despised red jelly beans.

Setting it down by the rutting elf's slippers, he hopped soundlessly around the bed and raised his head to study Santa's wife.

Anya was her name. Until this night, he had never really paused to appreciate her. She was a vision, this Anya. For all the tug and tussle of Santa and the Tooth Fairy, Anya in the pristine calm of slumber struck him as far more erotic than they. The shape of her head was so like a rabbit's, her hair so like soft white fur.

For the longest time, the Easter Bunny found himself staring at the top button of her nightgown. How breathtaking it would be, he thought, if she were to open those innocent eyes and, fixing him with a fathomless look of purity, undo that one blue button.

At last he looked away, a frenzy inside. The basket he pulled out of the void this time was usually reserved for spoiled starlets and the children of the filthy rich. Obscenely large and bound in gold cellophane, this Easter basket, whose crafted handweaving was itself a work of art, boasted all manner of fruit and nuts, in and out of chocolate coatings both light and dark; an extended family of bunnies, solid milk chocolate through and through save for hearts of marzipan; rich caches of jelly beans waiting to be discovered among the hand-painted Easter eggs and spun-gold chicks of marshmallow; and all of it bedded in the finest, most delicate strands of emerald green grass his machines could manufacture. This he set on the floor where Anya would be certain to see it on waking.

Then, rising to his full height and drinking in one last time the lovely Anya, radiant against the loathsome backdrop of jolly old Saint Nick locked in his fairy lover's embrace, the Easter Bunny turned to the window and leaped out into the night.

When finally she rose to leave, Santa grabbed her to him, kissed her long and hard, and said, one finger raised to admonish: "Next time, our love-nest in the woods."

She took his finger between her lips, tasted herself there, then cradled her face in his palm. "All right, my big fat fucker. But one request."

He raised a bushy eyebrow.

"Think about dumping her."

Santa scowled. "Incorrigible, aren't you?" He gave

her a smart slap on the rump. "Now for the love of God, let me get some sleep."

She threw him a look of pure chaos and, with a toss of her head, vanished into the night air.

For the longest time, Santa propped himself up in bed and pondered the duplicitous life he'd been leading. He ached for the simplicity and goodness of his life before Christmas '69. But he couldn't imagine abandoning his trysts with the Tooth Fairy. Finally, he cast a troubled glance at Anya, turned his back on her, and surrendered himself to sleep.

# *Chapter Five*

## *Mounting Frustrations*

Your typical rabbit—if asked and capable of giving intelligible reply—would choose a temperate habitat, an ideal mix of grassland and woodland, affording plenty of good grazing in tandem with dry, quickly accessible cover. But the Easter Bunny was not your typical rabbit, neither in size, nor in longevity, nor in his taste in living arrangements.

Save for Easter Eve and his nocturnal prowlings at bedroom windows, the Easter Bunny kept almost exclusively to his burrow, as dark and dank a hole in the ground as his Easter leavings were light and airy. He was there now, some six months after watching Santa betray his wife with the Tooth Fairy. Through the dimness of the low archway that separated Petunia's sleeping quarters from his, the metallic gleam of her eyes peered back at him.

"I know, I know, dearest," he said in answer to her weary look. "It's the end of October and I've been going on and on about this since April. So maybe you're right, maybe I am just a teensy bit obsessed. But God bless the jolly old bastard, Petunia, it isn't fair. The simpering Coke-drinker's got two mates, one for his lust, one for his love. I'm not even going to mention the countless copulatrixes he no doubt encounters on his rounds, wanton flibbertigibbets with too much eggnog in their noggins, waiting undraped by their fireplaces and dangling sprigs of mistletoe from their bellybuttons; I'm not even going to mention them. Let's confine ourselves, for the sake of my sanity, to the ones I *know* about. My point is, Santa's got two luscious ladies and I've got nobody."

Mistake. He glanced in at her and immediately wished he hadn't been so blunt. "Sorry, dearest. But we've been over this before. I love you, indeed I do. You're a good listener, you're compliant, you don't eat much, and you're no small consolation in a pinch. But let's face it, love, you just don't have what it takes when it comes to getting down and dirty. Both of us know that, though we like to pretend otherwise. I'm not blaming you, sweetheart. That's just the way things are."

No sense in being subtle. He squinted at her through the dimness. Clever little creature. If he didn't know better, he'd swear she was weeping. Fine, that was just hunky-dory with him. But if she was going to sulk about it, she could damn well sulk in private. Let her cry all the crocodile tears she wanted. "I'm off to survey my domain, Petunia," he said, trying to keep the anger out of his voice, "to look in perchance on the poultry." Now there were some females who knew how to move it. Petunia could do worse than take lessons.

If the archway had boasted a door, the Easter Bunny would have slammed it. Instead he turned tail, skritched some loose dirt in her direction with his back claws, and dashed from his quarters into the exercise area. There, with all the embittered zeal of one who works at having fun, he ran to and fro in the wide expanse of darkness, stopping on occasion to gnaw on scraps of bark or throw himself down and roll in the dirt, then leaping up again to resume his mad career about the perimeter. When he'd had enough, he sat in the dead middle and thrust his huge ears up to catch and amplify the burrow's activity.

Dull. Boring. Downright soporific.

His eyes pinched with envy. He pictured the North Pole as a place rich in sound: the prancing and snorting of reindeer; the shouts and laughter of elves at work and play; the chill night wind whistling in the chimney; the feathering of snow upon snow; the honeyed voice of Anya calling her husband home to supper; and then . . . the sounds of the bedroom. No! He pressed his paws to his temples and clamped his eyelids shut, refusing to upset himself again with that.

But here in his burrow, what sort of soundscape greeted him? From the sleeping quarters on the right, the sound of worms eating earth, of straw settling, of Petunia in silent pout. Ahead of him, where motes of dust drifted in the dim tunnel leading upward, the faint buzz of forest life, too far removed to distinguish its strands. At his back, the rhythmic weave and tumble of baskets being assembled, the gush and cut of colored grass, the counting-house clatter of jelly beans spilling into bins and hoppers, the dull hum of row upon row of candy-making machines: all of it set in motion by the Creator on the day He had made him the Easter Bunny, running unattended since.

And to his left, the sounds of the laying house.

The distant brooding of innumerable hens. That was the first sound that fired his ears when God created him. Crouched upon this very spot, his eyes not yet opened, he heard God resume a thought, speaking above a comforting wash of hen-sound.

"This burrow shall be your home, a place of rest and solace. And men shall call you the Easter Bunny. . . ."

His lids opened to effulgent light. His eyes were bathed in blessedness. He knew that moments before, he had been something other than what he was, a scaly thing, a thing of wind and bruises, a brutish sinuosity inlaid with pride, a reveler in . . . in what? The otherness slipped away faster than he could grasp it. Pure Easter Bunny filled the gaps.

"After the New Zealand White, a feisty breed and fair, have I modeled you. Yet, though your natural bent be rabbitlike, I have given you the stature and speech of men. . . ."

He leaped joyously into the air, feeling the surge of immortality in his veins. About his new-created home he flew, pausing to groom his coat or lie on his side in the straw with his hind legs stretched to their limit.

God laughed, a sound that made him weep with ecstasy. Then God walked with him, blessing with His presence every inch of the burrow. He enlightened room after room: the living quarters; the ever-replenishing food supply; the machines that ran by themselves; the exercise area; and, flinging back its doors, the laying house.

How easily impressed he had been then, he thought, slipping in now to observe the production of eggs. When he first beheld these thousands of hens, roosted tier upon tier, easing multicolored eggs from their nether regions, he had nearly fainted in awe.

But now, all that splendor looked prosaic and washed out. Not nearly as impressive as Santa's setup, he brooded. God's favorite saint had engaging elves to enliven his workshop with conversation and antics, a more opulent patch of real estate, and far greater freedom to vary his product lines.

Then there was the question of who, or what, he had

been before God had stolen away his memories and awakened him in this burrow.

Since April, the Easter Bunny had come to suspect that in all probability he had once been very important in the scheme of things; that just maybe he, and not God, had created the universe; that God—Whoever He really was—had filched his memories and now forced him to slave eternally in the bowels of the earth. Hurt feelings were not out of place, that much was clear.

He glared at the endless ovoids of color rolling and rumping along narrow troughs, at the gaping back fluff of countless hens, at the confused, quirky heads of Leghorns and Wyandottes, Dorkings and Orpingtons, Plymouth Rocks and Jersey Black Giants, Rhode Island Reds and Whites. At times he loved these creatures very much. But now, in the gloom of envy and resentment, they seemed little more than cogs in a machine.

Sometimes the fetid chicken-stench disgusted him. Sometimes it soothed him. And sometimes it turned him on. Even now, despite the depths of his emptiness, the close air and the seductive knock-and-roll of eggs brought his groin to life. He became aware of his testicles filling their scrotal purse. The vision of a dozing white-haired woman, a woman whose beauty made his heart hurt, floated among the feathers in the air before him.

No! Why waste time thinking about her? Anya was unattainable, a pointless fantasy.

Who then? He had tried one of the Leghorns once.

Snatching her one night from the bottom tier, he had carried her through the exercise area into his quarters. A sorry farce, that. Grunting low in his nose, he'd made to mount her. But she kept flapping out from under him. Despite the mismatch of parts, he tried time and again to jam himself into her. But whenever the tiniest bit of dicktip began to wedge its way upward, another emergent Easter egg would push it out. At last he released her in disgust, watched her meander back to the laying house—dropping eggs of red and green and orange as she went—and proceeded to lick himself all the way off.

Once, just once, he had tried a human female. Twenty years before, this eager young doe sat cross-legged on her mattress sucking dark-blue blotter squares with her boyfriend. Through the window of some dreary old brick dorm in Ithaca, New York, he had watched them. Before long, they were saying and doing odd things and laughing a lot over very little. His head buzzed with warm, fuzzy bees, his penis began to straighten up and poke out, and he found himself suddenly feeling amorous toward the young lady, very amorous indeed. After more inane jabber, the humans stripped, she opened herself up on the bed, her boyfriend wiggled into her and spent himself—"Cosmic!" he kept wowing—then he stumbled into the hallway looking for the john while she lay sprawled on the bed, one arm flung over her forehead and an endless string of feathery moans issuing from her lips.

He'd been overcome by the mood of the moment,

knowing it was foolhardy in the extreme (not in the least like his customary meek and mild self) and not caring one whit for the consequences. Passing through the window, he stole across the scuffed linoleum to the door and eased its lock shut. When, still invisible, he lowered his furry bulk onto her, she instinctively wrapped her legs around him. She had her eyes closed. A huge grin swam on the surface of her face. His back claws digging holes in her sheets, he gently licked her forehead, poised to thrust into her.

Then everything went wrong. Her stoned mate began to mewl in the hallway, jiggling the doorknob. When her hand brushed against his wet, quivering nose, she snapped open her eyes and discovered that she seemed to be embracing air only. She began to whimper and struggle. Worse than that, in the throes of impending orgasm, he lost his hold on invisibility. When he materialized—all three hundred pounds of him chittering and dripping like some Wonderland nightmare—she paid out scream after scream, plastering the walls with them. He leaped from the bed and zoomed about the room, displacing desks and chairs, bunching up throw rugs, and upsetting metal wastebaskets. Then he vanished through the window.

For weeks on end, he had cowered in his quarters, hearing nothing but screams. He lived in dread of a visit from God that never came. His heart shuddered to recall that time. He never found out what became of her, nor did he want to know. No, he wasn't about to attempt a human female any time soon.

Visions of Anya rekindled inside him. Dear sainted wife of a saint, betrayed in her own bed while she slept. If only there were some way to wrest her from Santa Claus, if only she would consent to live with him here in his burrow, go down on all fours, spread wide her knees, and graciously beg the inthrust of his bunnyhood.

"Wait," he said. A Wyandotte in mid-lay craned its neck around and blinked at him. "Who do you think *you're* staring at?" The hen turned away, looking perturbed, and laid a chartreuse egg. "Stupid chicken," he muttered.

Of course. There was nothing to stop him from paying a visit to the North Pole right now. Fairy-fornicator'd be in his workshop this time of day. He would hop boldly up the cottage steps, rap once, accept Anya's kind invitation to enter, and tell her—haltingly and with much feigned regret—what he had witnessed. Perfect. Expose the big blowhard, put Anya ever in his debt, then whisk her away, assuming she would have him.

Ah but that was pure fantasy. She would never have him, never love him as he loved her.

He would bring her flowers. Peonies were nice. Perhaps mums or snapdragons on the side. He pictured his precious Anya puttering about the burrow, bringing a woman's touch to it, making it more appealing. She would sidle up to him here in the laying house, stroke his ears or playfully twist his tail as they watched the hens, then go with him hand in paw, her eyes demurely downturned, to their quarters.

His back foot thumped excitedly on the ground.

Abruptly he stopped. His face twisted into a scowl. Bad plan. What proof could he offer of Santa's treachery? Who would believe his word against the word of Santa Claus? No one. Certainly not Santa's wife.

Envy lit a cauldron in his belly. He wanted to boil that fat little goody-twoshoes in it, singe his whiskers, make his balls swell and burst. God had made Santa Claus almost a god himself. He'd given him a winning smile, a wry wink, and an outsized erection. He'd set him atop the world and tied him to the birth of Christ. And who had he stuck with the death of Christ? Oh sure, he knew, all of that culminated in the resurrection. But let's face it, for pure appeal, no empty tomb, no death-defying corpse with a pierced side and wounded hands and feet could hold a candle to Baby Jesus in the manger. What else God had given him? One lousy burrow, one huge bunny body, one night's horrendous delivery schedule each year. And one raging confluence of hormones. No mate to share his love with, no stimulating companions of any kind to keep him from going crazy, and nothing to do during the rest of the year but peep in at bedroom windows.

Nothing to do . . . but peep in . . . at bedroom windows.

Watch Santa Claus fuck the Tooth Fairy.

Rouse the lovely Anya from oblivion.

Yes! He sprang six feet in the air, provoking a startled flurry of wings in the lower tiers. He dashed out into the exercise area and rolled back and forth in the dry earth, chittering wildly.

That's what he'd do. He'd camp out at the North Pole. He'd watch Santa sleep, all night, every night, studying his every toss and turn. And when he winked his lickerish eyes open, peeled back his blankets, and stole from his sleeping wife, there'd be invisible bunny paws following right behind him, tracking him right to that little love-nest the two of them had joked about. The rest was easy. Draw Anya into magic time, lead her to the hut, and stand beside her watching her husband's elfhood slide in and out of fairy flesh.

Goodbye Santa, hello Easter Bunny. That's what Anya would say. Then he'd have her. He'd have something that used to belong to jolly old Saint Nick. He'd have Santa's ex-wife. But would she love him? Would she have him? Oh yes, she would, she would! He scampered excitedly around the perimeter, drawing the thick woodsy air deep down into his lungs. Then he scurried into his quarters and poked his head around the archway.

"Petunia honey, I've got to have you now!" he said. She gleamed back at him like sex absolute. As usual, all was forgiven, they loved one another so. He hopped toward her, doing his best to hide the vision he was conjuring of Anya in his mind, a vision so vivid he was certain it splashed across the twin screens of his pupils. Not that he could fool dear Petunia, who knew of course his every mood and desire. Things just worked out better if they pretended they felt something genuine for each other.

Nuzzling her gently, he licked her about the neck and ears and forehead. She tasted so-so. No, wait. He shut his eyes and now it was Anya's forehead, wise with age and smelling as close and rich as a smooth block of cedar. He lingered there, exuding droplets of scent from the glands on his chin, letting them moisten her.

Time to move behind her. Turned on though he was, he paused to admire her great brown tail. There it was, upthrust and fluffed out above her lovehole. That tail had taken him months to get right, months more to perfect so that it would enhance their lovemaking.

He placed his front paws on her shoulders, readying himself to mount her. His left paw drew back sharply as though shocked. She was cold there. He saw, beneath her shoulderblade, the naked gleam of wire winking at him.

"Easily fixed, my girl," he said. Swiftly he bent his head between his legs, everted his anus, and voided a soft pellet into his mouth. Righting himself, he worked it flat with tongue and saliva and smoothed it into the upper edge of Petunia's wound. Instinctively he licked his mouth clean. Then down he dipped again. Up he came and jawed a second pellet into paste, working patiently at his mate's repair. It took thirty pellets to patch her up, but she looked grand when he was finished.

Now for his reward.

He ran in circles about her and pretended she was doing the same. What a dark beauty she was, all in all. There she crouched, hindquarters lifted, her chest and forelegs pressed eternally to the ground. He pawed away the dimness that separated them, mounted sweet Petunia, and closed his eyes to replace her with Anya.

It was Anya under him. It was dear white-haired Anya at his service, taking his bunnyhood inside her holy body and gasping thank-you's at every thrust. Upon her perfect back he drooled, imagining his dribble stepping down her skintight old-lady vertebrae one by one.

And then the great need came upon him.

In an instant, all thought dispersed. A chaos of feelings swept together and tightened into joy. And the buildup that could build no higher reached up one final inch and trembled there, poised to topple. With a thrust so vehement it brought his back feet off the ground, the Easter Bunny shot Anya full of seed and toppled over on his side, chittering and snorting in a delirium of joy.

# *Chapter Six*

## *Spilling the Beans*

The dead middle of the night at the North Pole. She dozed like alabaster perfection in the moonlight. One arm lying outside the bedclothes contoured the comforter to her curves. The other had draped itself idly across her breasts.

The Easter Bunny's eyes widened. A soundless chitter passed over his mouth. For an instant, that face made the image of a goddess flare up behind his eyes: before time began, a lone goddess standing—no, not standing, dancing, swaying, weaving—upon nothingness, her undraped contours fanning up a wind, fanning him up behind her, creating him out of chaos. But then his memory blinked away from that, and the bedroom was before him again, the big bed where lovely Anya slept.

He sighed. She would never be his. His fantasy would never come to pass. But if she couldn't be his, then she wouldn't be Santa's either.

When he passed his paw over her and twitched his nose twice to bring her into magic time, the breath flowed into her and turned her sculpted features to living flesh. She was stunning in her loveliness. "Anya," he said, gazing down at her.

Her forehead wrinkled and her face flinched, but she slept on. He had spoken too loud. Would she think him brazen, using her first name?

Softer then: "Mrs. Claus."

Her pupils glistened as her lids began to open. She inhaled sharply. The hand flung across her chest went to her face. With thumb and middle finger, she stroked her temples. Then, noticing him, she startled.

"Don't be frightened," he said.

Hugging the bedclothes to her chin, Anya shrank back against her headboard.

"It's all right," he soothed. "I'm not going to hurt you. It's me, the Easter Bunny. You know. Colored eggs and Easter baskets. I leave yours right here every year."

He pointed to the spot near her night table where he had set down the large basket on his last visit. But she was still only half awake. Her right arm shot out toward her husband, connected with bedding.

"Santa's gone for a little walk," he said. "In fact, that's what I've come to talk to you about."

Her breathing slowed and she squinted at him through the moonlight. "The Easter Bunny," she said, as though answering a child's riddle.

She snatched up the gold-rimmed spectacles from her night table and put them on.

His breath caught at her beauty.

Smiling, she shook her head. "You know you gave me quite a turn, you naughty creature. Old women are frail. We shock easily. And you're quite an imposing figure."

"Forgive me if I frightened you," he said.

She laughed and put a hand to her mouth. "The worst of it is seeing you talk. A six-foot-tall white rabbit is bad enough—"

"Eight, counting the ears," he corrected.

Again she laughed, then abruptly stopped, dipping her fingers into the collapsed comforter on her right. "Where did you say my husband was?"

The Easter Bunny worried his lip and looked out the window. Part of the workshop was visible, its bright red facade turned black by the night. Buttressed against it was the stable where Santa's reindeer now slept.

He felt an urge to go no further, to restore Anya to normal time so her husband could materialize next to her from one eyeblink to the next. Anya would, with the power of her husband's persuasion, be convinced his visit had been a dream.

Of course, if he did that, he would never be able to meet her again. There would be no chance for affection to blossom between them, no possibility that that gentle hand of hers would go roving through his fur. His mating would forever be confined to a doleful doe slapped together from shit and saliva. Enough of that, he thought. She was too good for him, she'd never go with him. But oh how precious she was and what pity she roused in him, lying abed in wifely ignorance, knowing not what dark deeds her husband was about. He owed Anya the truth. And he owed himself the satisfaction of seeing Santa toppled.

* * *

Anya was amazed how expressive the Easter Bunny's face could be. Her initial fear had swiftly given way to delight at his ability to talk, followed by astonishment at the emotional range his features commanded. At the moment, he was the very image of anguish and remorse, even to the downturn of his whiskers.

"Mrs. Claus," he said. There was a frown about his eyes and an inability to look directly at her for long that she found alarming. "Your beloved husband, whom all the world holds dear for his unbounded generosity, his irrepressible joviality, is, I regret to say, at this moment in the arms of another woman."

Anya felt a clench in her gut. Then it flew out into a dismissive gesture. "Stuff and nonsense." She hugged the blankets to her chest and laughed. "Not that it's any of your business, but Santa and I aired this issue twenty years ago and he vowed to be faithful. You may not know the value of a saint's vow, but I do."

"Long ago, deep in the woods beyond the skating pond, Saint Nicholas built a cozy little hut." It was as if he hadn't heard her, as if he had only paused for breath as she spoke.

"There's no hut in the woods—"

"A hut whose sole purpose is to conceal from you his adulterous goings-on."

There was something else in his eyes, something she couldn't quite read. It was alien, distancing, and cold. His assertions, absurd though they were, revived memories of the emotional devastation she endured when the whole Tooth Fairy business had surfaced. Thank God all of that was behind them.

"Santa Claus does not lie," she insisted.

"He's there now. Both of them are there now. They are"—he raised a furry eyebrow, shrugged as one ashamed, stared at the floor—"having sex." The Easter Bunny's words struck hard at her heart.

"What kind of cruel joke is this?" she said.

"It's no joke, I assure—"

"I think you'd better leave. I don't recall inviting you in and I'm not even sure you're who—"

"If you'll be so good as to come with me, I'll take you to their trysting place so you can see for yourself." There was a false note to his solicitude, an undercurrent that made her feel uneasy.

"Now what could possibly induce me to leave my warm bed and go hiking through the woods in the dead of night with a six-foot rabb—"

"Eight—"

"—with an eight-foot rabbit who claims to be the Easter Bunny but who might be something else entirely, for all I know, and whose motives may be less than honorable?"

To this, the creature raised one paw and gave a wry smile. Then he hopped—monstrous hops—over to Santa's closet, slid it open, and took out a pair of workpants. He reached a paw into one pocket after another, fishing for something. At last he stopped, drew forth a piece of dark cloth, sniffed at it, and flung it across the room. It landed on Santa's pillow, part of it spilling into the depression where his head belonged. Moonlight caught the red silk, the ribbons, the betraying shape of the thing. Anya's fingertips, reaching reluctantly to touch it, confirmed what her eyes had guessed.

Devastation claimed her heart.

"Fine," said Anya, clutching the red panties and tossing them away from her. They landed on Santa's side and slithered to the floor. She threw back the covers, anger flaring against her furry messenger. "I'll just put a few things on over my nightgown and we'll be off."

The whiff of Tooth Fairy, still potent after twenty years, nearly drove the Easter Bunny wild. He had to hold Santa's pants in front of him to conceal his arousal from Anya. She had flounced out of bed and now stood by her closet in a wash of moonlight. Feeling his right foot readying to thump against the hardwood floor, he crossed his left over it and jammed down firmly. His free paw he pressed to his mouth to keep from chittering. Then he tore the sexual thoughts from his mind and replaced them with forest images, as bland as he could conjure.

She was rebuking him, something about not believing for a moment his wild accusations and warning him not to try any funny business in the woods.

"You'll be perfectly safe in my company," he said. "I'm here to prevent your being taken advantage of. A woman of your caliber should not have to . . . let me say no more. By the way, if you prefer, feel free to change out of your nightgown rather than piling layers of cloth on top of it. I'm impervious to the charms of the female human form, you know. Doesn't do a thing for me."

"Forget it," she snapped back, delightful even in her anger. She moved like some rag doll, double-jointed and comical, reaching up for a woolen cap and jamming it over her ears, fumbling with the buttons of her fleece-lined coat, collapsing on the bed to reach down and zip up her snowboots. She tugged on thick mittens and stood up, her face flushed with defiance. "All right, rabbit," she said. "If we're going, let's go. I want to get this stupid little farce over with, throw you the hell off my property, and go back to bed."

Swallowing hard, he raised a paw to the bedroom door. "After you, lovely lady."

Anya stepped off the front porch and followed the Easter Bunny across the commons. Stars hung overhead, stipples of cold fire on a black backdrop. Underfoot, the snow squeaked and crunched in raucous cacophony. They headed toward the pond, scored with the stubborn scars of skate blades. Beyond it lay the elves' quarters.

Skirting the pond, they veered right and headed into the woods. Anya sensed a dread holiness about the place, as though the arching trees formed the ribs and splayed ceiling of some great cathedral whose white-vested prelate now guided her to its corrupt inner sanctum.

Endlessly they worked their way through the snow,

he hopping and pausing to wait for her, she moving one tired foot in front of the other. She wanted to believe he was lying, but the bootprints they followed engraved a message of betrayal on her heart.

When it seemed she couldn't walk another step, a wicked patch of orange light winked at her through the trees. The Easter Bunny took her mittened hand and led her into the clearing toward the hut he had spoken of.

His pink nose twitched. "I have the power to become invisible as the wind," he told her. "I've made us both so, though not to one another. They can neither see nor hear us."

He led her straight up to the blazing window.

The first thing she noticed, oddly enough, were his shiny black boots standing at attention by the fireplace. Beneath the bootheels, a pool of melted snow twisted with reflected firelight. Anya had never seen Yule logs burn so feverishly. They lay thick and numerous in the inner hearth, falling all over one another and flaming high and savage in the heat of consumption.

A vision invaded her head. *Darting through sunwash, him hot on her heels, her fir tree in sight, putting on a burst of speed, sweet balsam flaring in her nostrils, diving into the smooth gray bark, yanking her hair free of his fists as he sent up a volley of yowls outside.* Then the vision was gone, abruptly lost to memory.

Anya swallowed. She did not want to look at the bed. The corner of her eye had caught shapes moving there that confirmed all.

"See that little girl there?" He placed one paw on her shoulder, pointing into the hut with the other.

Involuntarily she followed it, saw for one instant her naked mate plunging into naked fairy, and beyond him, against the far wall, a tiny bed in which a little girl lay sleeping.

Anya let out a cry.

"She's not real." A whiff of bunny breath wafted against her left cheek. "I checked. She's just a doll with detachable teeth. It's how he summons her."

She shrugged off his paw and leaned into the window. Her beloved husband lay upon the four-poster, his knees and toes dug into the mattress between the splayed thighs of his lover.

Again the elusive vision swept in and out of her. *His lustspurt splashing her branches, that brute forehead pounding madly against her trunk until two conical gouges spilled drops of resin where his horns sank into her.* Again gone, again elusive, again a rollback.

When she could focus once more on the interior of the hut, Anya's eyes began to tear.

She remembered how it had been for them centuries ago when they were living hand to mouth, giving from their bones to prolong or brighten the lives of others. How God stepped down from the sky, enfolded them, and carried them to the North Pole. How He birthed each elf and reindeer out of the snowbanks in the commons, explored the grounds and buildings with her and Santa, and blessed their new home with effulgent grace. And she remembered how, with one all-giving sweep of His arm, God had granted them eternal life.

That first night of immortality had been so sweet. She had stood on the porch with Santa, listening to him address the elves, basking in their answering enthusiasm. Then he winked at her, ushered her inside, and, to the all-night warbling of elfin choirs, she and Santa made immortal love for the first time.

But now, he topped the Tooth Fairy, covering her fairy face with kisses and performing pushups with his pelvis. Anya lowered her head and wept.

"Shameful, isn't it," said the Easter Bunny, standing close beside her. "A man like that, with his reputation for kindness, for selfless giving—"

She looked at him through the steam on her glasses. "Why would he do something like this? I've been a good wife to him, I know I have." As her lenses cleared, the blur of his face resolved into furry eagerness. His stare chilled her, made her step away.

"Of course you have," he soothed. "Santa must be out of his mind to deceive a good decent beautiful woman like you with a wanton harlot like her."

Anya whipped her head about and again the horrendous sight assailed her.

A flood of vision consumed her, clearer than before. *Sapwood oozing for him, even her heartwood moistening at his heartache, relenting throughout her xylem and phloem, taking back flesh and blood, untreeing herself, extending her arms along her branches, rejoicing in the hot savagery of his delight, feeling his shaggy limbs engulf her, snake inside her, swirl her up into the sweep and surge of his ravening hunger.* It took longer to leave, ungraspable still, but her body tingled inside with a vitality that stayed with her. There was anger there too and a new restlessness in her belly.

"He's not going to get away with this."

"I wouldn't let him."

"I swear I'll get even. I'll show him what it feels like to hurt this way."

"Goose and gander, Anya," he said. "Tit for tat. *Sic semper tyrannis.*" He brushed his wet nose tentatively against an exposed earlobe.

Savagely she wheeled on him. "Don't touch me!" she said. Then she jammed her face against the pane, saw the flex of her husband's buttocks, heard his muffled screams of release.

An unstoppable surge of youth flooded her body *his meaty breath in her face, his holy sweat* and she couldn't understand it. The sight mortified her, yes, *the animal fullness of him thrusting at her loins* but it also shot hot life through her veins. Something was digging at her skull like a claw, raising all sorts of memories or ghosts of *his tongue licking her chin, licking her lips, filling her mouth with tickles of wine* memories flickering in her. It was obscene, that the sight of Santa's rutting could sweep away her bodily ailments and start wicked thoughts of her own spinning in her head, thoughts even of *a taste of nymph* she knew not what.

"I didn't mean to—"

Anya cast a contemptuous glance at the Easter

Bunny, who had retreated a few feet but craned now to see past her head. He had one paw over his erection, trying, or was he, to conceal it from her.

"I've seen enough," she said. She plunged into the bleak forest, tracking along their snowprints. The Easter Bunny hopped after, offering thinly disguised propositions veiled as mewls of apology. But her eyes saw only snowy depressions and her mind entertained nothing but wild and terrible revenge.

Halloween, 1990. Late Wednesday afternoon. Rachel McGinnis had taken the day off from work. She sat now at the kitchen table, hunched over her mom's reliable old Singer, putting the finishing touches to Wendy's costume.

She glanced at the clock over the sink. Almost time to pick up Wendy at school. Where do the hours go? she wondered.

Concentrating into the hum of the sewing machine, Rachel gathered net tulle onto a ribbon of baby-blue satin. She couldn't imagine why, but this costume made her nervous. Her daughter had seen the Disney version of *Peter Pan* recently and still remembered vividly her last viewing of *The Wizard of Oz*. She wanted to be a good fairy "with wings and a magic wand and pretty Tinkerbell eyes, Mommy."

Rachel raised the presser foot, pulled the material free, snipped the thread with her orange-handled Fiskars, and switched off the sewing machine light. She needed to apologize to Wendy, she thought. "Fairies don't have wings and they don't have wands," she had insisted, amazed at her own vehemence. She kept pressing the point, as if it were arguable, until Wendy burst into tears and Rachel regained a semblance of self-control.

But six-year-olds, thank goodness, forgive and forget with blessed ease. By the time Rachel arrived at the Montessori school her daughter attended, Wendy fairly leaped into her mother's arms. In the living room now, having pulled on her new ballet tutu over her sky-blue leotard and tights, Wendy stood patiently while Rachel made up her eyes.

"Kim lost a tooth today."

"Kim Rogers?"

"Uh-huh. I can move this front one a little I think with my tongue."

"That's nice, honey. Close your eyes. Okay, now let's tie those wings on." Rachel brought them out, crisscrossing the ribbons on Wendy's chest and tying them in back. Not bad, she thought, admiring her daughter's loveliness as she adjusted the wingtips. But beneath her calm, a dark premonition hummed. Absurd, she thought. It was as if she were afraid she might invoke some savage fairy by dressing Wendy this way. Yet everyone knew that fairies were creatures of myth, no more substantial than Santa Claus or the Easter Bunny.

"There." Rachel smiled. "Now stand right here and don't turn around."

"Why, Mommy?"

"You'll see." She went past Wendy to the tall hutch that had been her mother's, opened the middle drawer, and drew out the wand.

Wendy gasped and reached for it. It was nothing more than a dowel with a cardboard star taped to it and covered with aluminum foil, but Wendy loved it. Rachel delighted in her daughter's reaction, wishing that Frank were here to share it. His death had happened more than six months before, but she still woke in the night expecting to find his huge bearlike body beside her.

Wendy tugged her outside then and Rachel escorted her winged wonder from house to house, standing on the sidewalk while Wendy strode boldly up porch stairs to demand her due. The eerie feeling stayed with her during their hour on the streets. The shadows of bushes and dumpsters and alley-ways concealed not so much the human terrors she might dread on a normal night in Sacramento, as something unnameable that touched the nape of her neck with a cool hand.

"Look, Mommy," said Wendy, tearing down the steps of a house with a dozen blazing pumpkins grinning from the porch. "The funny lady let me reach into her bowl of steam and take two handfuls of candy."

"Did you say thank you?"

"Uh-huh," said Wendy, then raced to the next house. A heavyset man stood on the porch, watching what Rachel guessed was his son—a cowboy of perhaps four—hold out a pillowcase for a Tootsie Roll Pop.

When they passed her on the sidewalk, the heavyset man smiled at her.

Rachel liked the conspiratorial camaraderie that bonded Halloween parents. Except for single mothers like herself, it seemed that mostly fathers escorted their young ghouls and goblins about. There was something very attractive about a man who displayed his love for a son or daughter in this way.

It was even better when he was large and bearded like Frank. Her girlhood friends had watched *Batman* or *The Fugitive* and swooned over the Beatles. But Rachel's favorite shows had been *A Family Affair* with Sebastian Cabot and the short-lived *The Bold Ones* with Burl Ives, whose records she bought exclusively for two years solid. More recently, she had been drawn to William Conrad and Dom DeLuise and Luciano Pavarotti. Nothing thrilled her—indeed inflamed her with desire—like the sight and sound of the huge tuxedoed singer, absurd handkerchief in hand, caressing those liquid Italian syllables with all the love in his expansive heart.

"Mommy, my arms are getting tired."

"It's time to head home anyway," said Rachel. "Do you want to hit one more side street?"

"No, I'm getting cold. Mommy?"

"Yes, honey."

"Can I have a Snickers when we get home? I got three of them."

"Yes, but I'll need to look them over first. And then,

lovely lady, we'll get you out of that fairy outfit and into a nice warm bath. Sound good?"

Wendy gave an enthusiastic yes. As they walked home hand in hand, Rachel had a sudden urge to hide the fairy costume in the hall closet during Wendy's bath and bury it in the trash the next day.

And though she kept telling herself as she ran the bathwater that the idea was absurd, that's precisely what she did.

# Part Three

## Consequences

God sends meat and the devil sends cooks.

—*Thomas Deloney*

The prerequisite for a good marriage is the license to be unfaithful.

—*Carl Gustav Jung*

Jealousy is the greatest of all evils.

—*La Rochefoucauld*

# Chapter Seven

## *Anya Confronts Her Husband*

When Anya woke the next morning, her world had been transformed. She distinctly recalled the long trek back to the cottage. She had glared at the Easter Bunny as he sniffed the red panties and shoved them back into Santa's workpants. But once he had leaped through the window, all was a morass of vague thrashings and feverish dreams.

Her nightgown clung now to her back. She lay there stunned, her eyes roving, cataloging all things drab and diminished.

A dull stirring on her right. Something bulky rolled toward her, its arm heavy across her belly. A hairy upper lip brushed her cheek, a voice babbled alien words: "Good morning, Anya my love."

Whatever she replied seemed to amuse the creature beside her, for his eyes wrinkled up wet and demonic, and intermittent bursts of noise erupted from his lips like genuine laughter. She remembered laughter—what it felt like, what it meant. She wondered why this creature thought it necessary to perform such a pale imitation of it for her.

The bed shuddered when he rose. Then she was alone under the blankets, watching him move here and there, into the bathroom and out again, to the window for a hands-on-hips appraisal of the day, to the closet—Santa's closet, where red panties lay concealed in pants pockets. She fielded sound blips from him, tossed back blips of her own.

Thus it went that morning.

Over the weeks that followed, Anya walked about in a daze. She felt no great urge to re-embrace the myth of free will nor to begin making conscious choices. In fact she was moderately surprised—though she didn't show it—when she heard herself lie to Santa and knew at that precise moment that it was a lie.

"While you and the elves are busy in the workshop this morning," she said, "I think I'll drop in on their quarters and clean up a bit, maybe leave them a surprise."

"Wonderful, dearest," he said. "I'm sure they'll appreciate your thoughtfulness." He raised a bottle of Coke and smiled fatuously at her.

In the empty dorm, she straightened the sheets on a few beds, those belonging to the more voluble elves whose jabber would corroborate her story. Then she opened the windows to let in fresh air and set a potpourri beneath each pillow. When she was done, their quarters smelled like herb heaven.

To avoid being seen from the workshop, she slipped out the back, weaving in and out of the towering fir trees, deep into the woods. Not once did she falter in her steps, nor did the clearing where the lofty trees were thickest fail to appear as expected, nor did the dark stone hut refuse to rise from new-fallen snow like a rotten molar jutting up out of healthy gums.

She pulled off a mitten and touched the pane. *The kingdom and the power*. It was smooth and cold. *The glory and the ecstasy*. In the dim interior she made out the blackened fireplace, the four-poster dusky with shadows, the tiny bed with its dozing doll tucked snug under her coverlets. *The grape and the grope, the wild abandon*. Holding her fingers to the hut, Anya walked once around it, reading the rough stone of Santa's betrayal with her fingertips. *Encirclement by satyrs, goat hoofs in clover, their needy hands touching her breasts, their eyes transfixed by her vulva*. She tried the front door, opened it, felt the pull of youth and . . . something else tempting her inside. She closed it again, leaning against it until her head cleared. *Skin breathing on skin, polyrhythmic grunting, she being slowly spun and spindled, they like four rich flavors alternately sipped*. But when she returned to her original spot by the window, Anya, tears in her eyes, rapped sharply, slowly, repeatedly on the glass as if to rouse the little girl lost in slumber beneath the far window.

Fritz grinned into the mirror, turning his head this way and that to admire himself. His bunkmates Karlheinz and Max on either side of him fluffed their beards up around the red and green ribbons they had tied into them and flashed killer smiles into the glass. At the door to the washroom, envious faces, stacked like cordwood clear to the top of the doorframe, glared at them and shouted taunts.

"Simpering sycophants," growled one.

"Dumb luck for dumb clucks," sneered another.

"May you choke on a drumstick," cursed a third.

Fritz chuckled. Every year it was the same. The chosen three would elbow their way through a barrage of insult and invective to the dormitory entrance, link arms and stroll proudly across the commons to the jeers of their fellow elves, and be welcomed into the cottage to share Thanksgiving dinner with Santa and Mrs. Claus.

At first it was all they had dreamed.

"Max, Fritz, Karlheinz, my dear friends," boomed Santa. "Come in, come in, come in." Slaps on the back, warm hugs, and glad hands all round. The vestibule glowed with candlelight. The inviting aroma of roast turkey and honey-baked ham wafted in from the dining room. Then, a tinkling bell sounded in the next room and Mrs. Claus's melodious grandma-words: "Dinner's on the table!"

Karlheinz and Max, squealing with delight, dashed under Santa's arms and disappeared through the archway. Santa broke into a belly laugh. "Your bunkmates always were eager little devils, Fritz."

Fritz tried to look arch and disapproving. "Thank

God some of us know our manners. Shall we in?"

"After you," said Santa, sweeping as low as his bulk would allow, and Fritz passed at a measured pace through the archway, hoping that Santa's laughter was not at his expense. But when the dining room opened out before him in all its splendor, Fritz forgot his misgivings.

In the fireplace, subdued flames sizzled along three neatly stacked logs. From the large beam that stretched across the dark wood ceiling depended a simple but elegant chandelier. Two dozen beeswax candles rose slim and tapered from their holders, spilling soft light onto the great oak table below.

Fritz knew this table well. Long ago, he had been one of a score of elves who had helped Santa apply the finishing touches to it, planing and sanding and staining and polishing and buffing deep into the night so that Anya would have it in time for Christmas that year. Tonight, of course, the craft that had gone into its manufacture—the turnings, the friezes, the knees, the stretchers, the fluted edges—was covered, splendidly, in the finest damask.

But as beautiful as the tablecloth was from where he now paused, it paled in comparison to the spread of food that covered it. Mrs. Claus stood at the head of the table, a carving knife in her hand, a plump roast turkey on the platter before her. Steam rose tantalizingly from its gleaming brown body. The rich aroma that permeated the air nearly made Fritz swoon, it was so warm and full and inviting. Spilling out as though from Mrs. Claus's bountiful bosom were dish upon dish of cranberry sauce, fresh piping-hot peas and carrots, white whipped potatoes, fanned rolls and firm dewy pats of butter, breaded dressing barely contained by the rim of its serving dish, brimming gravy boats, and pumpkin stewed in a maple sap.

"Don't stand there gaping, Fritz," said Santa with a chuckle. "Come, sit beside me."

Santa placed himself at the far end facing Mrs. Claus and seated Fritz on his left. Fritz noted the empty chair across from him and its place setting. It was Santa's way of remembering the homeless and hungry. As he stood with his head bowed and his generous hands folded over the back of his chair, Santa asked the Good Lord to open the hearts of those blest with abundance so that they might know the joy of serving those less fortunate.

They fell then to eating and talking and laughing, to sharing precious memories, to hearing Santa regale them with stories of his nocturnal travels.

And yet throughout the evening, it seemed to Fritz that Mrs. Claus held back. She appeared at times to be observing them through an invisible sheen. Then she would interject a witty comment or a homily, or ask if anyone wanted another slice of breast meat, and Fritz dismissed his fancies.

The strangeness came on full force, however, when they had stuffed themselves fit to bursting and were all—the menfolk anyway—sitting back and letting escape exaggerated sighs of satiety. Santa held the sides of his belly and *ho-ho-ho'd* in sweet pain, then suggested they retire to the sitting room for a pipe.

"Gonna regale us wid yer exploits, Santa?" asked Max. He winked hawkishly at his bunkmates.

Karlheinz giggled, making fire with his fingers. "Oooh Max, you naughty elf, can you be suggesting that our innocent master—he's a saint, don't you know?—after spending all night reaching into his sack, might be so bold as to climb *into* the sack with some sweet single mom? Is that what you're implying, you little scamp?"

Fritz chimed in over them, feeling uncomfortable with the turn their conversation had taken. "Now, now, lads, no need to get indecent. There's a lady present. Let's do as Santa suggests and retire to the sitting room."

It seemed to Fritz that at this moment a sudden blast of air frosted his left cheek. When he turned his head, Mrs. Claus sat hunched over the picked bones of the turkey, her bloodless knuckles dug taut into the damask, her eyes fixed on her husband. "No," she said, "I think it's time for Santa and me to have a little talk, just the two of us."

Santa faltered, then laughed. "But Anya," he said, an index finger raised in gentle rebuke, "I always share a pipe with my co-workers after Thanksgiving dinner. You know that. It's a fine old tradition."

"Yes, dear," she countered, "and tonight we're going to break with tradition. Tonight you're going to see your guests to the door and then you and I are going to sit at this table and discuss our future together."

What Fritz saw in Mrs. Claus's eyes frightened him.

Max, sucking on a breadstick, seemed oblivious. He took it out of his mouth, screwed up his eyes, and said, "Pipe ud sure hit the spot."

Across from Max, Karlheinz stared down at his plate and said nothing. His hands were hidden in his lap like a little boy's.

Fritz folded his napkin and set it down. "Well," he said, "it's late and we really ought to be running along, thank you for a lovely evening, I haven't eaten this well in ages." He felt like he was fluttering too much, urging his companions out of their chairs, avoiding their hosts' eyes, moving his co-workers and himself awkwardly toward the vestibule.

"Fritz?"

"Yes, Santa?" Fritz had never seen him look less jovial.

"I enjoyed your company tonight, all three of you. It's a powerful pleasure working with you."

Fritz nodded. He ushered Karlheinz and Max to the door and together they started across the snow, stunned into silence at the strange turn the evening had taken. Halfway home, Fritz sent the others ahead and looked back at the cottage.

It sat there, thrusting up warm and fire-lit from the winterscape.

So cozy, so inviting.

But inside, something was happening that made Fritz want to shrivel up and die.

* * *

Santa waited for the front door to click shut. He wiped his mouth twice lightly with his napkin, then gazed down the table where Anya sat, her face buried in her hands. "Wife," he said gently, "would you mind telling me what that was all about?"

*(Oh shit, we're in for it now.)* The intruder was back. *(The sexless crone is on to us.)*

Anya looked up, her forehead resting on the palm of one elbowed arm, and gave a wisp of a smile. "I'm sorry, I just can't keep up the ruse one moment more. You see," she said, straightening up, "I know."

"You know?"

She nodded.

*(What'd I tell you. Can I call 'em or what?)*

*Yes. Yes I'm afraid you can.*

Santa stared at the crossed knife and fork on his plate, at the congealing pool of gravy out of which his fork tines arched. "How long have you known?" His initial flash of panic had yielded almost at once to shame. He also felt, oddly enough, a nearly irrepressible urge to break into a broad grin.

"Since October." She told him of her trek through the woods with the Easter Bunny. She told him about finding the hut and standing in the snow outside.

Santa listened with a growing sense of horror as she described what she had seen. "You watched us make . . . you watched us?"

Anya nodded, unable to look at him, her face fisted into a sob which she quickly stifled.

"Oh my Anya," he said, starting to rise and go to her. "My dear wife, how that must have hurt you."

*(Go ahead. Try it. What've we got to lose?)*

*Oh, shut up. Isn't there any decency in you?*

Her right hand shot out, palm pressed to the air. "Stay there," she commanded. "Don't you move from that chair." Then she brought her hand to her chest and asked softly, "How long have you been seeing her?"

Santa shrugged. "Not long. Maybe twenty years."

"I see," said Anya, fingering the ebony of her napkin ring. "In other words, when you swore twenty years ago that you would never sleep with the Tooth Fairy again, you were lying."

"I didn't mean to—"

"You broke a solemn oath."

"I tried to prevent—"

"Didn't you?"

"Now wait!" Santa slammed his hand on the table. Dishes rattled before him. "You've got to understand my position. I had been seduced, you were going all to pieces over something I had no control over—all right, very little control over—and I really meant to stop. But you don't know what it's like to be a man, to have all this . . . this copulatory energy building up inside all the time, and then to be set upon by the most ravishing seductress imaginable. My God, Anya, she's pure appetite. She wore my resolve down as if it were the thinnest veneer, and I swear to you it wasn't. My will was granite, thick and firm. But hers was diamond."

*(That's telling her, that's laying it on the line. Give it to her straight. Real men need pussy. She's got no right to keep you away from an open one if she plans to keep hers tightly sealed.)*

*I told you to shut up, you vile piece of filth.*

*(Ooh, hurt me, Santa. Hurt me with the truth.)*

"You lied to me, didn't you?"

Thoughts swirled in Santa's head, memories of those first encounters, of the Tooth Fairy's singlemindedness, of the overwhelming flood of carnality he willingly let wash through the calm landscape of his life. In the midst of the swirl, a golden ribbon of truth shone like sun through stormclouds. He grasped it now, felt it in his hand. "Yes, I did. I lied to you. In a moment of panic, seeing how much pain you were in, I vowed to be faithful even though I knew it was a lie. I'm sorry."

*(Wrong move, fat boy. Don't budge an inch.)*

Anya smiled at her hands, which lay before her on the table as if cupped over some prize. "I'm glad to hear you're repentant." Still looking at her hands, reasoning with them: "We could, of course, try to find out why you did what you did. We could poison our bliss by endlessly bickering about it. But I'm content, if you are, to let the whole sorry business recede into the past." Looking up at him now, attempting a conciliatory smile: "Maybe we can work together this time to fortify your vow, maybe we can confront the Tooth Fairy together, maybe—"

"Wait." Santa didn't like the way Anya was racing along the track of her own scenario. "I didn't say I was sorry for sleeping with the Tooth Fairy. In fact I'm not sorry for that. And I don't intend to give her up."

Anya's smile withered.

*(Yes! That's my man!)*

His vehemence startled him. "Not taking anything away from us, I quite enjoy the time I spend with the Tooth Fairy."

"But you just said she seduced you."

"At first," said Santa. "But I set aside my misgivings pretty quickly—all but one, deceiving you—and came to love the sheer carnality of what she offered. You know, in a way I'm glad we're bringing this out in the open. It feels so cleansing to talk about it." He was going to say more but caught sight of Anya's eyes.

"Cleansing? I'll cleanse your arse, you pitiful tub of guts." A hand went to her mouth. "Heavens, listen to me, I promised myself I wouldn't get mad, but oh you lying saint, you philandering shitwad, you . . . you jellybellied slutfucker." Each phrase dealt Santa a roundhouse blow. "God forgive my language, how dare you speak of continuing to carry on with that whore?"

"Now, Anya."

*(What's with this 'Now, Anya' crap? Slam into her. She's just a dumb fir nymph—)*

*A what?*

*(—she's got no right—the gall of her—to lord it over he who rules the—who rules her and the others—give one of them exclusivity and she turns possessive.)*

"How dare you assume I'd put up for one second with such an arrangement? Oh sure. Old worn-out

Anya's going to stand on the sidelines, wiping her hands on her apron and grinning good-naturedly, while her husband shucks off his suit and pokes away at some sleek young immortal with the sex drive of a rabbit and the morals of a rutabaga."

"Anya, you're not worn out," Santa protested.

"What chance do I have against someone with a body like hers?" Her eyes were glistening, her voice locked down tight.

*(None, sweetheart. Less than zero, you white-haired old bag of used-up gut and gristle, you dusty tunnel, you inflexible sleeve.)*

"It's not a contest."

"What does she give you that I don't?"

"Nothing!" he said. "It's just different, that's all. I've got enough energy for both of you. I need both of you."

*(Jesus, man, will you listen to yourself? What a wimp. You don't need this sack o' shit, tubby. You need to dump her's what you need.)*

*Enough!*

Her face pruned up at him. "Don't try to fool me, because I can't be fooled. You don't need me. I'm just a tired old woman who'd rather sleep most nights than give you the love you used to deserve. I notice you fondling yourself under the blankets while I read, don't think I don't. You want me to do that more for you, I will. You want me to mouth you more often than once a year—that's what men like best isn't it?—just say so, I'll do it."

*(Ooh, maybe dumping her's not something we want to rush into.)*

"Anya, please—"

"Only you've got to promise me you'll give up that homewrecking fairy slut of yours."

*(Oops. Dump away, Santa babes.)*

She folded her glasses and sobbed into her hands. It tore at Santa to see her go to pieces this way. But he couldn't let his love for Anya compromise his own integrity. Strange word to use, but it was right. The Tooth Fairy meant nothing to him, but she had taught him this much at least: that confining his sexual love to one woman was a betrayal of his deepest impulses, would make him less than he was meant to be. "Look," he said, "let me talk this out with her on Christmas Eve, find out how she feels."

"No, you've got to promise me you'll put a stop to it the next time you see her." Her tone grew insistent.

"I'm not going to promise that."

"Promise me right now." Her eyes pierced the air as she rose imperious from her chair.

"Don't give me orders, Anya," countered Santa with a patriarch's calm resolve.

"Promise!" she bellowed.

Anya's eyes burned into his face. Her hands groped the tablecloth. Abruptly the carving knife lifted into the air, slicing through the acrimony hanging between them. Along the table the sharp knife sailed, a flash of silver in the firelight. In the gold turnings of the chandelier above, its swift progress across bowls and dishes crusted with remnants of their feast was reflected fiftyfold.

Santa heard the *thunk* long after he felt the blade rape his chest, and it seemed to him—though surely he was wrong—that Anya turned pale and fled the room long before the steel point lodged in his heart. Through his tears he took in the bolster and web and the dark wooden handle with its three gold rivets. He gripped the handle with both hands and wrenched it out. Then he stared at his ruddy complexion in the blade, burnished red with blood.

His face seemed ancient, petulant, not jolly at all.

*(Getting closer, fat boy. Looking more like me all the time. Need a few more hints?)*

Had he cared to, he might have noticed the closing of the wound, the swift healing of his heart, the reweaving of immortal tissue carried on effortlessly in his body.

But Santa had other things on his mind.

He shut his eyes and wept.

Couples on the outs with one another tend to confine their bickering to hostility's natural habitat, the home. To the outer world, they display the cosmeticized face of marital harmony and bliss.

Such was the case with Anya and her husband.

In her public functions—of which there were admittedly few—Anya had nothing but admiring looks for Santa and affectionate little pecks on the cheek, which drew the cheers and whistles of his helpers. But behind closed doors, all was ice and fire, tempest and inferno, badly cooked meals shared in stony silence, and nights of troubled sleep in separate beds.

For the first two weeks, Anya tried—as did Santa—to come to some resolution of their problem through a round of early evening discussions. But as much as he professed to care for her, to love her deeply and devotedly, Santa refused to commit to giving up his affair with the Tooth Fairy. He sat at the far end of the couch looking stunned or smug by turns. While the fire hissed and popped on the inner hearth, she wept and raged and cajoled and pleaded, but Santa budged not one inch from his fortress of lust.

As often as not, Anya punctuated their evenings by bludgeoning her husband or by taking razors or knives or knitting needles to him. Her violence surprised her at first, but she quickly became inured to it. Santa's acquiescence in her mayhem—thinking, she could tell, that perhaps she would work off her anger that way and come to accept his affair—enraged her beyond endurance, so that at last she threw down her weapons, stomped off to her room, and slammed the door against him.

Then came the two-week, pre-Christmas rush. Santa spent long hours at the workshop and Anya had time alone to think. And the things she thought made her blush with the wickedness of them. More and more, she grew toward a certainty that she was capable of it, particularly given her newfound surge of youth. It was so unlike her, so naughty, it took her breath away. Yet there was a connection between what she now contemplated and her past, the past she couldn't quite recall; a connection that made it natural and (dared she say it) right. Worse, she knew in her heart that the elves—as devoted to Santa as they were—would take to her proposition as if it were second nature.

By the time of her husband's departure, Anya was in a welter of confusion about what to do.

After that peculiar Thanksgiving dinner, the elves kept a wary eye on Santa and his wife. At night, Fritz listened to his bearded co-workers trade gossip, craning over the ends of their beds to feed this or that twig of conjecture into the raging fire of rumor which swept through their quarters.

The work suffered. It wasn't so much a matter of not being industrious as it was a general enervation of the troops, the slightest surrender of spirit to the conqueror uncertainty. But at last, to Fritz's relief, the work came to a satisfying end and they found themselves once more in the commons, cheering as Gregor and his brothers led the caparisoned team from the stables and harnessed them to Santa's sleigh.

Santa seemed in high spirits. He gave each reindeer a hug around the neck and a cube of sugar. Then he made a rousing speech about giving freely of oneself, about the virtues of self-sacrifice, about respecting the core of one's beliefs and particularly that which makes each of us unique and peculiar and idiosyncratic, about not yielding one iota on issues that defined one's very nature, about how love always triumphs in the end. Fritz laughed and cried and cheered along with his compatriots, though he thought it odd that Santa strayed so far from his usual themes.

More fuel for the midnight fires.

Santa and his wife came into one another's arms and kissed long and lingering for the crowd. The elves went wild, as always, but wilder than they really needed to and longer in leaving off their cheers. Then Santa strode to the sleigh, pulled himself into it, picked up the weighty reins, chucked them across the backs of the team, and rose into the air, waving and laughing down at them like life irrepressible.

As always, Fritz and the others watched and waved until the diminishing spot in the sky winked out and the high jingle of sleighbells was but the memory of a memory. Hands dropped here and there in the crowd and heads turned from the sky. Fritz heard the general gasp first. Then he registered the drawn faces of Johann, of Friedrich, of Gustav and Knecht Rupert.

He followed their eyes.

There on the front porch stood Mrs. Claus.

Her peasant blouse—red and white and shot through with stitched green ivy—was unlaced and ripped open to expose the pink-tipped mounds of her breasts. Her skirts she had hiked up and tucked into her wide black belt. Below, she was naked as truth. While one hand teased her left nipple hard, the other moved in slow deliberate circles, rounding upon her sex like the fist of a yawning child at one puffy eye.

And when Fritz brought his gaze to her face, God help them she was looking out over the shocked multitudes with the hungriest old-lady eyes he had ever seen in his life.

# *Chapter Eight*

## *Vengeance and Lust*

Gregor stood at the stable door, an eternal humph of disapproval stuck to his face. Arms folded tight upon his chest, he gazed out through the buttercup light of magic time at an elfsnake whose long green body stretched deep into the forest, its restless tail tapering off at the middle of the skating pond. He refused to imagine the tomfoolery its head was engaged in. Every few minutes, another green-clad figure with his fly unzipped and his penis flapping right-to-left-to-right dashed out of the woods, kicking up snowdust in his eagerness to rejoin the line for another turn at Santa's wife.

"Disgusting," muttered Gregor. But as he said it, he wondered why he alone, of all the elves, had been able to summon up the willpower to refuse Mrs. Claus's outrageous proposal. Even his brothers, shy by nature, shifted under their clothing at the sight of her—as if a darkness long suppressed slithered up out of their bellies.

The whole wretched mob had grinned and nodded at her words, stamping and whistling their encouragement, until at last they stormed the porch and hefted her, half-naked, high above their heads. Gregor had just stood there by the stable, mouth agape, feeling as though he'd tumbled into a bad dream. Then into the woods they dashed, Mrs. Claus—acting suddenly as young and irrepressible as a schoolgirl—jouncing above and pointing the way.

Gregor missed his reindeer, their clear brown eyes, their animal honesty. He didn't much like these wild new elves with their demented looks and their taunts, these demonic doppelgangers. Some of them, before they rejoined the queue, dashed across the commons and waggled their willies at him. They laughed. They called him names. Albert did this, and so did Wilhelm, two of his dearest friends. He shut his eyes to stifle a sob.

What Gregor missed most was watching the elves wink in and out. Usually, at the moment Santa's sleigh passed through the protective bubble around his domain, those inside reverted to normal time. Every few minutes thereafter, a handful of elves would "wink out" of normal time into magic time, vanishing from their midst and reappearing soon after, exhausted and ready for sleep. It was no easy task, so they told him, to spend six straight hours transporting gift after gift from storage to loading where they had to be to replenish Santa's pack as he went from house to house. But now that Mrs. Claus, in her fury at Santa, had sustained the wrap of magic time about the entire North Pole, there was no need to wink in and out. There was only this ever-renewing queue of elves stretched into the woods, the now unbearable glowlight of magic time over all, and Gregor's interminable wait for the return of reason.

He rested his hairy forearms on the half-door of the stable. "A sorry time," he muttered. He watched Fritz, Mrs. Claus's appointed pander, march out of the woods with an air of self-importance, barking orders up and down the line.

A sorry time indeed.

From the shadows, the Tooth Fairy watched her lover pull presents from his pack and arrange them beneath the tree. As golden as her memory was of their time together, the reality never failed to outshine it. He was a better lover now—better because more giving—than in the old times, and he had been superb then.

"Santa," she said, low and husky. Her paramour gave the slightest start. Still on his knees, he turned to her. "Do you recognize the place?" she asked. She said nothing about his failure, for the first time in twenty years, to show up at her island; said nothing, though it stung deep.

"Of course." She didn't like the blank look on his face. "Our first time together," he said. "Twenty years ago, red lace panties, little Rachel Townsend's bed. I thought you might show up here so I scheduled California early."

"Like the way I look?"

"Radiant as ever." His eyes never strayed from her face.

"Aren't we the cool one tonight?" she teased, hiding her upset. "There's another little girl sleeping in that same bedroom tonight, Rachel's daughter Wendy." She clung to him and fingered his lower lip. "There's a delectable upper right lateral incisor lying beneath her pillow. Why don't we go in and . . . see what happens?"

"Anya knows," he said.

Ah. Things began to make sense.

"How?" she asked, searching his eyes.

"The Easter Bunny. He brought her to the hut. They watched us through the window."

She laughed. "Well, well. So good old Anya knows what we're up to."

"Yes. And it means we've got to stop."

Reluctance. She hadn't felt that from Santa for years. It unsettled her. "No need for hasty judgments, lover. Let's go in and look at Wendy, shall we?"

He hesitated, then agreed. "But no bedding down next to her." He raised an index finger. "We'll peek in at her. Then I'm off to the next house."

"Of course," she said, cozying up to him and making sure her right breast pressed against his upper arm.

Fritz did his best to seem in control. But inwardly he was a mass of conflicts, all of them bitter and none of them anywhere near resolution.

His penis. That lay at the heart of his problems. Before now, he had hardly been aware of it. It was just something you held onto so you didn't pee on your slippers. Funny soft droopy tubes of flesh, peripheral to their lives; they all had one, no big deal. But now this thing—all of their things—had stirred at Anya's words and deeds up on that porch. (She had insisted they call her Anya, not Mrs. Claus.) Suddenly, this hitherto inconsequential appendage had taken on great pitch and moment, nagging for female completion, refusing to let him think about anything else.

"Stay in line, men," he shouted to those nearest the hut. "Dicks at the ready. And warm them with your hands. Anya's orders." He stopped before a dole-eyed elf whose mittened fists hovered uncertainly at his belt. "Albert, for the last time, will you get your goddamn dick out?"

"Aw gee whiz Fritz, it's too cold," Albert grumbled. But he unbuttoned his pants and did as he was told.

Never before had Fritz's loyalty to Santa been at odds with his loyalty to Anya. "Fritz," she had told him after his first time, "I swear to you the next elf who fucks me deferentially gets tossed out on his ear. I want you diminutive cockwielders to wallow in my flesh like piglets in mud. Spread the word."

Lordy, lordy, why, he wondered, was he taking it all in stride? Why had all of them adapted so quickly to what they would rightly have seen as scandalous behavior scant hours ago?

And what would Santa think of all this?

But the horror—and the humor of it—was that, deep

down, Fritz didn't really give a shit *what* Santa thought. In her porch ramblings, Anya had spoken right to the heart of some depraved creature hidden inside him, hidden in all of them. It was rude and rowdy. It refused to be ruled. It stamped, it bellowed, it raged, and it craved precisely what Anya was offering.

Who, it demanded, was Santa Claus anyway? They had a new master now, a new mistress rather, a lusty old woman who seemed suddenly not so old at all, who had taken it upon herself to envaginate them, to bring them to a boil, to strip from them the sweet veneer of elfdom and wrench into focus a wilderness that surged unchecked within.

—•

Wendy's room silvered in moonlight.

As he gazed upon the little girl's beauty, Santa felt its mild reproach. Anya had been right all along. He had been bullheaded about the Tooth Fairy. One glance at the sleeping child was all it took to bring him to his senses. "Aren't they astounding?" he said.

"Mm." The Tooth Fairy's agreement was perfunctory. She was too busy munching on Wendy's baby tooth to say more. Swallowing it, she cupped a palm over her anus.

Santa kept his eyes fixed on Wendy's angelic face. His cheeks were burning. "Are you finished yet?"

"What's the matter, stud?" she taunted. "Afraid to see my cunt pucker?"

"You're being a little childish," he said. He saw her thrust a hand beneath the pillow, heard the muffled clink of coins. Her every curve and concavity was pantherish and provoking.

Without straightening up, she brought her fingers to her nipples and teased them out into hard tight nubs. Her eyes probed Santa's face. "Childish?" she said. With a sinking heart, Santa watched her right hand move down her belly into a thicket of curls whose every twist and turn he had by heart. "Is this the body of a child, Santa?"

In an instant he was behind her, gripping her wrist. He intended to scold her, to plead with her to honor the innocence of the child's sleep and leave him be. But she whirled about, planting a kiss deep in his mouth as she cupped and caressed his burgeoning desire.

And Santa let it happen, neither horrified nor elated, watching his body expend its lust, knowing that this time he had the strength to end it, and the resolve, and the best of reasons—his undying love for his wife.

Anya lay beneath Fritz, out of her mind with rage and desire. His prick was lodged up inside her. His balding head with its wisps of red hair rotated now at her breast, working like a horny babe at her nipple. His long bushy beard tickled her belly.

She couldn't believe how youthful she felt. What she was doing scared and exhilarated her. It seemed precisely counter to anything the wife of Saint Nicholas ought to be doing, yet it felt like something she had done countless times in some forgotten past—done and enjoyed, as now she enjoyed Fritz.

"You're improving, Fritz," she said. "Your first go was wretched, your second only so-so, but honey you've hit your stride with number three. Oh shit Fritz yes keep it up keep doing that don't stop don't break that rhythm."

In Anya's mind, each surge of pleasure Fritz evoked drew a razorline across Santa's face or scored a random whipwelt upon his bare back. Though she had thus far bled the jolly old son of a bitch dry thousands of times, she had thousands more to go before her vengeance would begin to approach anything like completion.

Anya gripped the sheets to either side of her, the same sheets that Santa had slaked his lust upon. Fisting them tight, she arched up to meet the moaning elf-body that pounded down on her. Wide-eyed faces packed tight the windows. Then orgasm bulleted through her and sent her screaming like a newborn, drawing Fritz along as well. He bucked and humped like joy and sorrow combined as she tightened about him.

"Anya, dear Anya," he gasped at his breath's end. He seemed, this detumescing elf, impatient to say something. For a moment Anya couldn't recall his name. "This isn't right," he blurted out, "what we're doing out here in the woods. We've got to start thinking about—"

Abruptly she raised herself on her elbows and glared at him. Then she hauled back and struck him, three hard blows. Fritz scrabbled off the bed and slumped, hands collapsed over his head, in a disarray of green clothing. "Don't you talk to me, you little shit, about right and wrong. We make the rules out here, me and my quim. Not you. Not any of you. Your job is to obey me. Mine is to hurt my sainted husband and to keep on hurting him until there's no more hurt left."

"But—"

"Enough!" she yelled. In an instant she was off the bed, her fingernails dug deep into Fritz's hairy shoulder. He clutched his clothing and winced, slunk in silence.

Anya rushed him to the door and swung it wide. Out he sprawled, naked in the snow.

"You! Inside!" she said, grabbing an elf at random. Then she slammed the heavy oak door on the unending line of little men stretched through the winterscape and fell to her knees, sucking fiercely at the new member, trying to identify its owner not by his face but by the taste and shape of him and by the feel of his buttocks through the chill green seat of his pants.

"It was awful when she found out. Plenty of bickering and hurt pride. Lick a little lower, would you? The knives came out too. Of course my feelings hurt more than my flesh. I stuck to my guns. You would have been proud of me. I tried to insist on having you both. But that's not going to happen, clearly. This has got to be our last time together so—oh Jesus God—so let's—"

The Tooth Fairy poked her head up. "Would you

mind not talking so much?" She ducked down and went on with her work.

"No, wait," said Santa, sitting up. "That's lovely, as always, sweetheart, what you're doing. But we've got to come to an agreement about this. Please stop for a moment and talk to me."

With a look of impatience, the Tooth Fairy shifted on his thighs. "What about?" She rubbed the head of his arousal along the soft line of her jawbone.

"About not seeing each other again." Row upon row of toys and books and stuffed animals climbed the wall next to Wendy's bed. Nearby lay Wendy herself, thralled in normal time and looking beautiful as only six-and-a-half can.

"Don't talk nonsense," she said.

"My resolve hasn't been worth much lately," he said, "but things have to change." He tried to sound forceful, but all he felt was ineffectual. The strength of Santa's resistance seemed to ebb and flow in counterpoint to the tides of not-Santa's passion, and just now his tide-pools were rapidly filling.

"Tell you what," she replied, leaning her cheek and temple along his erection and running her index finger around its tip, "I want you to remember what it's like to spend Christmas Eve without me. So you go about your giftgiving tonight, and me about my toothtaking. I'll wait for you to summon me. I'm betting your fidgety little hand will be shoved into Thea's mouth before the week is out."

Santa frowned. "You're not giving me the kind of cooperation I need."

"That's my best offer, big boy. Now shut up and give me that amazing snow-white head of yours." With that, she mouthed him again as deep as she could go, spun about like a noisemaker on his fat fleshy spindle, and smothered his face in fuzzy wet womanflesh.

During round five, emptiness began to tinge Anya's raging desires. She had as yet no name for the feeling. She knew only that it threatened her vengeance and that only copulation frequent and feverish would keep it at bay. The bleeding Santa she beheld in her mind's eye was weeping, yet he also grinned at her antics, grinned as if he had ordered them.

Gripping stray wisps of black hair that swirled about a bald spot, she wrenched up and peered into the bleary eyes of Wolfram, the workshop's master miniaturist with a cock to match. "Not bad, pindick. Now get off me and go. On your way out, send in the next two."

His jowls fell and the ovals of his eyes lengthened like soggy Cheerios. "Did you say two, milady?"

Anya lit into him then, snatching an andiron from the fireplace and whipping Wolfram's baboon buttocks out the door with its long hard length. Flinging it into the snow in spangles of sunlight, she reached out and tight-fisted two elfin erections. "You and you," she said, her eyes locking on the carnal gaze of Gregor's brothers. "Get in here and put these things to their proper use."

They complied.

* * *

Doubt bedeviled Santa.

For years he had lost himself in fairy flesh, first by way of seduction, then by design. It was elemental giving, this licking and stroking, this probing and enclosing. It stripped away his Santahood, yes. But it brought out a deeper urge to give, an urge beyond ego and tradition. And it brought out an urge to take as well, a grasping grope at exposed flesh and the joyous oblivion it offered.

But now that Anya knew all, now that he had spent a hellish month watching misery dwell in her, the reminders that he was Santa Claus would not be stilled. They nagged at him no matter how unbearably rhythmic his lover's hips rose and fell about him.

Santa he remained through it all.

The intruder—Santa's dark twin—had been eyeing him sullenly during this struggle, upset with his host's less-than-wholehearted attention to the pleasures of the bed. At the first hint of impending orgasm, he engaged him.

*(Okay, friend, the time for introspection is past. We're entering the homestretch here and I want your full attention on maximizing my pleasure.)*

*What you want no longer concerns me. This, I swear, will be the last time I sleep with the Tooth Fairy.*

Her fingernails tensed like claws at his back.

*(Swear and be damned. You and I understand the value of a saint's vow. We've heard enough of them. We've seen them broken like twigs. Pay attention,*

*damn it. She's starting to peak and so are we.)*

He took in the tumble of her hair, the switch and sway of her head as it tossed to the rhythm of their sex.

*Anya is my salvation, my anchor, my love. To her and her alone I hereby pledge my fidelity.*

*(What a wuss you are!)*

*Then there are the children. Sweet Wendy here, sleeping so soundly, shames me with her innocence.*

The blood throbbed in his head. His heart pounded to the surge of his lover beneath him.

*(Where's the shame? Humping is good. More humping is better. It's where kids* come *from, in case you've—)*

*They deserve better from Santa Claus.*

*(So* be *better. Be the* best. *Cease all this chatter and delve into the delicacy that lies before us—Tooth Fairy tenderloin en brochette.)*

The upward thrust of her hips came faster now, less controlled.

*To the boys and girls of the world, I vow no longer to dishonor them thus. And to my elves—*

*(Oh come now, you're going much too—)*

*—to my elves, faithful to me in all things, I owe this promise as well—to pull myself out of the foul mire of lust and regain my God-given purpose.*

Below, she gripped tight along the length of him. He began to tingle all over, inside and out.

*I'm rid of the Tooth Fairy. And I'm rid of you.*

*(Of me!?)*

*That's right. I'm putting you down, whoever you are. I don't need you anymore.*

Santa gave a sharp inward thrust that made the Tooth Fairy cry out.

*(Now wait just one—)*

*No need to wait! You're out of my life!*

A second thrust and a third. They pushed her over the edge, ramping and rioting into sweet oblivion.

But Santa's dark twin was less easily defeated. The battle raged fierce and furious right up to the moment of climax. And when it came time to scale the great orgastic peak, they bickered and fought like brothers all the way up the sheer face of the mountain. For every piton his dark twin's sinning prick drove into a rocky cleft, Santa snatched a dozen more from him and hurled them clattering down the mountainside.

At last, the saint gathered his resolve, put firm hands upon the intruder's shoulders, and shoved him screaming down the steep slope. Bleating a cry of triumph, Santa Claus reached one hand, then the other, over the topmost crag and pulled his huge bulk up onto the gasping heights of elemental orgasm.

In the frenzied feeding of Anya's revenge, two lovers became three, three became four, and four grew in kind. She dimly recalled Heinrich huddled about her, two of him taking turns at her mouth, two moving against her nipples, one each shoved into bunghole and cunt. But that memory lost its precision in the swirl of so many like it.

Long afterward, when she tried to focus on her bouts of passion, the recollection that shone most clearly was of every last elf packing the tiny hut to the rafters, though by any rational measure that could not have been. Yet there they were in memory—a host of Cupids grown old and bearded, leers of lust or bewilderment in their eyes; and loveshafts everywhere, thick and thin, lengthy and stubby, circumcised and un-. And somehow their slit pricktips all reached her as she lay there on the bed. Every pore was an orifice open to them, and their seed spilled forth rich and viscous, turning the mad swell of her vengeful flesh everywhere deeper, redder, wetter, until—while the Santa Claus that looked on and suffered in her mind's eye grew hardly distinguishable from the flayed carcass of some butchered porker—Anya grabbed all about her for love, bucking and ramping toward absolute forgetfulness.

Thousands of miles distant from one another, Santa and Anya came. Their climaxes were not joyous by any means, not the sort one is wont to replay to heighten the solitary delights of masturbation. Powerful as these orgasms were, they brought with them a terrible ambivalence and the first tentative turnings toward reconciliation.

Santa, pumping and gasping beneath his paramour, looked up and saw pure harpy, pure siren, pure succubus. If this creature, into whose womb tunnel the long arc of his arousal now curved, had anything more to her than insatiable desire, he failed to see it, now nor in the twenty years of their adultery. In the instant his flesh lunged into what it craved, the scales fell from his eyes and he knew that, unlike so many times before, he had the strength to keep them from growing back. For as much pleasure as he shared with this faery daemon, so much pain he now realized would his dear wife endure.

And that was intolerable.

As for Anya, there came a time when the lust she surrounded herself with transmogrified into some bizarre and meaningless flesh-machine and her ire against Santa turned to dust and blew away. Beneath mounds of humping elves, Anya found a certain stillness, in the midst of which stood her husband, whole and pristine and loving as always. There were roses in his cheeks and a twinkle in his eye. Smoke curled in white wisps from the bowl of his pipe, wreathing about his face like the fingers of a loving wife.

When she had come to herself, Anya rose from the bed and hurried two score bare-assed elves out the door like mice before a broom. The last of them—Helmut the clockmaker, whose mind, before this intriguing night, had been preoccupied with springs and flywheels—she collared.

"Send Fritz," she said, and Helmut nodded.

Fritz found her sitting on the side of the bed, staring into the flames. Uncertain of her mood, he wondered if he should tuck his engorged elfhood back inside his trousers.

"Mrs. Claus?" he ventured.

"Fritz," she said, glancing peripherally at him, "please help me into my dress."

"Yes, ma'am." He turned away, working with both hands to maneuver his stiff member beneath the fold of green cloth that fell from belt buckle to crotch. Given his tumescence, he abandoned the buttoning itself as a lost cause. It was all he could do to retrieve the torn peasant dress Mrs. Claus had tossed over the sleeping doll so long ago, carry it like a dead woman draped across his arms, and hold it out to her.

When she was dressed, he ushered her to the door and watched her take her silent way through a gaping sea of faces. In bewildered silence, the other elves followed Fritz out of the woods, past the skating pond, and across the commons to the porch. Those, like Fritz, who busied their giddy minds with renewed hopes of carnal easement, lingered there in the snow, watching the object of their obsession move from room to room, closing curtains. They heard her turn the shower on. Still they stood there in the snow, the lustful pure, in silent devotion. And when at last the distant hiss of the shower cut abruptly off, they took the occasion—all except Fritz—to disperse like whipped dogs to their kennel of calm, where elfdom damped down the satyr in them and all was right again with the world.

Sexlessness reclaimed them.

But it did not reclaim Fritz.

He stood there in the etched light of magic time, his clasped hands pressed against his erection, waiting for Anya to uncurtain her windows, to re-emerge on the porch, to give him some sign that his priapic adoration of her was not misplaced, that it had its parallel in the urgings of her own lovely sex.

On the long walk home, Anya felt nothing.

In the shower, nothing.

Beneath the comforter staring up at the ceiling, still nothing. The close of her eyelids and her swift drop into sleep came as casually and as unlooked for as a shift in the wind.

In dream, her naked body sprawled across the snowy commons. Her right thigh rested upon the roof of the cottage, her left upon the workshop. Both buildings were weather-beaten, broken-windowed, abandoned and badly in need of repair. So too the elves' quarters along whose ragged front eaves she ran an idle finger.

The winter cloudcover broke. The Lord God's hands parted the firmament. His face showered beatitudes upon her. Then, touching His foot to the earth, He crouched between her legs like the lowliest of His creation. His vestments were of rough bronze and leather. His beard, always feather-white before, had turned a mischievous brown shot with bolts of silver. His eyes rioted with typhoons. With the easy contrariety of dreams, Anya knew that this was how God the Father had come to them at the beginning of Santa's realm, even as He manifested Himself in robe and crown, fingers bejeweled and beard beribboned, with hosts of angels singing His praises.

Along the folds of her flesh, His tongue traced a path of healing. He flicked and swirled blessing upon blessing there until her soul felt so full of passion she wondered the wood didn't blaze up about them nor the snow sizzle into steam.

At first when He moved to cover her, she protested, craving more mouth. But where His divine flesh touched hers, He was all tongue. His private hair was a writhe of tongues, teasing, urgent, intelligent. And His unending organ of generation eased past the swollen petals of her womanhood and gloried inside. Ever deeper His divinity probed, absorbing heartache and radiating epiphany.

And when He kissed Anya's eyelids, she knew for one blinding instant what she had once been. The heady scent of mountain groves in moonlight came to her. Her chaotic queenship over the fir nymphs. Pitys, her name. After elusive chase she had turned to fir, felt Pan peel off a low branch and wear it as a chaplet, watched him kneel in supplication at the base of her trunk, suffered blinding white splashes of devotion against her bark, and at long last metamorphosed back and let him prick her to his heart's content. Thus to Pan and his satyr offspring did Pitys's fir nymphs thenceforth behave, eternally open to poking, giving back better than they got and falling upon each other when the males were spent.

God's love made Anya young again, locked that

youth into place. The barbs and burrs of old age softened and fell away. And when His climax came, it was oblivion as sweet as it gets, all-embracing, with a pleasure bearable only because her flesh had become divine.

When Anya's eyes opened, she lay in bed, the hushed light of magic time gilding the lace curtains. A gentle rapping sounded at the front door. A calm lay upon her, and a sadness. Her dream had evaporated—something about God and fir trees and copulation, something about how life had been for them in earlier times.

No matter.

Dreams were that way: elusive, tantalizing. Anya rose, a spring in her step, and wrapped her bright green robe about her.

She opened the door. "Yes, Fritz?"

He stood on the porch, bent slightly at the waist, hands behind his back, one toe sweeping an arc of shyness across the porch snow. "Um . . . I was wondering . . . that is I was hoping. . . ." Looking up from beneath a mop of red hair, he blushed.

"Come in," she said, opening the door for him, then closing it firmly behind, feeling a whoosh of cold air at her ankles.

Fritz crushed his cap to his breast. "The others, they all drifted away, they don't remember what happened in the woods, they can't understand why everything's in magic time. They look at me standing there in the snow with this bulge in my pants and call me crazy."

Anya shook her head and smiled. "My faithful Fritz," she said, "always so eager to please. It makes me wonder what you were in the other life."

"Other life?"

"No matter. Something I dreamed."

"Oh. Anyway I was wondering if you'd like to go back to the hut and—"

"It's over, Fritz."

"—and you and me, we could . . . what did you say?"

"Things are returning to normal. I'm Santa's wife again and only Santa's."

"Oh, no, don't say that. Please."

"You were there at the beginning, with the others. You saw God resanctify our marriage."

"But doesn't this count for anything?" Fritz took out his penis and held it as though it were a priceless treasure he'd found in his pockets.

Anya contemplated the ruddy column of flesh, its squinty eye, its wrinkled wrap of veins. Men were such children when it came to sex. All of their passion rushed to this hidden finger, the creature they kept in their pants whose primary function seemed to be to turn love into plumbing.

Now here was Fritz in her vestibule, surrounded by wreaths, spare overshoes, a pipe rack, and a dozen other reminders of his beloved master, and all he could think about was his elfin erection. She went to her knees and cupped him in her hands. Moaning, he caressed her face.

"This counts for much," she said tenderly. "These past many days, I've handled lots of these, Fritz, but none so beautiful as yours."

"Yes, yes, ooooooh that's nice."

"But this is what you gave up to be one of Santa's helpers. Surely the sacrifice was worth it."

"Never. Oh, Anya, please?"

Anya looked at the stiff rod she kneaded. Its tip glistened to Fritz's plea, like a lowly petitioner, naked and disarming. "You'll tell no one?"

"Not a soul." His head blurred with shaking.

"I'll drain you so dry, not a memory of any of this will be left in you."

"Fine, fine, just do it. Please." The way he said it, she knew he didn't believe her. The poor dear thought his newfound bliss would go on forever, that he would unseat Santa in her heart.

Anya bent then to the task of obliterating Fritz's memory, giving free license to her mouth to bob and weave as it would. But her thoughts were elsewhere. She scarcely gave ear to the increased volume and urgency of his groans, barely tasted the mucoid surge of his seed. She gave but passing notice to the confused look on Fritz's face as she buttoned him up, showed him the door, and waved the entire North Pole back into normal time.

Steadying herself at the porch railing, she watched Fritz stroll across the commons while elves here and there began to wink in and out. She wondered what her husband was doing at this very moment—and what would happen between them when he returned.

"Well."

"Well?"

"Well, it's over."

"Oh, fuck you, Santa. And fuck your precious Anya too. You're telling me you're never going to want to kiss these nipples, never feel the tickle of my breath on your balls, never again sail your longboat into the saline port of my sex?"

Santa gulped hard. Moonlight accentuated her lithe, lean, perfectly proportioned body. Spent as he was, the demon of desire raced about Santa's heart whenever his senses drank her in. He began once more to doubt his resolve.

"No reflection on you. It's just that I've got to get my life in order, and lust pure and simple is one emotion I've resolved never to act on again."

She seized him. "You see this meat? It's mine. I own it. In twenty years my tongue has given more life to this thing than Anya's whole body in the centuries you've known her. Admit it. See? It's stiffening up again. It knows what's best for it better than you do."

Santa removed her hand. "No more. We're finished." There, it was out, and it felt good. "You have to leave now. There's work to do."

At that, she swirled into a rage, hovering above the bed. "You dare deny me, fat boy? You'll pay for that. Next time you want me—and fuck the Christ child in the manger if it won't be before the year is out—I'm going to make you squirm and beg on your chubby little knees. I'm going to roll back the lips of my cunt like a baboon's mouth and turn my womb inside out right in your jolly old face, and all you'll be allowed to do with my glistening pink flesh is watch it, itching with all your heart and soul to touch it and stroke it and lick it and fuck it. You hear me, fat boy?"

Santa, softly: "If you want your panties back, look in my left pants pocket."

The Tooth Fairy's renewed display of fury took Santa's breath away. She spun in the air like a cat chasing its tail, giving a banshee wail. The enraged fairy whipped up storms of immortal anger, earsplitting peals of thunder, and clouds dark beyond ominous, from which forked lightning split apart Santa's skin and fried his innards. Then she was gone. Abrupt calm fell and Santa healed at once, though his body still tingled and thrilled at her outpouring of rage.

He pictured Anya, knitting and rocking by the sewing room window, and prayed to God it wasn't too late to save his marriage.

Santa looked down at Wendy, tiny fists poking out of the nightgown to either side of her body. "God keep you and all children from such furies," he said, bending to kiss her cheek. The sleeping child made him think of Rachel lying in this same bed twenty years before. And now Rachel had a darling girl of her own. Now she played at being mommy, asleep upstairs in her parents' bedroom.

On a whim, Santa gathered his clothes, tucked them under his arm, and headed upstairs. Rachel would provide closure. His affair would end with one loving glimpse at the girl who had been there beside them at the beginning.

From the door the sight of her, alone in the double bed, made her seem smaller than she was.

Santa entered her bedroom, taking in the nightstands of dark laminate, a matching dresser, a blond wood desk used as a catch-all for bills and stationery. Then he gazed again at Rachel asleep in the bed.

She was stunning in her loveliness.

Santa sat beside her, staring down in awe at the simple summation of humanity in her face.

"Dear, dear Rachel," said Santa. "How lovely you've grown since your first Christmas in this house."

And, God help him, Rachel's large hazel eyes opened just wide enough for Santa to fall into them.

# Chapter Nine

## Rachel All Grown Up

Santa was so astonished at seeing a mortal—let alone this mortal—open her eyes, that he quite forgot to snatch back the stray bit of magic time that had seeped out to claim her. Whether that straying occurred because Santa grew careless or because the events of Christmas twenty years before had opened Rachel to magic time, as the seconds ticked by and Santa ignored God's injunction to maintain the barrier that hid him from mortal eyes, any justification for vanishing from her sight grew less and less compelling.

It was the look she gave him.

A look that silenced his intruder, laid him in a box, and buried him deeper than profundity itself. New love, God help him, flowered among the blossoms of his love for Anya—a flora that complemented that love, not the choking riot of weeds his lust for the Tooth Fairy had given rise to.

The air in Rachel's bedroom seemed as heady as pure oxygen. He breathed it, and so did she. She looked radiant against the pastel columbines of her pillow. In the midst of panic at these new freshets of feeling, Santa's heart basked in a glow of peace.

"Santa Claus?" said Rachel. Part of her wanted to scream in terror, but the rest of her was remembering the details of Christmas Eve twenty years before as she took in the roly-poly phantasm sitting there naked, beaming down at her.

He gave a perfect nod and opened his perfect mouth. "Yes, Rachel," came his words, and their purity speared through her like sunlight.

"Jesus!" she gasped. "Turn down the gain!" She tried to sit up but it was difficult. Her skin tingled beneath her nightgown as though she had become one great heatlamp filament. Her womanflesh swelled and fretted, and a series of soothing orgasms giggled inside her like champagne bubbles.

"What's wrong?" said Santa. His caring voice set off a new round of climaxes, continuous as wavelets lapping at a shore.

"Not a thing," Rachel laughed, holding out her hands to deflect him. "It's just that you're a bit . . . overwhelming."

Santa touched his chest. He looked down at himself. "Oh dear, I'd better put something on."

"Don't," she said, touching his thigh with one hand, then snatching it back as though stung. His words she had begun to adjust to. But touching him had slipped her at once into a cauldron of climaxes. Had it not been so shudderingly delicious, the rush of them would have been painful. "You look fine the way you are."

"Are you sure you're all right?"

"Oh yes," she said, the sweat of delirium at every pore. She laughed. "Now I know how Leda felt."

Santa Claus looked away and repeated the name, trying to place it.

"Yes, Zeus came to earth as a swan and . . . and he slept with Leda, who gave birth to Helen of Troy."

"Oh, please don't think—"

"Of course not, I—"

"You're a beautiful woman, but—"

"It's just that you make me feel . . ."

"I make you feel how?"

"Well, very physical. You take some getting used to.

Everything you do feels like a caress." God, was she out of line? She lowered her eyes, though not looking at him was a torture. "An intimate caress."

"Really?" Santa seemed at a loss. "It's not too unpleasant, I hope?"

"Oh, no. Not at all."

"You see there's a reason, not one I'm very proud of, for my state of undress."

"You don't have to explain."

"I'd like to anyway. I need to tell someone." A moment's hesitation. "I want to tell *you*, Rachel."

And he did.

Reluctantly at first, fearing she would fault him for his adultery. Then, once he had gotten over the hump of telling her about his wife (her smile dimmed at that), he plowed straight ahead, relating more than he intended to about his sins these past twenty years, about the not-Santa that had plagued him and the lust that had tainted his giving.

Rachel was the perfect listener, condemning him for nothing, accepting him completely and returning unconditional love—in her encouraging nods, in the softness of her questions, in every gesture of head and hand. The impact of her presence amazed him. He wondered if an encounter with any mortal woman might tend the same way. Then he understood that Rachel was indeed special: free of guile, open, caring, lovely in her bones.

"Did Wendy see you with the Tooth Fairy?" Rachel's face registered alarm.

"Of course not," Santa assured her. "We kept the magic time strictly to ourselves, just as we did with you twenty years ago."

Rachel smirked. "I saw everything then."

"You didn't!"

She nodded. "Of course I had a child's understanding of what went on. And no recollection of it afterward, none. But now, I see it again as clear as can be." And she proved it, giving an exhaustive blow-by-blow of what she had witnessed as a child.

Santa felt odd listening to her. It was as if her account sanctified the lustful acts he had performed with the Tooth Fairy, honeyed over their vileness, and recreated them as acts of love. Beneath the clothing bunched upon his lap, there burgeoned an erection, and it felt good and pure and brimming with righteousness. When she was done, he said, "You were awake all right, though I don't understand how that could have happened. All I can say is that I think Wendy remained in normal time. You could always ask her in the morning."

Rachel chuckled and shook her head. "Unless she brings it up, I'll just let it slide. It didn't do *me* any harm."

"You're sure about that?"

Rachel shrugged. The way she did it made Santa break into laughter.

"Ooh, I like the way you laugh," said Rachel.

"It's my stock-in-trade," he replied, chuckling again at his own joke.

She had propped her pillows up and was leaning against the headboard, knees bent before her. Now she smiled at him and a sigh escaped her lips. A hand picked absently at the buttons that held her nightgown closed. Santa's flesh stirred again in his lap. Hackles rose at the back of his neck.

"Well, I suppose I ought to be going."

Her smile never faltered. She continued to toy with her buttons as if she hadn't heard him. When the top one popped open, her hand drifted lazily to the next.

God in heaven, thought Santa, this will never do. He had enough explaining ahead of him as it was. "Maybe next Christmas we can talk again."

Another button gave way.

"I want you, Santa," she said, "and I don't. Stop me if you like. I'll understand. But I feel so much love for you. And from you. This seems right as can be. I know I should be thinking about Anya, but the rules seem so pointless with you here. And me here."

Santa saw the smoky gleam in Rachel's eye, her moist tongue moving in her mouth, a moonlit V of skin at her sternum, her breasts straining at cloth, a tantalizing hint of nipple beneath.

Her fingers moved lower, ever working.

Rachel was in love. She had known mortal love, the hurt, the longing, the fulfillment. She had known puppy love, adolescent gropings, a full range of relationships.

And with Frank she had known the mingled joys of marital love. But everything paled beside Santa Claus. Santa beguiled, provoked, warmed her and completed her.

Had she stopped to reflect, her seductive ways would have seemed uncharacteristic. But with Santa before her, reflection was pointless. And so, her hands moved to free her breasts, fingers dallying there to entice this elf-man who had so swiftly captured her heart. "Help me undo this button?"

"Really we shouldn't."

"Put your hand here. Please."

"But, Rachel. What will I tell my wife?"

"I am your wife and you are my husband," she said, seeing clearly how things stood between them. "Tell your wife you love her. Do it right now. And do it again when you return to the North Pole."

He started to speak, then smiled and leaned toward her. When his fingers touched her throat and gilded along the open flaps of her nightgown to finish the unbuttoning, Rachel closed her eyes and shuddered.

Like a sunbather watching her eyelids redden and feeling upon her skin the wholesome heatlight of a cloud-emergent sun, so Rachel felt Saint Nicholas's face draw nearer. When she opened her eyes, his heavenly visage filled her sight. He was all there for her. There were no dark corners or ulterior motives as there always were with even the best of mortal men.

"I love you, Rachel," he said.

She gave a slight cry at that and gasped out that she

loved him too. His hand slid beneath the cloth and found her left breast. Her nipple grew hard and urgent beneath his fingers. She cupped the back of his neck and drew his lips down to hers.

It amazed her—the part of her mind that had room for amazement—that when she thought she had reached the height of sensuality, another plateau waited just above. Their kiss made her body surge up and explode anew. Yet every moment they prolonged it, the last explosion was but prologue to the next. Santa guided her through a land of ever-renewing orgasms, each more wondrous than the one before.

He tossed back the covers. His hands flew up the sides of her body and the nightgown vanished. Then he laid her down and she eased her legs open. Even with Frank, there had always been a residue of fear in that vulnerable position. But Santa was as gentle and all-caressing as a warm breeze, as loving as sunlight itself. Rachel opened everywhere, a flower heavy with dew.

He touched her first with his hands, those great expressive hands that gave without stint and gilded her every pore and orifice with the smooth and supple surety of a craftsman's love. Then he wrapped his hand about the barrel of his loveshaft and touched its hot moist tip to her, beginning at her toes and traveling by degrees up her supine body, lingering at her nipples, warming her neck with its radiant warmth, caressing her cheeks and chin and forehead, and at last brushing it to and fro over her mouth until its heady taste and aroma made her lips fall open around it. He lingered there to please her, stiff and undemanding; and when her jaws ached with the giving and she was ready to move on to new pleasures, he withdrew and brought his tongue into play. The gossamer of his beard acted as thrilling harbinger to his tongue, which darted down and licked her as if he painted her in healing and immortality. And when all of her had been licked clean of the mundane save her vulva, Santa swooped down upon it and made a divine meal of that drenched pouch of flesh, tonguing the folds of her labia and licking like life itself at her clitoris. Wave upon wave of divine love rolled through her until at last her hands insisted him up and around and he was inside her with his hot stiff goodness and she could taste herself on his lips and his heavenly flesh quite covered hers and they rocked and rolled and bucked and heaved their way into the shared joys of concupiscent release.

"Rachel, darling, you're so lovely," Santa said, lying beside her, unwilling to lift his hands from the evanescence of her skin. So delicate, so smooth. Hard to believe he and Anya had been like this once, possessed of a heart that must one day stop, lungs whose allotment of breath was recorded in God's logbook.

She touched his cheek. "You're crying."

He pressed a knuckle to his eyes and wiped his vision clear. "It's because you make me so happy," he said.

"Ohhh," she said. Moving full against him, she

rested her arm along his back and snuggled her nose into his beard.

With one finger, he traced a line along the daring curve of her hip. He knew one thing only. He wanted the nightscape of that hip beside him in his bed always; not just here and intermittently, but back home in his cottage every night of every year for all eternity. He wanted to bend down and tongue the elemental epicenter of her lower depths whenever the urge took him after a long day in the workshop with his colleagues, a look-in at his reindeer, and a fine dinner prepared by Anya.

Yes. Anya. That was the sticking point. He loved her no less than before. He loved her fully and deeply, with all the love and affection a husband ought to feel for his helpmate. But he loved Rachel now as well, and he loved her just as much as Anya, though Rachel's uniqueness called forth that love in a different way, as the twist of a kaleidoscope tumbles the same bits of colored glass into new patterns of brilliance.

He despaired of Anya's ever understanding that, she whose reaction to his affair with the Tooth Fairy had been so unreasonable. But this love was different. The Tooth Fairy had been the antithesis of Anya. She drove all thought of Anya out of his mind, and when he did think of Anya, it was in a resentful way. But Rachel, lying warm in his arms and redolent of sex, paradoxically sanctified and made stronger his love for his wife. They were, these two women, multifaceted gems which juxtaposed reflect one another's beauty and so become more beautiful themselves.

"Rachel." He had to chance it.

"Mmm?" She toyed with the curls at his ears.

"I want you and Wendy to come live with me at the North Pole."

*Good lord, what are you doing?*

*I'm asking the woman I love to live with me, that's what I'm doing. Any complaints?*

*Can't think of a one, except her name be Anya.*

Yes. Anya. A formidable bridge to cross. But this felt right to him, just as Rachel had said it felt right to her. She was his wife indeed and he would not live without her. This time, he would be totally above board. And Anya would simply have to come around to his way of thinking.

A stiffening of Rachel's spine, an intake of breath, a still finger encurled. Then she pulled back to look him square on. "You're not serious."

"Never more."

A thousand thoughts raced through Rachel's mind. To give up her home, her job, all her friends was out of the question. She had no winter clothes. She hated cold weather with a passion. What of Wendy's school, the car payments and the mortgage, all the things she owned and loved? Then there was the question of Santa's wife. The image of a wronged woman clutching a carving knife loomed before her, red-eyed hordes of faithful elves glaring out from behind the woman's skirts at Rachel and a terrified Wendy.

"Does your silence mean yes?"

She rested her head upon her hand. "I need . . . it's not an easy decision, you know . . . I need some time to think." She laughed. "God, I can't believe I said that. Santa Claus invites me to the North Pole and my mind spins off into fear, uncertainty, and doubt. But what about Anya? How will she react to this?"

Santa lowered his eyelids in thought, then looked up at her. "I don't know. There could be some difficulty at first. But I think, once she meets you and has a chance to adjust to the idea, everything may work out fine. We can hope so, anyway."

Rachel read serious doubt on his face. She let her eyes laze and glide over the fantastic fat man in her bed, knowing from the sheer corporeality of his flesh that she wasn't dreaming. *Or if I am*, she prayed, *let me never wake*. Her senses, gently orgasmic still at the look and feel and sound and smell and taste of Santa, trumpeted like red brass their Yes and Yes and Three Times Yes I Will. But there were other considerations: the thousands of annoying encumbrances that went with modern life, the call of her profession, the ties of friendship reluctantly broken; but over all, there loomed the face of Wendy, whose love sustained her like no other love she had known and whose welfare was her chief concern. This was not a decision Rachel could in good conscience make on her own.

"You're beautiful when you ponder." Santa softly

chuckled. His hand moved on her arm as he bent his great white head to kiss her shoulder. His soft beard brushed her left breast. Inside, the light of passion brightened by a lumen or two.

Touching a hand to his neck, she said, "I'm already taking next week off from work, and Wendy has no school until January third. Could we try it for a week? See how it goes? Subject, of course, to Wendy's approval."

He kissed her throat, her cheek, her lips, which opened to welcome his tongue. She curved a hand along Santa's rotundity, knuckling the riotous curls of his private hair and taking in hand the thick rod of his love. Caressing it, she broke their kiss and pulled back to murmur her question once more. "Just for a week?"

Santa's fingers nippled her left breast. "I think," he said, "that a one-week trial period is a great idea."

She sensed that his thoughts were more complex than his words, but for the moment none of that mattered. There were rising urgencies in both of them that called for their immediate attention.

And attend to them they did.

Perched not at all precariously on the second-story ledge outside Rachel's window, the Easter Bunny drooled invisible drool down the windowpane. Below on a modest patch of front lawn, Santa's reindeer stood stolidly in the Sacramento night, snorting and stamping on the grass, eager to resume their night-journey. He wondered what Lucifer and his antlered friends would think if they could witness their beloved master in action, betraying Mrs. Claus first with the Tooth Fairy in the bed of an innocent child and now upstairs with the child's mother. Hours of magic time the jolly old bastard had spent in this house, a juicy two or three with the Tooth Fairy, twice that much with Rachel McGinnis. If his count was correct, Santa had climaxed three times with the immortal, seven so far with the mortal woman, and the rutting swine showed no signs of letting up.

The Easter Bunny's pride still smarted from Anya's rebuff two weeks before. He had opened her eyes and she had treated him like slime, not even offering a word of thanks. He'd gone back to his burrow and stared at the walls, feeling emptier and emptier, eaten up with envy at the thought of Santa enjoying two lovers while he bore his lonely lot with the likes of Petunia.

Now Santa had added a third woman to his stable of lovers. He appraised her, as much of her as he could see beneath Santa's fat frame. A compact little slip of a thing, tawny and lithe and fully into the rhythm of the hump. This Rachel wasn't some passive Petunia suffering fleshly intrusion. She welcomed Santa into her body as if she needed him for completion. Her hands roved freely.

He liked that in a woman.

He liked it very much.

A dangerous confluence of concupiscence and anger swept his thoughts in bizarre directions. And out of those swiftly flowing waters surfaced an idea, fully formed, that bobbed and held and rode the thudding rapids through the black night. The idea caught hold of him, thrilled his heart, made him turn unthinkably away from the sacred acts of copulation unfolding before his eyes and hie himself westward out of Sacramento, moving swift as darkness out over the ocean.

# Chapter Ten

## Invitations Accepted

Needling his way in and out of an immense gloom-gray blanket of cloudcover, the Easter Bunny strained to pick out the tiny island from the vast wash of ocean. It had to be close by. There was no mistaking the ill winds weaving fiercely for miles now, nor the blind rage that shot through those winds, a rage whose precise counterpart he had seen spill out of Wendy's bedroom when the Tooth Fairy reared up and blasted Santa Claus above the child's bed. Banking low out of the clouds, he saw, no more than a mile ahead, the unmistakable sliver of land rising like a rude welt on the bare buttocks of the ocean.

She squatted upon the sand at the island's northern extremity. Near her hunched a cedar tree. Tattered strands of seaweed hung from the twists of its limbs; broken seashells lay like shattered bone about its base.

At its top he saw the torn half of a starfish, as blue and lifeless as the hand of a dead Morlock. The Tooth Fairy's elbows locked her knees rigidly together. Her arms shot straight out, ending in tight claws turned up to the sky. Her eyes, shooting dread far out to sea, burned into a wall of gray that seemed continually to be thudding down upon the horizon.

With caution and cowardice, the Easter Bunny touched paw to sand fifty yards off and hopped closer on a zigzag, pretending to sniff curiously at the stiff dune plants, at driftwood, at strewn clumps of seaweed which marked the limits of the last tide. Her stillness spooked him. Were it not for the nearly imperceptible rise and fall of her necklace of teeth and the dreadful in-out-in-out of her belly, he might have thought her transfixed into statuary.

But despite her apparent calm, there was something unsettling about this ravishing creature's vital signs. Being near her had set up resonances in him, echoes from some dim time, the time before God made him the Easter Bunny, the old time when he had been more in control of his life, and perhaps of the universe itself. His brain hummed dangerously. He suddenly wished himself safe and snug in his burrow with Petunia, whose passivity covered not some smoldering fireball of fury but more passivity, passivity pure and simple.

His heart nearly gave out when she turned her head and demanded: "What do *you* want?" Leaping straight up, he collapsed into a heap of confusion and cowered in the sand, emitting a faint high-pitched squeal like a cornered piglet. She watched him with cobra eyes, waiting for an answer.

Swallowing his fear, the Easter Bunny hopped closer and sat back on his haunches. "I watch at windows," he began. "I watch acts of copulation. It excites me." He fell silent, though his jaws twitched, wanting to go on.

"Is there a point to this?"

He shut his eyes for a moment and forced his neck to bend forward. When he opened them, he was looking at the animal perfection of her midriff, tight and smooth-haired and kissable where it disappeared behind a muscled arc of upper thigh. "I watched you tonight with Santa Claus. After you—"

"You did?" Rising inflection and a razor-thin edge to her voice.

"Well," he said, losing air, "yes I suppose I did. It's harmless really. Just something I do. At windows. But when you—"

"And did you like what you saw?"

"When you left, he—"

"Answer me, you little shit!"

His glance shot to her eyes, then darted off. Why had he come? Things were always easier in the planning. Reality always tumbled out whichever way it liked, wild and out of control. He swallowed with difficulty. "Yes, I did. I liked what I saw, very much. But I don't think *you're* going to—"

"What in particular did you like?" He was sure she

had not yet blinked. Her eyebeams bored like lasers through his left cheek.

"Well uh, I guess when, when you uh, crouched over his face and, you know, moved your hips real slow so he could see your, your fairyhood all wet and swollen, and you fingered yourself until your juices gathered and grew into shiny droplets and splashed onto his beard. That was, that was really"—(*Good God, stay on track!*)—"but as I was saying, after you left, Santa went—"

Her voice cut in like acid. "And what specifically did you like about that?"

"Well . . . you know."

"I'd like you to tell me."

"It's obvious."

"Not to me it isn't."

Some hot hard thing spread upon his mind, twisting his words: "Well uh, I don't know, the glisten, the slickness, the openness of it, it's hard to say, maybe it's seeing it move and shift, knowing he's watching it and taking the abrupt fall of your fluid on his lips and running his tongue over them and reaching out for you and pulling you down onto his mouth, feasting on all those gathering juices, maybe that's it; but—(*Duck out from under!*)—Santa went upstairs and spent twice as much time in bed with Rachel McGinnis—"

"You—"

"—and he told her he loves her and wants her to come live with him at the North Pole." He rode the last tumble of words out over her, pitching them louder and faster and feeling feverish and tight-chested beneath the oppressive cloudcover.

Pure stun beside him.

He became aware of the waves schussing at the shore, at the shore, the shore, shore. Overhead a seagull flew, high and white. The sand felt cold and gritty beneath his haunches.

He took a deep calming breath.

When at last she spoke, her voice was low and flat, but full of points and edges. "Tell me everything they did and said, Mister Rabbit. All of it, right down to the last detail."

And that's what he did. He chattered every bit of it out before her like a pagan worshiper laying the fruits of his labor at the feet of an idol. He not only reported every word and deed, but also volunteered precise contrasts between Santa's interaction with her downstairs and with Rachel upstairs. He scattered before her there on the beach the exact words of love Santa had murmured to the mortal woman. These he lingered over like a jeweler contemplating a velvet of diamonds, then set beside them the dead sheen and roughcut facets of Santa's endearments to *her*. Upstairs, he told her, every thrust, every caress, every lick, clip, and cuddle carried special meaning, special caring. Downstairs, all was, by his account, an impressive display of divine animality, a slickening into sweat, a desperate feasting on body parts—a feasting with its own sensual integrity, to be sure, but one which paled beside identical acts done out of the love Santa had come quickly to share with Rachel McGinnis.

As he spoke, the Easter Bunny's eyes grew bold. They drifted over the Tooth Fairy's flawless body, settling in to linger upon cheek or chin, nape or nipple, thigh or cunt or rump-lovely buttock. She was daunting in her ways, this fairy woman. But he wanted her more than he had ever wanted anything. His verbal recounting of her intercourse with Santa brought back into his groin all the passion that had typhooned out of Wendy's bed and washed over him as he watched them. His erection now rose thick and red, right out in front of the Tooth Fairy. He felt no need to conceal it.

"The longer I watched, the more indignant I grew on your behalf," he said. "So when they'd got in their last licks at one another and said goodbye, I took to the sky and crossed the ocean to inform you of Santa's perfidy, knowing that vengeance might interest you, and, if I may be frank, hoping that your sense of gratitude would allow you to . . . to see your way clear to . . . well to—"

But before he could weasel out his oily proposition, his innards began to rumble and pound like thunder. He glanced over in alarm at the Tooth Fairy, who remained in her impassive squat on the strand, staring out to sea. A fist of fury seized on his guts, twisted there with an anger not his own, and splayed open its fingers. He quickly yielded to it, letting it own him and move him, feeling it entwine so with his lust for the Tooth Fairy that it turned into a monstrous meld of emotions, which stood his fur up with rage and sexual need.

"Vengeance?" she said. "The world of men and elves does not yet understand the meaning of the word. But I understand it. And I can see you do too."

"Yes, yes I do. Now please—"

"We feel it in our bones, don't we, you and I?"

"I'm possessed by it, oh believe me I am. But I also need to, to possess, to be possessed by you. Look at the state I'm in and pity me." His head throbbed. His brain felt near to bursting with desire. It didn't help matters to touch a paw to his erection; that felt like the closing of yet another high-voltage circuit in his body.

The Tooth Fairy fell to her knees, her back arched as if to bay at the moon. Her breasts were magnificently pendent. Her fingers dug deep into the sand like gnarled tree roots. At his words, she glanced his way: first a flash of contempt, then a longer look at his privates, a mix of bemusement and loathing and curiosity and some perverse form of reverence. "You want me to give this prick," she reached out and wrapped a rough hand around it, "what it so richly deserves?"

Colors deepened at her touch. Sounds too. "Oh God, yes, anything you say. Please, make me your slave."

"On your back, bunny." She pushed him down onto the sand, leaping upon him like some savage panther and skewering herself on his stiffness. She was dry and harsh there, coarse sandpaper against his tender dick-skin.

"Wait, oh Christ, that hurts," he yelped, tearing her

thighs to ribbons with his back claws. Splashes of blood spattered the sand behind her.

"Shut the fuck up!" A backhand seared across his face. Never letting up on the bone-dry coitus below, she thrust her hands into his mouth and wrenched his jaw open, straining his facial muscles to their limit. He gave a series of high-pitched squeals and opened deep wounds in her flesh with front claws and back, lacerating her breasts and buttocks until they streamed with gore. But his attacks only turned her on. Her face fisted smack into his mouth and she bit into his huge front teeth, punching through the enamel to the pulp and wrenching at them like a dog worrying a rag, until at last their roots could hold no longer and they broke free of their sockets, drawing fountains of blood after them. She grabbed his front paws and pressed them down into the sand, munching, cheeks full, glaring at him and flaying his dick with her dry tight vagina. Bunny blood embittered his mouth. His jaw muscles throbbed in agony, but shoots of tooth grew back where she had taken her bloody harvest. Down below, sprung sperm coiled up like whomps of flame through his erection, defining it in his mind as one raging column of torment. Every spasm opened a raw wound. Each wrenching spurt dug another barbed hook into his balls. And then she was off him. Blessed healing visited him as he reeled there and her anus opened and dropped gold-foiled coins of chocolate onto the blood-stained beach.

"Did you enjoy that, Mister Rabbit?"

"No, I mean yes, that is I . . ." He was overwhelmed and tingling everywhere.

"Now listen," she said, gripping his testicles and squeezing hard, "I don't give a shit whether you enjoyed it or not, but you'd better get used to it because that's going to be what it's like as long as we work together. And we are going to work together, you and me, aren't we?"

"Yes, ma'am," he gasped. His claws unsheathed into the sand. He hurt everywhere. But by God the pain proved he existed, and my how she thrilled his senses even as she drove them beyond their limits. No, he would gladly give up a ba-zillion nights with Petunia for one eviscerating evening with the Tooth Fairy.

"Be my eyes and ears, bunny rabbit," she said. "I give the fat elf one year to wise up and reclaim my love. I want to know his every move, what he says and where he goes, who he shares his bed with. I want to know every eyeblink, every wink, every sigh. You'll do that for me, won't you? You'll spy on Santa Claus for me?"

Slowly nodding, his eyes wide with pain: "Whatever pleases you." One raised paw. "But what if he doesn't want you back?"

"Why then, my friend," she said, twisting his balls until he beat the sand with his back feet and screamed for mercy, "you and I are going to hurt the fat little bastard like he's never been hurt before."

* * *

Rachel hugged Santa tight, not wanting to let him go, but understanding that she had to share him with the rest of the world. "I'm going to miss you."

"You won't wake Wendy until I return?" he said.

"No," she agreed.

Santa told her he'd be thinking about her everywhere he went. Over and over he said he loved her. She echoed his words. The glow of his presence remained with Rachel long after he withdrew the magic time from her and vanished like pixie dust into the night. But depression also claimed her. The bedroom seemed empty without him, as if the sun had blinked out and plunged the earth into unending pitch. It took a middle-of-the-night walk downstairs and a silent vigil at her daughter's bedside to restore her spirits.

As for Santa, his rounds that night took on renewed meaning. These sweet children of earth, as dear as they'd been to him before, seemed more precious than ever. His and Anya's mortal lives lay so far back in the past that humanity had come to seem almost a race apart. Rachel had reestablished a lost link.

Having reached one last time into his pack and set the last gift beneath the last Christmas tree of the night, Santa bounded off the front porch of the Hansen household on Maisonneuve in Montreal, leaped to his sleigh, took up the reins, and shouted, "No Tooth Fairy's island this year, my patient steeds! One last stop to pick up a dear friend and her daughter, and then we're homeward bound!"

At this, the team sprang into the sky with unflagging

zest, galloping through miles of winter to set down once more on the lawn of the old Victorian on K Street. Santa wrapped Rachel round with magic time and roused her from sleep with a kiss. She embraced him, and when they broke their kiss, she sighed and said, "If it was a dream, I guess I'm at it again."

"No dream, dear Rachel. I'm here, my sleigh awaits, and all that remains is to obtain Wendy's consent and hop aboard."

Worry marks crimped her forehead. "Oh, my love, you make it sound so simple. But there's Anya to think about and you know it. Let's not gloss over the problems we're going to face."

"One step at a time," said Santa, soothing with his gentle hand her troubled brow. "Let's live our life together day by day, and let the future unfold as it will. Do you still want to come?"

She pursed her lips, looked down, nodded.

"One week's trial?" he asked.

"Yes. Subject to Wendy's approval."

Memories of the sleeping child came to him as he had last seen her, oblivious in normal time, her light-brown braids framing her face, the flowered, ruffed sleeves of her nightgown lapped over the backs of her hands. A good little girl, he knew; one he would be proud to call daughter, if she'd have him as a father. "Shall we wake her?"

Rachel smiled and said yes.

* * *

Wendy lay deep in dream. It was a warm cozy dream with Mommy and Daddy and Mrs. Fredericks and Wendy's best friends from school all holding hands and staring up in awe at a Christmas tree that climbed like a beanstalk beyond the clouds. Then Mommy's voice spoke from outside the dream (because her dream mommy's lips didn't move). Wendy, she said, Wendy, Wendy; and her voice was soothing and solid, as solid as the ears of a chocolate bunny at Easter.

"Are you awake, dear?"

Wendy groaned and rubbed her eyes in protest against the harsh light spilling in from the hall. Her mother's comforting shape sat beside her, her loving hand along the side of Wendy's face.

"I have a surprise for you."

"Wanna sleep s'more, Mommy," she said through a yawn. Then she remembered it was Christmas and the sleep drained from her like darkness fleeing light. "Has Santa Claus come yet?"

"Yes, honey. That's part of the surprise."

Raising herself, Wendy saw the sharp outline of someone standing behind her mother, someone large like Daddy. For a moment she thought it might *be* her daddy come down from heaven, but this man walked in a different way and pure beams of happiness came rushing into her like fresh breezes from the fat black hole he made in her room. Then he moved closer. Moonlight painted his face and the bright red and white of his outfit, and Wendy was at once scared out of her wits and giddy with excitement. Such joy filled her as he approached that she threw herself without hesitation into his encircling arms. "Santa!" she said. Above her hug, his beard softened against her forehead.

Santa's voice tickled her insides: "I'm delighted to meet you, Wendy."

"Santa has asked us both to the North Pole for a week's visit. I told him that all depended on how you felt about it." It seemed as if her mother was trying to hold back her own glee but not succeeding very well.

"When would we leave?" Wendy asked.

"Right away, dear one," said Santa. "My sleigh is waiting on the front lawn and my reindeer are eager to reach home."

"Goody! Oh, but when will we open presents?" She didn't think she could stand waiting a whole week until they got back, no matter how wonderful their visit to the North Pole was. The whole time, she would picture the packages waiting under the tree, aching to lay her hands on them and tear off the wrappings.

"Well," her mother began tentatively, "we could—"

"We'll take them with us," said Santa, laughing. "My pack is empty. There's plenty of room for gifts."

Wendy's tongue knocked against the blank space in her front teeth. "Oh, I nearly forgot." Breaking free of Santa's arms, she pressed her pillow against the headboard. Five dark discs swam up out of the dim gray sheets. Wendy closed a fist around them. "Look, Mommy, the Tooth Fairy was here too!"

"Yes, she was." There was something odd in her mother's voice.

Santa crossed through the moonlight to her shelves and returned with Mister Piggy. "Better bank those dimes, young lady." She dropped them in carefully, hearing the clatter of metal against ceramic.

"Well then, Wendy," said Santa, sitting back down and giving her another astounding hug, "shall we be off?"

"I . . . I guess so."

"You guess so?"

"I'm worried about Mrs. Fredericks. Won't she miss us at Christmas dinner? And what about the potholders I made for her at school?" She pictured the floppy package under the tree, wrapped in pale yellow paper that showed kittens clawing balls of yarn.

"Tell you what," said Santa. "While the two of you pack your things, I'll put your gift under her tree and leave her a long letter explaining where you've gone and when to expect you back. Then you can bring her something extra special from the North Pole, how does that sound?"

It sounded fine and Wendy said so, though she still missed Mrs. Fredericks and was sure that Mrs. Fredericks would miss her and Mommy.

The rest of the night was a dream Wendy never wanted to wake from. She bundled into her warmest clothes while her mother packed a bag for her and Santa gathered up the presents. Then it was downstairs into the night-smell of pine needles and out the front door. She laid a wondering mitten on the huge gentle head of each reindeer as Santa introduced them. Then he lifted her into his shiny black sleigh. And when the nine great beasts pounded silently the cold night air, raising the sleigh effortlessly into the sky, Wendy giggled at the flutter in her stomach and held on tight. Cities passed beneath them in miniature and cirrus clouds wisped by, but Wendy felt not the least bit cold. Even when they sleighed into the far north and snowflakes danced upon her cheeks—the first snow she had ever seen—and, further still, the icy wind howled in her ears and thick frost formed on the team's bobbing antlers, even then, Wendy felt nothing but warmth and comfort as she sat beside Santa.

Across frozen tundra they flew. In the distance, poking out of endless ice and snow, Wendy saw tiny points of green which, as they drew nearer, shot up into tall trees that kissed the sky. The sleigh's runners brushed the tops of them, leaving a wake of powdered snow that swirled up into the air and drifted down onto the woods below. Ahead, Wendy saw a clearing with bright angular juttings of red and blue and green—buildings out of which now swarmed, like herds of caribou, tiny green figures who Wendy guessed had to be Santa's helpers. Clearer and clearer they became as the sleigh spiraled slowly downward. They were shouting something, but their voices were swallowed by the raucous jingle of sleighbells.

"That's my workshop, Wendy," said Santa, pointing with a child's pride. "And the blue building next to it? That's the reindeer stable." His voice went weird for a moment, then returned to normal: "And look, there's

Mrs. Claus in front of our cottage. That's where you and your mommy will be staying."

Wendy clung to Santa's arm and nodded happily. On the porch of the bright green cottage stood a white-haired woman waving up at them. She had on a festive red dress frilled in green and yellow. It reminded Wendy of Shirley Temple's dress in *Heidi*.

The clamor of the elves mingled with the *tzing-tzing-tzing* of sleighbells as down they drifted, spiraling clockwise into a counterspiral of little men. Many of them pointed excitedly at her and Mommy. They waved up at her and she waved right back at them. She had a feeling she was going to like the North Pole a whole bunch.

In the master bedroom, Santa marveled at how lovely Anya looked, despite her upset. "Would you mind telling me who these people are and why they're here?"

Anya's fingers lay rigid and cold against his palms. He was robed in red terrycloth, fresh from the shower. Through the walls came the sounds of Wendy and Rachel settling into their quarters: a closet door rumbling along its track, the muffled piping of Wendy's voice rising in question, Rachel's soothing alto answering her.

Santa led Anya to the bed, seated her there, sat beside her.

"First," he said, "you'll be relieved to know I've broken it off with the Tooth Fairy."

"No backsliding?" Her eyes were cool.

"Well, we slept together one last time," he admitted reluctantly, "but I put my foot down at last. She's out of my life for good."

Exasperation sharpened Anya's eyes. She looked away, then suddenly back, like the steel tips of a cat-o'-nine-tails stinging him across the face. Then her eyes grew soft and a smile glimmered on her lips. "It hardly matters," she said quietly. "I took my revenge while you were gone."

"What do you mean?"

"I slept with all of your elves. Many times over. All but Gregor. They've reverted since then for some reason. They don't remember a thing. But I did it and I'm glad I did it and now I just want things back the way they were. Now will you tell me who this McGinnis person is and why she's here?"

Santa had begun to laugh, but his laughter dissolved when he realized Anya was serious. She really *had* opened her loins to his elves. "Well, in the process of breaking up—" he faltered. "You couldn't have. Surely they would have stopped you."

"They didn't and I did. But that's ages ago and all my demons are exorcised," she said dismissively. "Now get off that subject. You can agonize over it later all you want, but right now you're going to tell me about this McGinnis woman."

Air seemed suddenly in short supply. Santa was sure his face had gone pale, even unto his rosy cheeks. "How dare you boss me around?" he muttered, knowing it was a mistake to let his anger show, but not caring.

"What was that?"

"I said how dare you boss me around? And how dare you take advantage of my elves that way?"

"Keep your voice down."

"I won't," he shouted. Then lower: "Yes I will, but for their sake, not yours." He sprang from the bed and paced before her. "All right, it was a mistake to carry on for so long with the Tooth Fairy without your knowing about it and it was a mistake to sleep with her tonight, though you've got to believe me I did try to resist her, I really did. I got to thinking about you out there and how much you mean to me and so I vowed to end it and by God I did end it. It was a relief to rid myself of her and it was . . . it was comforting to picture you waiting by the fire, rocking and knitting and glancing out the window at the elves cavorting on the commons."

"Tell me who she is."

"Instead I discover you stripped yourself naked and fucked the living daylights out of my co-workers. My God, Anya, what did you expect me to do? Nod sagely, give a sly wink, and say, That's nice, dear?" He caught sight of himself in the mirror over Anya's dressing table, pacing back and forth with his huge bear-like feet ankling out of his robe while his wife sat sad and defiant on the bed. "Oh Anya, my precious one, listen to me carry on. So much pain, so much anger. It feels wrong. But all of that we can let go of. We're husband

and wife. We can renew our vows. I love you, after all, and that's all that matters. And you love me, don't you?"

"Tell me who she is, Claus."

He sat beside her once more, feeling frantic and elated and talking much too fast. "Yes, as I was about to say: When the Tooth Fairy stormed off—Lord, she was in a towering rage, you should have seen her!—I went upstairs to look in on Rachel. It was her house you see and she'd been an exceptionally well-behaved child in years gone by. But I guess I got sloppy with my magic time because her eyes opened and she caught me. And she was so . . . so fascinating that I let it continue and got to know her and—now I know you're going to be tempted to take this the wrong way, but please try not to—I fell in love with her. Not that I love you any less, because of course I don't. No, it's just a different kind of love. But anyway the upshot was, I asked her to come live with us at the North Pole and I really think you two will hit it off. We're going to give it a week's trial and then she'll decide whether to stay or not." He paused for breath, feeling like he'd been jabbering for hours. Anya sat next to him, head bent, hands picking at each other on her lap. "I mean it will be a group decision of course, whether she goes or stays. She and little Wendy and . . . and all of us will decide."

"She'll go." Anya spoke with a quiet finality, not looking up. "I'll make it clear to her she's not welcome and she'll go."

Wonderful, thought Santa. Now she's playing the long-suffering wife. "There, you see? You *are* taking it the wrong way," he said, his voice as winning as he could make it. "Look, I know this will take some getting used to, but give it a chance, won't you? At least promise me you'll be on your best behavior when Wendy unwraps her Christmas gifts and takes the grand tour."

She looked up at him, her eyes red and moist. But he guessed it was too hard for her, because she looked away, rested her hand on his shoulder, and stared into the back of it. "Claus, my big little boy," she sighed, "when are you going to grow up? It seems we were once creatures of questionable morality. That much I learned while you were away. But we're the Clauses now and this world depends on our being faithful to each other, on foregoing lust—however lovely the feeling—for the sake of love."

"Anya, it's true I felt lust and nothing but lust for the Tooth Fairy," said Santa. "But what I feel for Rachel is different. It's love I feel, a love as right and good as the love I hold in my heart for you, and the two loves can co-exist, I know they can, if you'll let them."

A tiny knock came at the door and then Wendy's voice called his name.

"Yes, Wendy?"

The handle turned. The little girl's head poked in, brown braids flying. "Hi. We're all unpacked and

Mommy says I should ask you if it's time to open the presents yet."

"Give me five minutes to dress," he said. "You and your mother make yourselves at home by the Christmas tree. We'll be right along."

Wendy agreed excitedly and vanished.

Santa rose from the bed. He pulled a comfortable cambric shirt and a pair of pants from his closet and tossed them over a chair. Long red flannel underwear and two thick red woolen socks joined them out of his dresser drawer. He sighed audibly, unable to look at the silent figure of his wife on the bed. He hung his robe in the closet, pushing his shirts aside so it could dry properly.

Santa paused naked by the chair. One hand rested on the red shirt draped over the chairback. "Are you . . . are you all right?"

"Oh yes," she said slowly, not looking up. "Never better."

"Just try," Santa pleaded, feeling strange in his nakedness but standing there anyway, exposing himself to her, hoping the undeniability of his flesh would turn her around and sweep her along to his conclusion. "Try just a little. That's all I ask. Will you do that for me? Will you give it a try?"

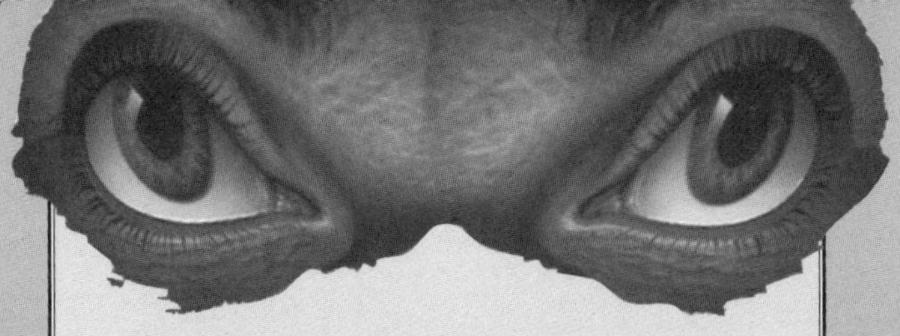

*Experience the Ultimate in Fear Every Other Month... From Leisure Books!*

As a member of the Leisure Horror Book Club, you'll enjoy the best new horror by the best writers in the genre, writers who know how to chill your blood. Upcoming book club releases include First-Time-in-Paperback novels by such acclaimed authors as:

*Douglas Clegg   Ed Gorman*
*John Shirley   Elizabeth Massie*
*J.N. Williamson   Richard Laymon*
*Graham Masterton   Bill Pronzini*
*Mary Ann Mitchell   Tom Piccirilli*
*Barry Hoffman*

**SAVE BETWEEN $3.72 AND $6.72 EACH TIME YOU BUY. THAT'S A SAVINGS OF UP TO NEARLY 40%!**

Every other month Leisure Horror Book Club brings you three terrifying titles from Leisure Books, America's leading publisher of horror fiction. **EACH PACKAGE SAVES YOU MONEY. And you'll never miss a new title.**

# *Part Four*

## *Trying Times*

Even in civilized mankind faint traces of monogamous instinct can be perceived.

—*Bertrand Russell*

Here's to our wives and sweethearts—may they never meet.

—*John Bunny*

So heavy is the chain of wedlock that it needs two to carry it, and sometimes three.

—*Alexandre Dumas*

# *Chapter Eleven*

## *Modus Vivendi*

Fritz had never been happier.

The exchange of gifts between Santa and Mrs. Claus on Christmas morning was traditionally a private affair. But now, on top of the arrival of Wendy and her mother—an event which spun Santa's helpers into a leaping tizzy of joy—Fritz had been one of a handful of elves singled out to join them on this special occasion.

The Christmas tree dominated the living room. It had to be the tallest, greenest, branchiest tree Fritz could recall, riotous with ornaments and icicles, colored lights and unending strings of popcorn.

On the floor to Fritz's right sat Gregor and his brothers, friends again, though the reason they had fallen out in the first place escaped him. Indeed all the elves were somewhat hazy about what had occurred during Anya's magic sway over them. What remained from that time were vague stabs of pleasure and guilt, a sudden waking on the commons, and delight at Mrs. Claus's newfound exuberance.

Upon the couch, somewhat obscured by branches and stepped towers of gift, sat Wilhelm and Siegmund and Karl, specialists in the subtleties of kiln and glaze and brushwork on plateware or piggybank. Their excitement at being in Santa's living room was palpable. Fritz felt it himself, a joy radiating from the pit of his stomach. He needed suddenly to hug somebody, so he latched onto fat Josef, Gregor's younger brother, and squeezed a tight *oomph!* out of him. Then a door clicked open down the hallway and a young girl's high excited whisper filled the air. At once, they shrank back tight and eager-eyed into their best behavior.

Wendy, puffed-sleeved and lovely in white, appeared in the archway. She gazed at them, her wide eyes unsure at first. Then she crinkled into a broad grin, reached back for her mother's hand, and pulled her into the room.

Fritz liked Rachel McGinnis lots. Her face was fresh and open, and there was something bouncy in the way she moved. But now, despite the glee with which she took them in, she seemed to be holding back an essential store of treasure. She dropped into a chair and gave them all a warm smile.

Her daughter homed in on the couch and thrust out her hand—"Hi, I'm Wendy!"—to an astonished Wilhelm. His hand seemed to rise on its own like a seedpuff in the wind, but he sat there, mouth ajar, saying nothing, until Siegmund knuckled him on the shoulder and began the introductions. Then the others on the couch chimed in, followed by Fritz and Josef and Gregor and Englebert sitting on the floor, and suddenly the room was alive with cheery banter.

At first it focused on Wendy. But when Fritz sensed that Rachel was feeling left out, he spoke up: "That's a lovely dress Wendy's wearing, Mrs. McGinnis. Did you make it, by chance?"

"Yes, I did," she said, "last week in fact. Oh and please call me Rachel." Fritz could tell she appreciated his gesture. Her smile generated a warm, baked-bread glow in his heart.

Everyone reached out to finger the cloth and admire the hem-stitches, telling Wendy, who beamed, how fortunate she was to have such a skilled seamstress for a mother. "Yes and she writes very fine computer programs too," Wendy said, and they at once praised Rachel for that talent as well.

Then Santa burst into the room, trailing Mrs. Claus behind him. "Merry Christmas, everybody!" He swooped Wendy up and charged about the room, glad-handing and hugging each elf in turn. Fritz noticed, as Santa descended upon the crowded couch, that Mrs. Claus slipped silently into her rocking chair by the fire.

Her hands clung tight to its arms.

"Fritz, old friend!" Santa's booming voice washed like goodness into his ear, warming him inside and out with the spirit of giving. The jolly old elf's strong red right arm hugged Fritz to the bulge of his belly and to Wendy's thin bony legs where she rode in the crook of his left arm. Hasty kisses to his cheeks, a glimpse into Santa's animated face (but was there something false in that animation?), and Fritz watched him hurry past his wife and deposit Wendy on her mother's lap. Then he sank with a sigh of pleasure into the far end of the couch, lit a long thin white ceramic pipe, and enjoined his elves one by one to retrieve and deliver gifts.

The ensuing orgy of dissemination swept them all into a sweet oblivion of wrappings torn asunder, boxes unlidded, and tissue paper parted; of squeals of delight and unending thank-yous and you're-welcomes; and beneath it all, like the bowel-stirring pedal point of a Bach passacaglia, the hearty boom of Santa's laughter thundered forth. Fritz found most of his deliveries going to Rachel or Wendy—they had, after all, brought their cache of presents with them—but some he held out to Santa, and others to Mrs. Claus, who, while decidedly less old-ladyish in her movements than at past celebrations, looked at him with the fretted eyes of the elderly. But it was hard to focus on Anya for long, what with the level of excitement whirling about the room and the wonder of having actual mortals sitting here in the same room with them.

And when the last gift had added its contribution to the colorful mountain of torn wrappings and ribbons, a sly grin spread across Santa's face. "Dear me," he said, "I nearly forgot the best present of all." Fritz saw the slightest flicker about Santa, the telltale discontinuity of magic time kicking in. Leaning forward, he brought forth from behind his back two mewling kittens, one black and one white. They hugged two or three of his fingers with their front paws and let their back legs splay, claws out, to either side of his wrists.

"Oh, they're so cute," said Wendy. "What are their names?"

"That's up to you, Wendy," replied Santa. "They're yours."

From the look on Wendy's face, Fritz understood for the first time why they were in the business of delighting children. Nothing in his experience could compare to watching Wendy's eyes light up. "This one has got to be Snowball," she said. "And this one I'll call Nightwind."

"Snowball and Nightwind," said Santa, holding the kittens to his rosy cheeks. "Say hello to Wendy." With that, he placed them carefully in her lap and knelt beside Rachel's chair watching the little girl glide her hands in wonder along the fur of their tiny bodies.

When Fritz chanced to look up, Mrs. Claus's rocker, now empty, was rocking back and forth on its own.

A timid knock sounded at Anya's sewing room door. Setting down her knitting, she removed her glasses and wiped her eyes with the back of her hand. Then she put them on again and picked up the knitting needles. "Come in," she called.

It was the little girl, alone, her hand lingering at the brass doorknob. "Can I talk to you for a minute?"

"Of course, my dear. Close the door and come sit

by me." Anya gestured to the footstool with the embroidered reindeer on top. She felt ashamed. Part of her—a small but vile part—wanted to strike Wendy with such violence that her hated mother would keel over and die. The rest of her wanted to take this dear young child to her heart and hold her there forever, tight and warm and loving. It surprised her that there could be any mitigation to her rejection of Santa's latest folly, yet the little girl filled a vacancy in her life she hadn't been aware of.

Wendy sat down. "This is a pretty room."

"Thank you, child."

"My mommy is teaching me to knit."

"That's nice. Do you like knitting?"

"Oh yes," said Wendy. "Um, can I ask you something?" Her voice took on a conspiratorial air.

Anya smiled tightly as her hands danced before her through the clicking of needles and the slow sweatering of yarn. Somehow her bout with the elves—as crazy as it had been in other ways—had instilled new youth in her, right down to her now nimble fingers. More precisely, it had taught her that the illusion of age had been her choice all along. "Yes, my dear," said Anya, "you may ask me anything you like."

Wendy stood beside the rocker, her white dress pressed against its arm. When she put her hand on Anya's shoulder and leaned in, Anya, delighting in her touch, turned an ear to receive the girl's confidence. "Mrs. Claus," Wendy whispered, "why don't you like me?"

Anya pulled back at this, noting the deep runnels of concern on Wendy's forehead. "Where did you ever get such a silly notion?"

"I'm very observant," Wendy said, a trace of pride in among her concern. "Just like Nancy Drew and Miss Marple. I guess it was mostly how you looked up at us when we flew in. The way you hugged me when Santa lifted me down from the sleigh, like your shawl was doing most of the hugging for you. And the way you sat by the fire and watched me. Stuff like that."

Anya felt her temples pounding. She set her knitting down on the basket beside her and patted her lap. "Young lady, be so good as to sit here," she said. And when the child had allowed herself to be lifted up and was nestled comfortably against Anya's bosom: "I want you to listen very carefully to me. Will you do that?"

Wendy said she would.

"Good girl," said Anya, gently rocking and placing her hand upon Wendy's nape. She did not at all like the streak of jealousy that urged her to do violence to this innocent creature. As she told Wendy how she and Santa sat here on top of the world with their hearts full of love for every boy and girl on earth, how they felt like special godparents to them all, the savagery of the green-eyed monster made her throat seize up. But for the child's sake, she narrowed her attention to herself and Wendy, two orphans with no connection to anyone else in the world.

And Anya's core of benevolence triumphed. Her

love touched the child's love and she found herself sobbing and hugging her and kissing her, this frail mortal creature on her lap whose beauty was as the beauty of fresh meadow grass. Once more she welcomed Wendy to the North Pole and this time she meant it. She promised to teach her all the tricks she had learned about knitting and needlepoint and crochet and macrame, and how to coax culinary magic out of grains and vegetables.

"You mean just like my mommy does?"

Anya smiled. "Maybe even better than your mommy does."

Deep in the dark recesses of the workshop, with the smell of manufacture all about and the firm give of foam beneath them, Rachel felt Santa's lips upon her cheek, the thick goodness of his penis nestled like an infant inside her. Her eyes, drifting into the darkness above, could make out only the dim outlines of lighting fixtures and an impression of laddered shelves lofting upward. Cavernous yet comforting this place was, even in the dead of night.

Santa sighed. "That was beautiful," he said. "You couldn't begin to guess how much I've needed you."

Rachel ran her fingers idly through his soft white beard and smiled. "Mr. Claus, you are the most amazing lover I've ever had."

"So glad you enjoyed it, Ms. McGinnis."

Then it was time to be serious with him.

"We need to talk," she said. "About Anya." There.

It was out. She hated being the other woman, particularly when Santa's wife had been so kind and loving to Wendy and was clearly as dear and sweet and attractive in her own way as Santa was in his. There were oblique reminders—in the sway of her hips, in certain vocal inflections and turns of phrase—of Rachel's fling at college with Rhonda Williamson, whom she still remembered fondly. "You and I have been exchanging looks for three days now, hoping things would improve. But they haven't. You know they haven't."

"You're right," Santa admitted. "When she deigns to look my way at all, she gives me that withering stare. It's worse for you, isn't it?"

"Yes. It's like a blast of winter licking at my heart." She laughed. "That sounds a bit melodramatic, but it's the truth. Yet when I'm with you or your elves, everything is wonderful again."

Santa, thoughtful behind the sparkle of his eyes, soothed her brow. "Thank goodness she's not taking it out on Wendy."

"She's the only reason I've held on this long. I've never seen her happier or more continuously excited about anything. She grows wiser and more mature and more beautiful every hour she's up here. But we've really got to go home. Tomorrow."

"Give it time," he pleaded. "I love you so much. Wendy too. I don't want to lose you. You've been my salvation. I haven't thought once about the Tooth Fairy since we met, not a whisper of illicit lust."

His warmth enwrapped her. "You're such a dear

kind soul," she said as though it were a complaint, and hugged him as tight as she could. Suddenly she was sobbing with her whole body, freely like a betrayed child, making the moonlit workshop ring with wailing. Santa kissed her and comforted her and promised he'd talk to Anya first thing in the morning. With his words he assured her, with his kisses, with his caresses, and, down below, with the gentle movement of his manhood, which eased like a mage's healing touch along the troubled walls of Rachel's vagina, soothing and arousing her.

And for a time, Rachel knew nothing but the joyful oblivion of their makeshift bed.

After kissing Rachel goodnight at her bedroom door, Santa stole into his bedroom, doffed his clothing, and slipped beneath the covers. He lay there wide awake for hours, idly listening to the paced breathing of his wife lying as far away from him as she could. Down the hall, he heard the low muffled beat of the grandfather clock he had built eternities ago. It patterned his thoughts, granting them an orderliness they otherwise lacked.

But that sense of order wasn't enough. He felt no optimism about the coming confrontation. While his dear adversary slept and rested, Santa fretted the night away until dawn began to engray the black, gradually wedging under its oppression and easing it aside.

When Anya rose into the pale morning, Santa feigned sleep. His eyes followed her to her closet. She put on a robe over her nightgown, cinched it tight, and headed for the bathroom.

"Anya?" he spoke up.

She stopped. "You're awake."

"We need to talk things over."

She blinked once, then nodded. "Not here. In the woods. I need a shower first." She paused, her face still impassive. "Why don't you join me?"

Before he could stop himself, he said yes. In the past, sharing the shower had usually meant lovely sudsy sex, but there was no such intent in Anya's eyes now, none at all. She smothered his rotundity in suds, lathering him with the rough hands of a mother grim-set against grime. And he let her treat him so, like a little boy guilty of one too many wallows in mud. She stopped soaping at his belly, glanced at his drooping manhood, thrust the bar of soap into his hand, and said, "You can clean that yourself." Then she turned away from him and bathed her breasts with sperm-white, sperm-thick liquid soap, rubbing it into a rich lather, moving handfuls of foam down her belly and working them through the white wonderland he loved to rove in. When he moved to touch her, her eyes warned him to keep away.

Later, he followed her into the forest just beyond the workshop. The snow lay thin there and the evergreens, though full and lofty, grew far enough apart to let in lots of sunlight. When they reached the clearing the elves called the Chapel, Anya half-sat against a long flat outcropping of granite known as the Altar, and said in a voice carefully expunged of emotion, "You have something to say?"

Santa groped for words. "Are you . . . are you still dead set against . . . I mean are you feeling any better about our guests than you did a few days ago?" A rotten way to start, but those damned eyes of hers were locked on him as he paced before her.

"I can't stand the presence of that woman in my home. It makes me ill, knowing what you've done with her and how you claim to feel toward her. It's all I can do to keep from flaying her face with my fingernails."

Her reply seemed measured, as if rehearsed, as if she only half-believed it. "Anya," he said, "as messed up as our lives seem to be at the moment, I know in my heart that bringing Rachel here was the right thing to do. And meeting her seems to have put to rest, finally, the lust that drove me to the Tooth Fairy."

Anya laughed. "There doesn't seem to me a whole hell of a lot of difference between them. Birds of a feather. And both of them have driven a solid wedge between us."

"It doesn't have to be that way."

She looked up archly. "It surely doesn't."

"That's not what I meant. I need Rachel, dammit. And I need you."

"Oh? Whatever for? What could you possibly need me for when you've found yourself a sexy young widow eager to fall at your feet and worship the great Santa Claus?"

"You're being unfair to her. She's a mortal—"

"She's a mortal homewrecker is what she is," Anya broke in, "and far worse than most—she has the gall to ride in, arm in arm, with my philandering husband and peddle her wares right under my nose." The woodland hung dreadfully still around Anya's rising passion. "Don't go talking to me about fairness, Mister Tell-Anya-It's-Over-But-Screw-The-Tooth-Fairy-Anyway."

"Anya, must we dredge that up again?" he pleaded. His wife's arms were tense, right down to the mittened hands poised against the rocktop of the Altar. "Who slept with a thousand elves while I was out on my yearly rounds, picturing my loving wife rocking and knitting by the fire when all the while she had her skirts hoisted, her legs parted, and her womanhood splayed open for the delectation of my helpers?"

"I did, that's who. And I'm glad I did it, not that I had much choice in the matter. It cleared things up for me, or seemed to until you . . . you . . ." Anya broke off, blinking back tears. In that instant, Santa wanted to take her in his arms, kiss her tears away, and assure her of his love by doing precisely what she wanted. But Rachel rose to mind, so perfect, so full of love, and it was impossible.

"So," he said, "we've reached an impasse. I want Rachel and Wendy to stay, to blend in, to become part of our family. You want them to leave."

Then, for the first time, Santa saw the hardness in Anya's eyes soften. "Well," she said, staring down at her boots and thrusting her hands deep into her coat pockets, "I'm quite taken with the little girl. I don't know if I could bear to see her go."

It stunned him. "What are you saying, Anya?"

"That there's room for compromise." She attempted a smile. "A few days ago, I would never have said such a thing. But Wendy's so precious. I love watching her with the elves. I love teaching her things. She brightens my life."

An image came to Santa: Wendy beside Anya in the kitchen, stirring a pale-green bowl of cake batter with a large wooden spoon, Anya steadying the bowl with one hand and resting the other on the little girl's shoulder. They looked wonderful together.

"So it's not hopeless?" he ventured.

Anya glared at him. "Not in the way you mean, you old satyr." Santa had never seen her this touchy about anything. "I will never welcome Wendy's mother into our home, and you and she had better get used to that. That's not about to change. No, if she's not comfortable around me, you'll have to put her up somewhere else."

"Where?"

"That's your problem, not mine. Build her another cottage if you like. You seem fond of new buildings for your paramours. All I know is I plan to avoid her and I hope she'll have the good sense to do likewise."

Santa wondered why he still felt defeated, despite Anya's assent to their staying. "There are bound to be times when you two are together, holiday gatherings, that sort of thing."

"We can work around them. I'll promise not to look daggers at her if you two promise not to make a public spectacle of your affection for each other. Oh God in heaven, listen to me. It makes my throat hurt just to think of it!" She slapped the flat rock silently with her mittened palm and gritted back tears. "And don't expect me to . . . there won't be any relations between us as long as she's here. None."

"Are you sure you'll be able to live with that?" he said, feeling a chill inside.

"The question is, can you live with it?" A pause, then quieter, "I always thought you were such a kind and generous soul. Now you've chosen another woman over me."

"I'm making no such choice," he protested. "I love both of you. Why can't you accept that? No, don't bother snapping back at me. It's obvious you can't. And I guess I've got to honor your feelings and accept you as you are. All right, then. I'll tell Rachel what we've talked about and see what she thinks."

Anya nodded. Her eyes were moist.

"Shall we walk back?" he asked.

"You go," she said. "I want to stay here a while and collect my thoughts."

"All right," said Santa. He raised a hand to touch her sleeve, then thought better of it. White head bent, he turned away and trudged back through the woods. The glare of sun on snow made everything red when he blinked: fallen branches, rocks dusted white, Anya's bootprints pointed off determinedly in the opposite direction from the fresh tracks he now made.

It was a wonderful year for Wendy. Midway through their first week at the North Pole, Rachel, tucking her in, had asked whether she would mind staying longer. Wendy flung her arms around her mother's waist and said she wanted to stay forever, going on and on about the reindeer and the elves and Snowball and Nightwind and Mrs. Claus and dear dear Santa. Her mother seemed both happy and unhappy, but she hugged Wendy and cried tears of joy, and the next morning Wendy woke to find that Santa had built them their own cottage.

Wendy came awake knowing that Santa stood beside the bed looking at her. Nightwind and Snowball raised their heads from the blankets. Santa lifted a finger to his lips and said, "Can you keep a secret?" Wendy nodded and he took her hand and led her to the living room window and pointed across the commons. Santa's workshop made its usual bright red sprint across the snow, but now, beside it, stood the dearest little cottage she had ever seen. She clapped her hands in delight and promptly dubbed it the gingerbread house, and so it was called ever after.

It had a kitchen and a sewing room, just like Santa's cottage, its own Christmas tree in the living room, and the best bedroom a girl could wish for, with plenty of shelves, a workbench for her art projects, a lovely bed that precisely fitted her, and a huge picture window opening out onto the commons. Her mom's bedroom, at the back of the house, had a perfect view of the wooded hills rising from the far side of the workshop. For days, the gingerbread house was the talk of the community. There was a lot of tramping in and out, much elvish gawking and grinning in at windows, and that first night a ceremonial toast shared by Santa and Wendy and her mother and a few dozen lucky elves. But Mrs. Claus did not come, nor did she ever visit the house afterward. Whenever Wendy asked her why, she pretended not to hear, or she changed the subject, or she told her she would surely have to do that some day—and Wendy soon accepted it as how things were.

Wendy's life that year was filled with wonder and instruction. From Mrs. Claus she learned and perfected the arts of handstitching and macrame, tie-dying and stained glass, quilting and needlepoint and cream etching on glass. She became her helper in the kitchen, growing intimate with spices and spatulas and the magic of putting together meals that brought rare smiles to her mother's lips. Most of the time Wendy ate at the dinner table with Santa and her mother, carrying out each course when Mrs. Claus called from the kitchen that it was ready. But sometimes, and more often as the year advanced, she ate with Mrs. Claus at the old oak table in the kitchen, sharing the day's experiences and waiting to see if Mrs. Claus would wink at her and reach into the pantry for some special chocolate treat she had prepared just for them.

Once when a fox darted from behind a tree and

nearly tore poor Nightwind's throat out, the elf who responded to Wendy's cries of alarm chased off the attacker and rushed the broken kitten to Mrs. Claus. She swept Nightwind up into her arms and licked at the bloody flesh and fur until he was whole and purring again. "It's a special talent I have, dear," she said, and Wendy was suitably impressed.

Santa and the elves taught her, more by example than explanation, the intricacies of toymaking. Their simple love and respect for the tools and materials they used were abundantly clear. Every task they put their hand to they carried out with sensual joy, and this approach Wendy learned and applied as diligently as she could to her own tasks.

But what she liked best was to climb up on Santa's lap each evening in the living room of the gingerbread house, feeling on her scalp the warm glow of the lamp beside them and listening to his deep voice thunder forth stories of dragons and kings and monumental quests from a heavy leather-bound book he held open in front of them. And when her eyes grew heavy and the thundering images took on distance, Santa carried her to her bed, tucked her in warm and snug, and touched his lips to her cheek.

Still, from the way the grown-ups acted, her visit to the North Pole did not feel at all like forever. So she was disappointed but not surprised when her mother took her aside a few weeks past Thanksgiving to tell her that they would be leaving after Christmas. Wendy acted as brave as she could, giving her mother gigantic hugs and assuring her that things would be all right (though just once, late at night, she cried her eyes out on her giant teddy bear's shoulder and felt better for it).

"Besides," she added, "Mrs. Fredericks has probably missed us a whole bunch."

"That's my big girl," her mother said, giving her a squeeze. Wendy had smiled back and worried her loose tooth with her tongue.

Despite the happy times, Wendy had noticed her mommy's growing sadness. She had been okay at Easter, standing beside Santa watching Wendy and the elves hunt for eggs in the snowy commons while the cats sniffed curiously at the Easter baskets, batting at bits of grass. But by Independence Day, a chronic anguish lay upon her face. Despite the fireworks Santa set off above a skating pond full of whirling elves, sadness lifted in waves from her mother as they watched from the porch of the elves' dormitory.

Even Santa couldn't lift her mother's spirits when she was sad. Wendy noticed his unusual way of trying, though. She would sometimes waken in the night and hear Santa groaning at the back of the house; then her mother, higher pitched, joined in. When she asked them about it, they smirked at one another and mumbled something about making love, assuring her she would understand when she was older. But it didn't sound much like love to her—she had never heard anything remotely like it when Daddy was alive, and he had certainly loved Mommy. No, Wendy was convinced they were just trying to make the sadness go away by bringing it out in the open and sharing it with each other. But she knew it wasn't working because of the way they kept at it and the way the groans never seemed to ease up; they were, if anything, louder and more insistent. By the time autumn came, her mother had begun to sob quietly afterward. It made Wendy sob too and feel cold inside her skin, despite the thick blankets that covered her.

So she accepted Rachel's announcement with all the stoicism of a maturing seven-year-old and felt pleased at her mother's relieved look. When Santa came in and hugged them both, Wendy brightened at his promise: he vowed to bring her back to the North Pole for a visit every Christmas thereafter.

She knew better than to ask if her mother would be coming with them.

"Please try to understand," Rachel pleaded. "It's nothing you've said or done." Through the window, she watched her daughter, scarfed and mittened and booted, being pulled on her sled by Fritz and Heinrich from one end of the commons to the other.

"Then why are you leaving?"

"Because I don't want to be your mistress. I want to be your wife."

"But dear one, you *are* my wife."

"You say that, and I know you mean it, and we both know it's true. But as long as I'm a problem for Anya, I don't fit in here the way I want to. She's been fine.

I'm not faulting her. But all she can do is avoid me and expect me to avoid her. Your helpers feel that tension. So do the reindeer. Even my own daughter treats me like the outsider I am."

Santa chuckled bitterly and ran his fingers through her hair. "You're not an outsider, *liebchen*. Or if you are, it's only because you worry yourself into that role."

"The reason's not important," she said, kissing his free hand. "When we're together, just you and me, it's wonderful. But that can't make up for the rest of it."

"Please reconsider." There was pain in his throat. "I need you. You saved me from my own weakness—"

"You did that—"

"No, Rachel, it was you. I could never have stayed away from the Tooth Fairy if I hadn't met you. If you go away, I'm afraid the not-Santa will return and drive me back to Thea's mouth."

"Don't you see, that can have nothing to do with my decision. Fight him if he returns, and triumph over him. But Wendy and I have to go."

Santa held her for a long time without saying a word. Closing her eyes, she let the touch and the smell of him invade her senses.

The first indication she had of Santa's heartache was the sting of a tear, cold and shocking, tumbling down his cheek where their faces touched. Then he began to shake and Rachel opened her eyes to find Santa Claus sobbing in her arms. The sight was heartrending. From the surprise on his face, she doubted that Santa had ever had occasion to cry before.

At her ear: "Shall I . . . visit you at Christmas?" What he was asking was clear.

"No," she choked out. "I couldn't bear it. Take Wendy with you if you like, but let me sleep."

He nodded against her shoulder, then made to pull away.

"No. Come with me," she said. "Wrap us in magic time." And Rachel led Santa, wet-faced, to her bedroom, where—while Wendy and her friends froze in frolic—they made the most dolorous love the world will ever know.

"They're going then?" she said.

"It seems so, yes."

"I'll miss Wendy."

"So will I." He paused. Anya said nothing. She stared into the fire, mindlessly rocking. "At least," he said, "we can look forward to her visit at Christmas."

"Yes, there's that."

"Anya, I'm scared."

"I know you are."

"I'm afraid about what may lie ahead. About our future."

"I am too, Claus."

"We've grown apart, haven't we?"

"There seems far less common ground between us. It's sad."

"I'd like you to hold me."

Nothing. Just the soft steady protest of the rocker.

"Will you hold me, Anya?"

"Not yet. Not now. Give me time. Let it heal."

Anya had triumphed. But as she stood at the counter kneading dough, hands white with flour, she wondered why she felt defeated. Less than a hour before, her husband had lifted off into the sky and his wave had seemed empty, mere ceremony. She punched the dough and pursed her lips, feeling that the world would never be right again.

She no longer blamed Rachel for that. She didn't even blame Santa. A goodness had fled from their lives, and it seemed as though it might just be a symptom of the world's decay, not subject to reversal no matter what they did.

Footsteps sounded in the dining room. A light knock tapped at the doorframe to soften an entrance. Anya turned and saw Rachel.

"Where's Wendy?" Anya asked.

"She went to help Gregor and his brothers freshen up the stables, I think."

Anya turned back to the cutting board. The dough was nearly ready for the rolling-pin.

"What are you doing?" asked Rachel.

"Making gingerbread men with raisin eyes. It's Santa's favorite cookie."

"More of a favorite than Oreos?"

Anya smiled over her shoulder. "Oreos don't even come close. Want to help?"

"Sure." She went to the sink and washed her hands, drying them with an embroidered dishtowel hanging by the refrigerator.

A comfortable truce had grown up between the women since Rachel's decision to go, even though Santa continued to spend his nights in the arms of his mortal lover. Anya was glad she and Rachel were ending things on a positive note. Although she hadn't the least desire to visit the gingerbread house, she had pretty much opened her doors to Rachel, and Rachel now spent most of her daylight hours there. Something about being nearer the heart of things, she had said.

"The cookie cutters are in that bottom drawer there," said Anya, nodding. "Trays are under the stove."

"Right."

While she rolled out the brown dough, Anya gave half an eye to Rachel. Her light blond tresses curved like wraps of sunlight about her face. Her breasts and hips Anya found disarmingly lovely beneath her heavy wool sweater and long skirt. No wonder Santa had been taken with her. Indeed in these final weeks, while they had tiptoed about one another, Anya had noticed how engaging Rachel was in her own quirky way. It was unfortunate, she thought, that Santa's having cast them as rivals for his affection had precluded their getting to know one another better.

She would sorely miss Wendy. But in an odd way, she would miss Wendy's mother too.

"All right," said Anya as Rachel finished waxing a cookie tray, "I think it's thin enough to—"

A sharp rap fell upon the front door, loud and not at

all like the knock of any elf. "Good lord, who could that be, and me with my hands all doughy?"

"Don't bother, I'll get it," said Rachel. In an instant she was out of the kitchen and moving through the house, Snowball and Nightwind at her heels.

"I'll be right there," called Anya.

She plunged her hands under the faucet and grabbed at a towel. She was still wiping them off when, shouldering her way through the kitchen door into the dining room, she heard Rachel scream with terror, and saw, looming in the doorway at the end of the hall, the furry white figure of the Easter Bunny holding in one paw an enormous bouquet of red roses and pink carnations.

# Chapter Twelve

## Blood and Passion

The Easter Bunny strode in, unasked, and kicked the door shut behind him. He stared hard as nails at Santa's new fuckmate, clothed for a change, cringing back against the hall mirror, shock splashed across her face. A sweet morsel she'd be, this Rachel woman, once she calmed down and extended freely the warm sleeve of friendship to him. Santa's wife, a feisty old biddy full of dark fire, was drying her hands on a dishtowel and frowning at him from the archway.

"Ladies," he protested, "is this any way to greet a gentleman caller?" He clutched the bouquet tight to his chest, keeping his other paw concealed behind him.

Anya glared. "I don't recall inviting you in. What are you doing here with your eyes shot red and your fur bristling out in all directions? You look a fright."

"Just dropped by to give this lovely bouquet to the fair Ms. McGinnis"—he thrust a pawful of flowers under Rachel's nose and she fumblingly took them, holding them in both hands like frozen fire—"and to offer you, my peppery Anya, this exquisite treasure."

Here he brought forth his prize, feeling its burning luster fuck and refuck his paw, the tiny orgasms coursing up his arm like wavelets lapping at a golden shore.

"An egg?" She was mesmerized. Her arms fell to her sides, the dishtowel dropped to the floor.

"Not just any egg, Anya. From the way you gaze upon it, I can see you appreciate that. Yes, Rachel, you too. Come closer, there's nothing to fear." As they stared in wonder at the pulsing pink ovoid, he skittered his lust over the soft curves and concavities of their bodies and told them how, one thousand Easters after Christ rose from the dead, while he (the Easter Bunny) was out making his rounds, his most lackadaisical layer (a Wyandotte who was the butt and scorn of the other hens) blinked open her astonished eyes and, protesting every inch of the way, brought forth from her nether regions four divine eggs, blood-pink and perfect, dropped to form the corners of a square, and a fifth egg, this one, at their center. With the fires of heaven they throbbed, and God had stepped down from His high throne upon the Easter Bunny's return and adjured him to keep their quincunxial pattern unbroken until the last trump sounded.

"But for you, sweet Anya, to buy your carnal favors, I now break the pattern. Go ahead, touch it. As amazing as it looks, a thousand times more wonderful is the feel of it upon your flesh."

Anya's hand rose, hesitant. How lovely her elderly fingers were to his eyes, those fingers he'd seen fondle into full flower so many elfin genitals the year before. As irresistible as the Tooth Fairy was, the prospect of yet another bout of knock-down, bone-dry sex had lost much of its perverse charm. And when he'd stood in the snow at the rear of the gingerbread house, watching Santa plunge into the wide-open meat of a soft, wet, yielding Rachel, he ached beyond the ache of gonads. How soothing that moist warm tunnel of flesh was going to feel hugging his abraded organ, which now rose painfully to full tilt. His nose twitched. He sniffed the interwoven woman-stench of Santa's lovely wives, who drifted ever closer under the unrelenting lure of the quintessential egg.

Anya's scalp tingled. The hallway had grown suddenly dark, as if night seeped through its walls to cup the precious egg in its palms. And the egg? It gave off a glow, pink and powerful as sunset across a howling tundra. Rising to a gentle dome above the two clutching paws, it looked like the unslit tip of the perfect lover's penis, the pink and perfect skin of its glans waiting, tight as a drumhead, for her fingers, her lips, the opening flower of her womanhood. Now the hallway closed around her like a hothouse, rich with the aroma of warm damp earth. Longing to loosen her garments, she let the fingers of her left hand move upon her breasts, toying with the cross-lacing there, as her right hand floated closer to the egg.

She watched Rachel reach out and finger the eggtip, then heard a spike split open her throat and unholy orgasm seize the mortal woman. Anya broke from the egg and jerked her head up to gaze into the mad reddish whorls of the Easter Bunny's eyes.

For the first time, Anya saw him clearly. This was a rogue bunny now. Something had gotten to him since they had last met, eating away at his restraint until there was nothing left but death and madness.

She snatched the egg from the Easter Bunny's grasp. "Here's what I think of your gift, Mister Rabbit!" she said, and hurled it hard toward the hall mirror. As lights once again flared in the hallway, the egg's pink twin came rushing to meet it, kissing with a loud crack its cracking double and dribbling yolk and bits of shell down the glass. The cats grew wide-eyed and raced out of the hallway.

But before she could turn back and throw her unwanted guest out, the Easter Bunny slammed into her and she fell hard upon the floor, buried beneath white fur and raking claws. "Stupid cunt," he screamed, his bunny breath rank as weeds, "I'll teach you!" Her spectacles flew off and clattered across the floor. Razors seared her face. Then he was grinding her skull into the carpet. Her neck strained from the twisting and she saw out of the corner of an eye the hard pink pads of his paw, and her blood dripping from the curve of his claws. His long bristling ears whipped furiously above her. He rent her bodice with his teeth, taking skin as well as cloth. Below, his back claws tore her dress to tatters. He wrapped his powerful legs tight around her lacerated thighs, prying them apart and doing his best to thrust his huge red erection into her. Past his shoulder, Rachel was pummeling his furry back, her face knotted in anger, her mouth hurling harsh words.

Now shock gave way to rage, and Anya's fury knew no bounds. Strength surged back into her arms and legs and she bit into his paw, tasting bunny blood. She twisted a knuckled fist into his underbelly. When the swiftness of it made him momentarily loose his hold, Anya pressed her attack, digging into his throat with one hand and twisting mercilessly at the pinched tip of his prick with the other. Rachel, she saw, was tugging on his long upright ears, wrenching at them and making them stretch. Good for her!

"Jesus Christ!" yowled the Easter Bunny. Suddenly he was out of Anya's grasp and off her. The cool air of the hallway slapped at her wounded body. She raised herself on her elbows, looked about, and swore. Rachel, full of useless protest, had fallen victim to his attack. Bits of bloody sweater flew free of her torso. Her skirt hung in tatters about her hips. Long thin slashes cut across her inner thighs and burbled over with blood. Then their attacker was inside her, thrusting and chittering, and Rachel, screaming and struggling, clutched her bleeding breasts, dark red dripping from a deep gash across one cheek.

Anya staggered to her feet. She had to act quickly or the mortal woman would die. But time hung heavy about her. She waded knee deep in it. The crazed rabbit drove himself home again and again as Rachel's blood-laced arms flailed helplessly at the air. Between the Easter Bunny's hind legs, translucent brown skin cupped his pink kidney-shaped testicles. Anya hauled back with her right foot and slammed her shoetip into his crotch. He fell with a shocked yelp onto the carpet, glared at Anya through his pain, snarled, made a weak swipe at her with one claw, and vanished.

Gone into magic time, Anya supposed. But pursuit was the furthest thing from her mind. Though Anya's wounds had healed completely, Rachel would be dead in minutes if she didn't act swiftly to save her.

Without a thought regarding their late rivalry, she began at the deep gash on Rachel's face, tonguing around the ragged edges of it, making her way lick by lick to its harsh red center. If she tasted its bitter tang, she paid it no heed. Rachel had lost a great deal of blood. Her wounds had to be closed at once.

Face looks fine now, thought Anya. Thank God he left her neck alone. Ugly lacerations across the chest. She straddled the unconscious woman and licked in haste at the torn left breast, taking the aureole and nipple and skin into her mouth and tonguing it all back into shape. Then one by one she soothed and erased with her healing saliva every bloody clawtrail the Easter Bunny had blazed across Rachel's torso. The victim, she noted, though still unconscious, was breathing easier.

But there was no time to let up, no time for Anya to give a care to the ruins of her own clothing, which fell away as she ministered to Rachel. Worse mayhem lay below and Rachel was hemorrhaging badly. The fiend's back claws had shredded her skin, laid bare the muscles of her inner thighs, de-lipped the very organ he proceeded to violate. Anya plunged her face into the carnage and licked to save Rachel's life. Though the taste of gore filled her mouth, she shut her eyes and let instinct guide her, keeping her tongue moving back and forth over the mortal woman's belly and thighs, ministering to her, healing where hurt had sundered flesh.

Soon the taste of fresh blood no longer met her lips and Anya opened her eyes to behold the smooth expanse of Rachel's flawless white body, no wounds anywhere, not even a scar, her blond private hair mottled now with shades of russet under Anya's fingers where the blood had tinted it. There was a new taste on Anya's tongue, a taste she very much liked. But mingled with it was a vile drop of rabbit semen, and she knew that one task remained if Rachel were to be truly healed. Down she dipped, her mouth against the mortal woman's sex, tonguing deep inside her, as deep as she could probe, and sucking with all her might. The rapist's bitter seed halted its mad hurtle wombward, beaded protesting backward down the walls of his victim's vagina, and passed out of her labia into Anya's mouth. Resisting the impulse to gag, Anya leaned aside and spat out as much of the rank fluid as she could. It puddled like pale pus on the blood-soaked rug.

A gentle hand touched her leg. Anya gazed up from where she crouched over Rachel, past the riotous blond curls shining like angel hair in the lamplight of the hallway, and saw her large hazel eyes open and glowing. "How are you feeling?" Anya asked.

"Don't stop," whispered Rachel and reached out with her other hand to urge Anya's head gently back down.

Throughout the attack, it seemed to Rachel that she had fallen into a tangled mix of her worst nightmares: smotherings, helplessness, unbearable cold, monstrous clawed beings invading her and stretching out her death through an eternity of pain. Then it no longer boasted even the soft ameliorating edges of a nightmare. It felt everywhere hard and sharp, and she knew she was bleeding to death.

But abruptly the relentless slashings and impalings ceased and a benign goddess began pasting her face back together. Rachel's eyes fixed idly upon a rectangular lake: a chandelier hanging sideways above it in the walled sky found its double beneath the ice, which shone mirror-clear save for translucent skids of yolk and egg white and scattered shards of eggshell.

Then the goddess's mouth went to her chest, her teeth tearing away wrappings of pain. Her swift tongue stanched the bloodflow, replacing throbs of hurt with the pulse of healing. The lake resolved into a mirror indeed, the goddess into Anya. Rachel felt her kind lips, insistent with life, close upon a nipple. Through half-shut eyes, she pictured Santa's wife wrestling with death, who now conceded Rachel's torso but shifted his firepower to her loins, a wide battlefield of trauma and devastation.

Letting her eyelids fall, Rachel saw a distant light, alluring beyond this earthly plain of suffering and sadness. She drifted toward it, feeling the hooks lift free of her body. It would be so easy to cut loose of the torment, so much nicer to go into the light, to join Frank there. But down below, the waves lapped against the shore of her thighs, thudding down insistent beneath the moon that hung like a huge breast in the night sky. That moon opened its mouth in a sad O and spoke to her of womanly matters—of childbirth, of tides, of desires long kept under. The rhythmic slap of waves sounded below. Foam fizzed and sizzled against the shore, glistening silver in the moonlight.

Rachel opened her eyes to Anya's naked flanks where she knelt beside her, one knee resting warm against her ribs. The older woman's arms angled along either side of Rachel's hips. Her head was lowered to Rachel's parted thighs, the bun of her hair tightly curled and circling. Inside, the unbearable pain of violation still seared. But now, it felt as if Anya's healing tongue stretched clear up into Rachel's womb, licking away all traces of suffering.

Life surged anew into Rachel's veins. Life, yes, and something more: an impelling desire for physical love, to affirm life, to tie her more completely to it after nearly losing it. She rested a hand upon Anya, below the rounded curve of one buttock.

"How are you feeling?" Anya's glasses were gone and she looked ancient and beautiful. Her face was rusty with blood, Rachel's blood.

"Don't stop," she whispered. She felt whole again and glowing, and her vagina throbbed now for completion. She caressed Anya's neck, gently coaxing her back down between her legs as she had often done with Santa when he teased her with stopping. Down went the tight white head and again Rachel felt the amazing gift of Anya's tongue on her sex.

Rachel felt doubly weak, from loss of blood and from her gathering arousal. Yet it was as if Anya's healing tongue were speeding the manufacture of new blood as well as stimulating the old. Life surged through her from her moistening nexus. Running her fingers along her savior's lovelips, Rachel coaxed Anya's parted thighs down over her mouth and feasted on the fluids that flowed there. Dark and rich their flavor, like blended herbs steeped on stone hearths, an elixir for all the world's ills.

For an eternity, naught existed but licking and being licked. Anya's moans mumbled upon her labia. When climax claimed them, it brought with it for Rachel the sweet painful wrack of rebirth. Stretching every limb beyond its limits and gasping gloriously for air, she felt at once born out of her own birth canal and out of Anya's, washed head to toe in a glow of sweat and lovejuice.

At last, they rose and threaded their way past dark puddles of gore and torn tufts of fur, washing the blood off one another in the shower, and spending hours of magic time in bed. Rachel apologized over and over for the suffering she had caused Anya, to which Anya tearfully regretted her own stubborn jealousy. Then both of them praised to the stars Santa's exquisite taste in women and dove into one another's arms for more.

"You know what I can't wait to see?" Anya asked as she fondled Rachel's right breast.

"What?" said Rachel, offering up a silent blessing to God for inventing nipples.

"The look on Santa's face when he finds out."

As Santa neared the Pole, his sleigh passed abruptly from the blizzard that whipped furiously about him into the mild winter of his domain. But he paid the transition no mind. His shouts to Lucifer and the others, his *pro forma* whipsmacks over their heads, unfolded on automatic.

There was far too much else to think about.

For one thing, the Tooth Fairy had not shown up once on his rounds. He had braced himself for his worst trial yet, certain that this time he would withstand her wiles. It unnerved him, her not attempting to seduce him along his route. The Tooth Fairy was not, he knew, the sort of creature to give up easily.

Then there was the sorry situation awaiting him at home, his two lovely wives who ought to adore one another but did not.

It hurt Santa's heart, the sadness of it all.

Wendy and Rachel's impending absence shrouded him in gloom. God knew how long it would last, that gloom, and how Anya would respond to it. Would their marriage ever be whole again? Did it matter?

The sleigh's runners skimmed the tops of snowy pines, throwing up clouds of mist that sparkled like diamond dust in the sunlight. Out from the elves' dormitory swarmed hundreds of dark dots. The dark dots did a slow curl around the skating pond, then scattered everywhichway across the commons. As Santa swooped lower, they grew greener and sprouted distinguishable legs and heads. More came tumbling out of workshop and stable, all of them headed for the expanse of snow before his cottage.

There on the porch was Wendy in a bright red dress, waving wildly up at him. Beside her on the railing sat Snowball and Nightwind, legs tucked under, patient black and white pods.

Behind them stood Anya and Rachel, holding hands and waving like twins, broad smiles lighting up their faces. Santa dropped the reins in shock, then groped forward and grabbed them again.

When Wendy leaped into the roil of elves that

swarmed the sleigh, Santa lifted his radiant stepchild out of the turmoil—as though he plucked a holly berry from a cluster of leaves—and squeezed her tight. Her kisses warmed his cheek. Then his helpers closed in and one beloved face after another came into focus. Hearty handclasps and hugs besieged Santa on all sides. Wendy laughed in his arms and clasped him round the neck.

"We're staying!" she shouted.

When the green sea finally parted, Santa's wives were waiting on the porch. He bounded up and hugged them both, Wendy giggling as he crushed her against her mother. Anya he kissed first, tasting a new flavor of frisk and frolic there that pleased him greatly. Then, still puzzled, he bent to Rachel; her full lips parted and her lovely scent captivated him anew.

In the commons, the crowd went wild with cheering.

Later, in the living room, Santa heard the laundered version of what had happened. "Mommy got attacked by a giant animal," Wendy blurted out. Then, skirting around the details they later provided, Anya and Rachel painted the broad picture of what had occurred and how it had brought them together. Santa had noticed the bare floor in the hallway and the dried trail of egg running down the mirror. "Several of the elves have volunteered to weave us a new carpet," Anya told him, which left the larger question unanswered, "and the egg residue simply refuses to yield to conventional methods of cleaning, so we're leaving it there for now. More on that later."

When he had showered and was robed in red, soft black slippers hugging his feet and a long thin clay pipe wreathing aromatic wisps of smoke about his lips, Santa sat back in his easy chair and let Christmas unfold before him. On his return trip, he had dreaded this final round of giftgiving, the funereal mood that would surely pall every attempt at merriment. Now it was all he could do to keep from laughing out loud, things having fallen out as he had always dreamed they would. There was Wendy in a beautiful gingham dress Anya had sewn for her, once more assuming responsibility for delivering the gifts, pausing before him once to stick out her lower jaw and wiggle her first loose tooth in more than a year. ("Be sure to let someone know the instant it comes out," he cautioned.) There was his dear wife Anya, rocking and knitting and beaming as he hadn't seen her beam in ages. And there was Rachel, young and zesty and full-breasted, an arm draped over Heinrich's nearest shoulder where he sat, all six of him, bunched up on the couch, barely able to contain his glee.

At long last, after the eggnog had vanished but for a filmy residue at the bottom of the cut-glass bowl, and the large plates piled high with gingerbread men held only a stray crumb or two, Santa put on his holiday best and they adjourned to the elves' dormitory for festivities and giftgiving that lasted until dusk.

By nightfall, Wendy began to nod and Santa brimmed with a delicious mix of curiosity and lust. She drifted asleep in his arms as they watched elf after elf whiz by on the ice. With a twinkle of his eye, Santa summoned Fritz to his side.

"Fritz, I think you understand how much Wendy and her mother mean to me."

"Of course, Santa," Fritz assured him, watching the sleeping girl's head loll against the crook of Santa's arm as they made their way across the commons. "All of us, to the last elf, feel the same way."

"Good. That's good, Fritz. Now I want to tell you something. Get the door, will you?"

Fritz opened the front door of the gingerbread house, turned on the hall light, and stepped aside to let Santa through with his precious burden.

"Now, Fritz," said Santa while the sleepy girl was in the bathroom brushing her teeth, "Wendy and Rachel are not like us. They can be hurt. They can be killed."

"But Santa," Fritz scoffed, "who'd want to hurt—"

Santa held up a finger. "Never mind who. I'm afraid they may be in danger of further attack. You saw the rug. You heard what happened."

"Yes, but—"

"Then you know as much as you need to know. Keep an eye on Wendy tonight. Don't relax your vigilance for an instant. Will you do that?"

Fritz, puzzled and frustrated, stood by the picture window and looked out across the commons at the skating revelers. "She'll be safe with me, Santa."

"Thank you, Fritz."

Tucking Wendy in, Santa laid a fatherly hand upon

her brow. "Go back to sleep now, darling. Fritz is here to look over you, and I'll see you in the morning." He bent down and kissed her.

"I love you, Santa," said Wendy with a yawn.

"I love you too, Wendy," Santa replied. "Sleep well, dear one."

Wendy smiled and her eyelids closed.

Santa paused at the door, his face soft but fearful. "Remember," he whispered to Fritz.

Fritz mouthed renewed assurance, and Santa headed back to his wives.

Hours later, when the festivities were over, Anya took one of Santa's hands and Rachel took the other and they led him beguilingly to his bed, stripped him naked, and demonstrated beyond the power of words how much love they had in their hearts for him and for one another. Hour after hour they dallied, these three, exploring with delight the new instance of matrimony they had become. Three hours shy of dawn, his arms full of contented woman, Santa drifted off at last into sleep, feeling safe and cozy and warm, drained and happy and, by any measure, complete.

"G'night, Fritz," Wendy said. The next moment her eyes blinked open and everything was dark and silent except for the soft glow of her nightlight and the breezy snores of her guardian elf curled up in a chair by the window. Snowball and Nightwind lumped dim and immobile at the foot of her bed. Outside, snow stretched in a silent blue roll across the commons past the gleam of the skating pond.

Too much hot apple cider. She needed to go tinkle. She had to leave her warm cozy bed and lift her nightgown above her waist and sit on the cold potty seat. Yes, but then she would get to nestle back under the covers again and that would feel wonderful. Nothing to be done. Wendy angled back her blankets and stepped down, chill air upon her ankles. She eased open her bedroom door so as not to disturb Fritz, crossed the hallway, and snapped on the bathroom light.

Loud knock of potty cover against the bright white tank; white seat cold on the backs of her legs; a sudden spray of tinkle hitting the water, and the easing of her discomfort within. Nightwind craned his head around the door and yawned up at her. Wendy worried the loose tooth with her tongue. She felt it give. Raising a hand from the seat, she brought it out.

It glistened between thumb and forefinger, jutting up thin and white and almost smooth, a pinched drop of red at its root end.

In her mouth she tasted blood.

She wiped herself and flushed the potty, then stood at the sink. Santa had said to let someone know if it came out. Should she wake Fritz? She set the tooth on the countertop and stared at it. No need. She was fast approaching eight, a big girl. What had Mommy done the last time in their old house? Stood next to her, an arm around her shoulder. Suggested she rinse her mouth out. Set the tooth beneath her pillow and tucked her in.

Anya told her often what an independent young lady she was becoming. They would be proud of her the next morning when she told them she had taken care of things herself. There might even be more dimes in it, assuming the Tooth Fairy rewarded such efforts. It was worth a try, anyway.

Wendy sloshed warm water about in her mouth and spat out the pink fluid, washing it down the drain. She did it a second and third time. Then she closed her palm around the tiny tooth, flicked off the bathroom light, and ushered Nightwind back into her room, shutting the door as quietly as she could behind them.

Fritz snored. He looked cold, Wendy thought. She tipped up the pillow and centered her prize beneath it, then pressed it firmly down around the tooth. She lifted a confused Snowball off the bed and set her on the floor. "Sorry, Snowball," she said. Her top blanket, light blue and pilled with age, she took off, draping it around Fritz and tucking it behind his shoulders so that he looked as if he had fallen asleep in a barber chair. A smile came to his lips. At last, Wendy crawled beneath the covers, savoring the mommy-like warmth that wrapped her in its arms, and drifted down into deep slumber.

# Chapter Thirteen

## The Tooth Fairy Takes Her Revenge

When immortals dream, death and disfigurement come surprisingly often into play. And yet not so surprising when one considers their indestructibility in waking life. Upon the deadly playground of a dreamscape, the agonies of separation and irrevocable loss are theirs at last to claim and be claimed by.

Because God had given Santa and Anya memories of past mortality, their dreams frequently took up these themes. In a typical scenario, God reached down in displeasure to peel away the veneer of immortal life from this or that inhabitant of the North Pole. There followed many tearful visits to the victim's deathbed, an elaborate burial scene in the woods, and after a heartrending period of gloom and mourning, at last a reversal: God forgave all, the grave belched forth its victim amidst a rain of flowers, and joy returned tenfold to every heart.

This night, however, Santa's dreams took an atypical turn. He floated blimplike above the world, an earth made not of rock and soil but of mattress, white with feathery blankets and pillows of snowdrift. Lying legs akimbo in every direction were vast expanses of women, naked and swollen-lipped. Down he drifted into the embrace of each of them, dipping into her ready flesh and leaving liquid gifts inside her. Glancing back, Santa watched them belly up and birth out girl babies, who blossomed swiftly into womanhood, their limpid gaze inviting his return.

But when he closed his eyes to savor his bliss, a blast of chill air suddenly assaulted him. Peeling his lids back against the wind, Santa found himself falling precipitously toward an island engulfed in flame. One twisted cypress burned, as did the ash trees racing up a mountain slope. Beaches of sand and rock roared with the ferocity of a furnace. Into this inferno he fell, skin scorched, lungs scandalized. And this isle—which was somehow the Tooth Fairy herself—rose to seize him. She held out inflaming arms, hugged him to her fiery bosom, sucked his prick into her pit of love, and pressed it to white coals until it sizzled and blistered like a hotdog on a grill.

"Santa." Her demonhood gripped him. "Look into my face. Behold what once you were, what realms of bliss you lorded over in days past." Through the wash of flame, her skin cleared like a pool and he witnessed scenes of forest abandon, heard reed-pipes endlessly rippling. His head fell forward into hers and the goatishness surged within him, wild and gamy, clever in chase, rough in capture, rude in ravage. Raising a hairy arm, he splashed wine down his throat and the spirit of pressed grape filled him. "Nymphs," came his command, "pleasure me!" At once, out from the trees—ash and oak and lofty pine—they flew to him. Lips moistened, grandly flush between the thighs, they grabbed at him, smothering him in tongue and cunt, nippling his lips with full milk-yielding breasts.

She thrust him up from her flaming face, tearing the vision away. Pain seized his limbs and worse pain gripped his sex. "But you gave that up long ago, fearing to die. Hoodwinked by God into a life of selfless giving, you are no longer worthy to wield such a lovely weapon as this." The blazing pit of her vulva, sprouting teeth and tongue, parted its jaws and inched around the tight pouch of his testicles. Then her teeth dug deep and incisive, severing his genitals with one savage chomp. As he screamed, her vaginal jaws munched away at their prize. Then she tossed him upon the hissing sea, straddled his head, and irised open her anus. Out fluttered flurries of currency, all colors, shapes, and sizes. Engraved presidents and kings and queens slapped across his face. Monetary excrement blinded him. So thick and furious came the defecation of banknotes that no air was left for breathing. With his last gasp, he found enough breath to scream, scream for his life . . .

. . . but suddenly he was awake. And it wasn't his scream he heard but Rachel's. There by the bedroom door in the moonlight stood the Tooth Fairy, her strong right arm thrown savagely across the shoulders of Wendy's torn nightgown. Wendy's head whipped from side to side in protest. Ringed in a ghastly red, her torn and toothless mouth sobbed open.

* * *

When Rachel saw the look on the intruder's face, she knew at once why this hellspawn stood at Santa's bedroom door, hurting her daughter. In the same instant, she saw Wendy's terror, her face a fist of pain, and Rachel's love for her took over.

"Let her go!" Flinging back the bedsheets, she leaped at the vengeful demon before her.

"With pleasure," said the intruder, hurling Wendy with a loud smack against the wall and turning to embrace the charging mortal.

"Mommy, a big bunny rabbit took Thnowball," she heard her daughter cry out, but then Rachel's ribcage snapped like a rack of twigs in the Tooth Fairy's brutal hug and the creature's jaws suddenly gaped far wider than seemed possible. Rachel inhaled sharply, astonished at how much pain went with the puncture and crush of internal organs. Then the Tooth Fairy's head sprang forward and her teeth lit into Rachel's face, and Rachel knew no more.

Blond bitch tastes halfway decent, came the thought. But there was no time for thinking, no time to savor the woman's flesh; time only to bolt it down. First the head, face and teeth and tongue, shove the skull in, crush it, gulp down bones, brain, and all. Then the torso, ripping into it like a hungry shredder pulping a treetrunk, taking in shoulderflesh and clavicle, arms and elbows, wrists and fingers, breasts and breadbasket. Finally she heaved the rest of the woman up into the air (a swirl of motherblood slapping across the whimpering girl's nightgown), ate away at innards and cunt and buttocks, stuffed down thighs and legs and feet, gulped flesh and bone and blood in quick triumph.

She was in high spirits, the Tooth Fairy. She'd been in the room ten seconds tops, her feast had taken no more than three, and Santa and his wife lay wrapped in shock. Already she could feel her insides working over her meal. Her belly bulged and she rose into the moonlight, hugging her knees to her breasts, ready to mint the mortal bitch.

She screamed at the pain.

Her anus gaped wide, straining at all sides. The milled edges of the coin came first, accordioned over three or four widths' worth. It fanned out as it emerged, gleaming golden. Faster and faster the impacted metal issued from her, hurting her even as it fed her pride. Like a flat balloon, it filled out huge and round and golden. On the upturned side, she made out the mortal woman's breasts and hands and anguished face. When its last serration had been shat, the huge disc stiffened in the air like swiftly tempering steel and clattered to the hardwood floor, digging deep dents in it.

The sound roused Santa to action, but the Tooth Fairy rocketed over to Wendy and swooped her up, screaming and kicking, by the waist.

"In the name of God, put her down!" Santa shouted as he leaped from the bed.

She threw him one last look, then folded herself and her victim into magic time and was gone.

* * *

Still cocooned in shock, Anya watched Santa race to grapple with the Tooth Fairy.

Too late.

The moment his moon-white arms began to close on her, she winked out, Wendy with her. Santa slammed full force into the wall. A long, wounded howl issued from him. He struck it with his fist and crumbled against it, weeping.

Anya went to Santa. Turning at her touch, he hugged her. "Good God," he sobbed, "what have I done?"

"There, there, Nicholas." He blubbered in her arms. Anya fought away her tears, shutting out the terrible images of her loved ones bloody and dying, so as to tend to her husband.

"I could have stopped it. I could have held Rachel back. Don't you see, Anya, I could have gone into magic time and saved her."

"That's enough," she replied, looking him straight in the eye. "It happened much too fast for either of us to stop it. Now pull yourself together. You've got a child to save."

"Yes, I must think of Wendy." The catch in his voice tore at Anya's heart. "But how will I ever find them in time? They could be anywhere. Wendy might already—"

"Wendy is not dead," said Anya with more conviction than she felt. "But she's out there somewhere, hurting, and you've got to find her and rescue her." An image of Lucifer sprang to Anya's mind, his antlers glowing bright as neon.

"Claus, do you still have those red panties?"

* * *

Back in his burrow, the Easter Bunny's brain was buzzing. The Tooth Fairy had tossed him a sop for his conscience, this vigorous young she-cat, this Snowball. An insult to his dignity, a blatant bribe. And a prize worth having. It didn't by any means erase the sight of that little girl's mouth being savaged. He had almost leaped in to stop it, screeching at the Tooth Fairy to quit hurting her. But she had looked death at him and shouted, "If you value your balls, you'll stay the fuck where you are and shut up!" And he, God help his wormy soul, had prized his accursed genitals above the well-being of a child in trouble. Where had his virtue—what little there had been—gone in the last year? He grimaced. He knew the answer. Right into the Tooth Fairy's quim, that's where. She had sucked it clean out of him. Yes, he thought bitterly, casting a baleful eye along the walls of the exercise area; and he hadn't lifted a claw to stop her.

He hung his head and felt chills of regret course along his spine for the degenerative spiral he had hopped down since last Christmas.

Snowball meowed up at him.

"What's that, my pet?" he said. "You'd like to see the rest of the burrow?" He stroked her smooth white fur, at which she lifted against his paw and piano'd upon his chest in approval.

At his groin, a stirring.

"All right, my precious little Snowball. First I'll show you where the candy is made and where the baskets are assembled. Then we'll go watch the hens lay Easter eggs, won't that be fun?"

She purred.

"And then I'll show you my bedroom."

Lucifer was dreaming about Bambi's girlfriend Faline again: her gangly legs, her white wiggly paintbrush tail, and below—what Disney dared not draw—her puckered anus and the sweet wet furrow along which Lucifer eased the tip of his buckhood.

But then the stable door's sharp creak and the harsh gleam of Gregor's lantern robbed him of his cartoon lover. He looked up in annoyance to see Santa all suited up; Mrs. Claus in bathrobe and slippers; Prancer and Blitzen poking their heads over the sides of their stalls, blinking in curiosity; Fritz standing alone, looking stunned; yonder, Gregor lifting a saddle out of an old trunk and wiping the dust off it. All of them were bathed in the soft glow of magic time.

What in blazes was going on?

"Lucifer, old friend," came Santa's voice, with an edge of desperation that frightened him. "I need your help."

At once, new vigor came into the lead reindeer's limbs. He rose from his straw bed and cocked his head.

In the glow of Lucifer's antlers, Santa's face shone like a violent blush. "The Tooth Fairy has taken Wendy. We've got to find them and get her back, and it must be done quickly." Fumbling in his pocket, Santa brought out a bunched handful of red silk and lifted it to Lucifer's nose. "Can you track her from this?"

The reindeer shut his eyes and inhaled.

He had once thought it strange when Wendy carried her kittens into the stable one morning, teasing them with a catnip mouse Mrs. Claus had stitched together from scraps of calico. It had amused him, how they dizzied about their prize, sniffing it and batting it and pouncing upon it. Now he understood. Now, with the aroma of the immortal seductress rising in his flared nostrils, by God he understood.

"Easy, Lucifer!"

Great Christ, his antlers flared at once into flame, straight out to the tips. Down below (Jesus in a manger, how embarrassing) his sex suddenly stiffened, her fairy hand stroking him there. His hoofs beat out a tattoo on the stable floor and seed shot from him in gleeful jets and spurts.

"Gregor, for God's sake, help me hold him! Anya, stay where you are!"

Strong elfin arms steadied him. His brain felt energized, as if there were networks of bright white Christmas lights everywhere agleam along its folds and runnels. He shook his great antlers and snorted. Then, looking at Santa, he nodded sharply.

Santa smiled. "Good boy! All right, Gregor, saddle him up. Make haste. Watch where you step." While Gregor placed a blanket across his back and cinched him into the jingling saddle, Lucifer watched Santa exchange a parting word and an embrace with Mrs. Claus by the door.

Then they led him outside into the sleeping snowscape, where he caught her scent, faint but unmistakable, in the air by the cottage.

With Santa riding him, he bounded away, speeding southward, tracking his prey on her zigzag path through the night, down across the frozen reaches of the Yukon, swooping low over sleeping cities sprawled the length of British Columbia and Washington and Oregon, straight on toward the gleaming heart of the Sacramento Valley.

Wendy had no more tears and very little fight left in her. Her gums throbbed and it hurt something fierce when her jaws accidentally jarred shut. But the images in her mind hurt much more—the sudden appearance of the hard-faced fairy in whose grip she now flew, jolting her out of sleep and digging her fingers again and again into Wendy's mouth; Nightwind's mewls of protest; Fritz frozen in normal time; the gigantic white rabbit who just stood there and Snowball's sharp yowl when she was snatched up and tossed to him; and worst of all, her mother vanishing in a sweep of blood down the Tooth Fairy's throat.

She bleared down at the frosted lights of yet another city. So many cities she had passed over, so many homes strung with color, full of warm beds and dozing children.

But this city, wet with rain, they began to descend toward. Twin pinpoints of light inched along ribbons of highway, enlarging into small circles that threw before them glittering scoops of yellow.

They banked sharply and her nemesis pointed down. "That's where we're headed, right there. Recognize it?"

Wendy saw a wrought-iron gate in a tall dark fence that ran for several blocks. A dimly lit road branched out from the gate, meandering along wide patches of earth. Here and there, trees gloomed up like glistening broccoli. The only sign of life was a lone lit windowpane in a tiny building near the gate. The place nagged at her, as if she had seen it in a dream. But she shook her head.

"You will soon enough," came the harsh voice. "Keep your eyes open."

Wendy looked. Below them, black teeth thrust up through the earth in serried rows. A certain stand of oak trees moved into place about a rise in the landscape, and it dawned on her. She moaned anew as they circled in on her buried father.

"That's more like it," said the Tooth Fairy, pausing in the air above Frank McGinnis's grave. "Now I want you to read the words on this tombstone." She fingered the wet cold stone along the engraved X in XAVIER. "My spies tell me you like to read. Be a good girl and tell me what it says."

"Read it yourthelf!" said Wendy defiantly.

But the Tooth Fairy's fingers clenched like steel calipers around her cheeks and bore down. "Do I have to tear the words out of your mouth, young lady, or will you do as I say?" Wendy nearly fainted, but she managed to hang on until the hurtful fingers withdrew at last. "Now read!"

She lisped painfully through her father's name and the numerals engraved beneath. Born 1933. Died 1990. Knuckles of rain rapped upon her skull. She wished Daddy were alive to rescue her. Or that she could die now, escape this cold and rain and torment, and be held by his strong arms forever.

"Now this part, the phrase below."

Wendy didn't need to look but she wiped her eyes with the back of her hand. "Beloved huthband and father," she muttered, choking on the last word.

"Good girl," said the Tooth Fairy, who flew Wendy to the grave opposite her daddy's and sat her atop a fat blocky marker. "You understand what 'beloved father' means, I suppose? Well now, I'm going to show you why your mother called him 'beloved husband.' "

As Wendy watched, the Tooth Fairy beckoned toward the carefully tended mound with outstretched arms. The moist earth rumbled. Wendy heard slow scraping sounds that grew stronger and faster. Then a sharp wrenching. The earth sifted like dark wet flour beneath the incantatory hands of the Tooth Fairy, who cackled in triumph as she lifted free one gnarled grasping remnant of a hand, then another.

By the time her father's head emerged from the mound and his muddy eyes blinked open, Wendy had retreated far inside.

* * *

"And this," he said, "is where I sleep. Do you like the pretty straw?"

Snowball meowed.

"Yes, of course you could share all this—if you treat me right. Oh and just beyond my nice soft bed is the opening to the sleeping quarters of a very special friend of mine. Let's knock, shall we? Oh Petunia, we have guests. Are you decent? She says she is."

He stroked the pure white cat from head to raised rump. Petunia's room, as always, was dim and dank. But he sensed something new in the air. A whiff of jealousy, perhaps? He hoped not.

"Petunia, I'd like you to meet Snowball. Snowball, Petunia. That's right. Give her a good sniffing. She likes that. Now Snowball, I have a question to ask you."

The cat looked up quizzically.

"Do you think you could get into that same position for me?" He licked his lips. "Right now?"

One moment Frank's mind was one with the Eternal Hum. The next, a strong pull from somewhere grabbed him off the line and stuffed him back into bones.

Like an angry surge of bees, a superhuman strength rushed through him. The pine lid splintered in his hands. Rising through churning clods of earth, he shut his eyes against the yielding mud and clawed upward until he felt . . . a hand. Two hands. They helped him rise. At last his head crowned out of the soil, and his shoulders followed. Cold sweet air. He tried to breathe it. In vain. Then he opened his eyes and saw his benefactress: naked but for a necklace of large white teeth; white of skin but muddied where she had touched him; pure-breasted and pure-thighed, pure everywhere.

A face that bewitched.

She had been talking to him for some time, but until she swam into focus all he heard was a soup of sound. As he regained language, he understood and obeyed. "That's right, lover boy. Lie back and let momma attend to your needs. My, my, you were a chubby one, weren't you?"

He managed a loud prolonged vowel, which he paid for in vicious hurt inside.

"Still plenty of you left, though. And I'm delighted to see you're mostly intact down here. Let me help you stiffen this right up. Will you do that for your lover? Will you go all hard, Frank darling?"

She smiled sardonically at him, kneading him where he couldn't see. But the ghost of old thickenings arose. He had forgotten what it was called, that piece of flesh her fingers sculpted. But its name didn't matter. Only the feeling of life resurgent mattered.

"Yes, that's the way momma likes it, Frank. Thick and juicy."

She mounted him. She closed around his muddy member and rode him, looming full-breasted and red-haired above. It pleased Frank immensely, despite the voracious hunger in her eyes.

But in an instant, all of that changed.

That was the moment when a high-pitched filament

of sound, faint at first, grew louder and resolved itself into the insistent jingle of bells.

That was also the moment when Frank saw the wounded figure of a little girl seated upon a tombstone and knew at once that it was his Wendy, that she had been watching him, and that she was in terrible pain.

The Easter Bunny held Snowball's front paws together and wrapped them tight round with baling wire. She tugged hard against it and *mrrrrrowl*'d up at him.

"Now, now, little one," he muttered. "You'll only hurt yourself that way. And that's my job, wouldn't you say? Just a little joke, precious. I want you to enjoy yourself too, stick around awhile, make this a habit for both of us." He found a gnarled branch he liked at times to whet his teeth on and wired her back legs far apart at its opposite ends.

Snowball's claws curved full out. But as she had no room to maneuver, he felt quite safe. Her yowls were loud and incessant now, the way his lazy Wyandotte might sound laying an abrupt succession of angular eggs.

Stooping, he placed her upon his bed of straw. Her hindquarters waggled violently back and forth. Her saucy target made "pay-me, pay-me" movements beneath her puffed-up tail. "Take it easy, sweetie pie. I'll try to make this as pleasant as I can for both of us."

His paws floated down his belly and found plenty to grab onto, lots of stuff to stiffen there.

* * *

As they flew in over I-80, Santa brought them out of magic time. The stuck traffic below resumed its dark hurtle east and west. He assumed that Lucifer would alight at Rachel's home. To his surprise, they passed it by and headed south. From his mount's angle of descent, Santa sensed their journey was nearly over. He prayed to God they weren't too late.

*(He-he-he, you can pray to God all you want, big brother, but you're the one who's responsible for this mess, and you're the one who has to clean it up.)*

*So. You're back.*

*(Never left, really. Just laid low.)*

*Rachel told me I should fight you if you returned, fight you and triumph.*

*(That's crazy, bubba. I'm part of you. Hell, I am you. What you used to be before the big man in the sky turned you into Santa Claus. You know who I am, don't you? Why not just out and say it?)*

Santa, staring down at the shiny roofs below, heard wet tires peel back pavement. *Pan*, he thought simply, letting it out for the first time.

*(Ooh yes, that's right, that felt good. Let me hear it again.)*

*Pan. I used to be Pan.* His head felt strangely airy all of a sudden.

*(Feel that rush? That's yours truly, the old goat-god himself, feeling his oats. Trust me, bro, all right? Don't deny your deepest self.)*

*You got me into this mess, you and your lust!*

*(Hey, mea culpa, okay? What can I say? I like to*

*fuck. We both do. Couple of old rutters from way back. But listen, I got the goods. You can feel the power knocking against your ribcage, right? Pounding in your pecker? Beating at your skull? I can give you the strength to best the bitch.)*

*I'll do that on my own, no help from you.*

*(Shit, man, you're trembling like a leaf. You want to fight fire you use fire, not milk and cookies.)*

Santa was on a cusp. He knew it. He ought to refuse the intruder, to deny his Pan side. But doubt clouded his judgment, and: *So be it, then. Do your worst.* And the thing slipped into his heart, hardening it like a cock and turning his thoughts dark.

As they banked over tall trees, Wendy came first into view, pale and thin and white, a ghost perched upon a tombstone. Then, her father's gaping grave and Frank McGinnis's muddied corpse writhing under the Tooth Fairy, who glared defiance at Santa as he descended.

When Lucifer set hoof to ground not ten yards away, Santa bounded off and made for Wendy.

"Not so fast!" The Tooth Fairy pointed a finger at Wendy, who cried out in pain. Recalling how she had split open his skin in just this way, Santa halted. The dead man, a fat rotting caricature of Santa himself, pleaded for his daughter from the muddy depths of his throat.

"If you know what's good for you," boomed Santa, "you'll give me the girl." His tone struck him as odd indeed. Stentorian, commanding, ruthless, threatening mayhem. He didn't like it one bit.

*(Good one! That got her goat!)*

The Tooth Fairy looked momentarily stunned. Then she laughed, her buttocks thick with mud where she straddled the dead man's lower body. "Idle threats? That doesn't suit you, lover."

"Why are you doing this?" said Santa.

*(Oh, come on, man. Let me through. Tell her you don't make idle threats, tell her you're going to whup her ass.)*

"That's not at all like Santa Claus. He's so kind and generous. Everybody knows that."

"Please," he said. Lucifer gave a troubled whinny of protest. Santa took a step toward the awful copulation. "In the name of all that's decent, let me take Wendy away from this."

*(Please and decent, right. Sure got her on the run now, don't ya? Must be time to break out those Pat Boone records, pound the last nail into her coffin.)*

"And interrupt her lessons in lovemaking?" She cast a steely glance at Lucifer, then hurled it into Santa. "Would that be fair? To show our little lovely the joys a man and woman can share and not allow her to indulge in them herself?"

"You're insane."

She tossed her head back. "You betrayed me, you jolly bastard. I'm going back to my dear wife Anya, you said, be faithful, and fuck nobody else. Then you went upstairs and latched onto another tasty piece. Did you really believe I'd let you get away with that?"

"We fell in love," he pleaded. "What you and I had

was never love. It was animal lust pure and simple. But that's over now. You've murdered my Rachel. Now you're killing her daughter, my daughter. Please. She's hurt. She's in shock. She's freezing to death. At least let me cover her with my coat." Santa tugged at his top button and took another step toward Wendy.

In a flash, the Tooth Fairy was upon him, twisting muddy fingers into the clean cloth of his suit, grinding her groin against his belly. "You want the girl, you can have her." With a wicked grin, she ground her cheekbones into Santa's face and tore at his beard. "You can have *her*—if I can have Lucifer."

"What?"

"You heard me. I want that large studly buck over there, the one with the big stiff furry handle poking up beneath his belly. Yes, that's what this bad little girl wants for Christmas, Santa. She wants Lucifer, the jolly old elf's favorite reindeer, ready to do her bidding for a year."

Santa pried her off and hurled her into the air. She floated like a wind-wraith before him. "That's out of the—" he began.

Enraged at his rebuff, the Tooth Fairy hauled back and blasted Santa's mouth with a thick gout of flame. It scoured the flesh off his upper palate and charbroiled his tongue.

At once, Santa gave Pan free rein. The goat-god pumped up Santa's body into a fighting machine, planting his boots like hoofs in the grave-ground, feeling the chthonic solidity root him deep in the earth.

He gave a blast of sound so bellicose that it ripped straight down the Tooth Fairy's front, whipped the skin off her like a winding sheet, and sent it flapping and fluttering into the night sky like an albino bat hellbent for heaven.

Undaunted, she oozed new covering out of her bloody flesh. Her necklace clacked as the skin re-wrapped her, clattering like miniblinds. "So you want to play rough, eh?"

Her fingers danced about her head, pointing this way and that. Flowers lifted from grave after grave, flying straight into Santa's face. Into his lungs they flooded. They filled his belly, made it swell up. A button popped. Another.

Gathering his rage, Pan-Santa puked out the impacted petals and thorns, shaping the projectile with his mouth. It shot forth thin and hard and sharp as wire.

The weapon speared straight through her. It claimed several vertebrae, leaving her lower body dangling until self-healing regenerated what was missing or damaged. But she was too full of fight to wait for that. She flew to Frank's tombstone and grappled it from the earth, lifting the thick slab of granite and hurling it at Santa with all her might.

Frank's marker whumped into his body, driving him to the ground, snapping bones. Then healing erased the trauma, reshaped and knit his broken bones. Pan-Santa shoved the stone away and went for another, this one twice the size, twice the thickness, of Frank's.

By Zeus, he thought, he'd beat her at her own game.

Then Santa saw the inscription: TO THE MEMORY OF MY BELOVED WIFE, ELLIE MARSH JEFFRIES. 1914–1987. MAY SHE REST IN PEACE.

*Good God, what am I doing? This is sacred ground.*

*(Can it, Santa. We're doing what needs to be done.)*

*But this isn't right, I—*

*(Shut up and grab the fucking tombstone!)*

But a loud whinny, close by, cut him short.

Lucifer nosed Santa's armpit from behind and threw him off-balance. Turning, he saw the eager eyes of his lead reindeer; the fiery filaments of his fur; his antlers swaying with the high winds of desire.

The Tooth Fairy laughed. "Out of the question, is it?" she said. "So do we strike a bargain, or do you feel like ripping the whole goddamn cemetery apart?"

Santa turned to his nemesis. There was no time to argue the point. Lucifer was willing. And Wendy might die if he didn't spirit her away quickly.

"He must be back at the North Pole one week before Christmas."

"Done."

"In perfect condition."

"Spanking clean and ready for action."

"So be it," said Santa. "He'll arrive on your island before daybreak. And Wendy—?"

"She's yours." The Tooth Fairy gave Lucifer a wicked look and twisted about to delve into her dead lover.

"One thing more," Santa said.

"What?" Impatience thundered in her face.

Santa tugged off his coat, wrapped it snug around Wendy, lifted her from the tombstone, thrust a hand into his pocket, and took out his prize. "You can have these back. I'm finished with them."

Hissing at him, the Tooth Fairy snatched the red lace panties from his fingers and pussied down onto her lover's aroused putrescence, twisting the wispy garment about his exposed neckbone in a grim parody of sexual strangulation. Santa's last glimpse of her, as he settled his precious, unresponsive burden before him on Lucifer's back and lifted into the air, was of her necklace knocking like a rattle of dice against the screaming corpse's chest as she bent to bury her teeth in his skull.

Between his paws his bunnyhood grew rigid. His back right foot had begun to pound the packed earth of his burrow. The sharp high-pitched *meowls* coming from the bed wove a stirring counterrhythm across the boom and thud of his thumps.

He felt good, very good indeed.

But just as he bent to touch the fat red tip of his sex to Snowball's pink privates, the earth rumbled. At once he straightened, perking up his ears. A ringing sang in his head, a jangling that made him slightly nauseous.

Then thunder sounded and the burrow shook. Giving out with a high treble squeal, he dashed wildly about, making for the door, hoping to reach open air before an earthquake swallowed his home. But as the archway gaped to let him into the exercise area, a flash of brilliance flared at the mouth of the burrow, growing in intensity as the jangle of sleighbells shrilled louder.

Through a pulsing ring of light burst the figure of a fat red rider on an antlered steed. Light swept in with them, swirling about them. And he saw that it was Santa Claus glowering down from Lucifer's back and looking like no Santa he had ever seen—harsh, shifty, full of muscle and meanness, not the soft and fuzzy elf he'd grown used to. The pale unseeing face of Wendy McGinnis poked up out of Santa's coat.

Terrified, he skittered backward into his bedroom. But the bells started up again with a raucous jangle and the solid wall of earth which kept him from his invaders dropped away like a curtain of dust. Lucifer charged through glowing motes of earth, bringing his master and the little girl through without a spot. The Easter Bunny cowered against the outer wall, trying to stay out of the vast corona of light which splashed through the bedroom, trying to avoid the fat elf's piercing glare.

Santa's eyes swept the room and whipped back to sting him with righteous wrath. The great hands lightly flicked the reins they held. Then Lucifer dashed into the air. Flattening himself against the wall, the Easter Bunny felt the sharp tip of an antler sear a line of fire across his face and the quick vicious punch of hoofs—front, back—pounding at his belly, bringing blood and pain welling up there. Santa swiped across the bed and lifted Snowball, unrestrained, up into his lap.

Holding his belly as the blood burbled from between

his paws, the Easter Bunny sobbed bitter tears. "I'm sorry," he blubbered. "She made me do it. I'll be good from now on, I promise."

Santa reined in, hanging in mid-air, and looked back in scorn. "Shame on you! May you roast in hell for this!" Then he put bootheels to the sides of his mount and he and the girl and her still-protesting pet dashed away in a blur of color.

Gloom descended then upon the Easter Bunny. Dread, despair, emptiness. For hours he stood against the wall, sobbing and chittering as his flesh—but not his spirit, no never his spirit—healed. When at last he moved, it was beneath a weight of misery that would not be shaken off. He looked upon his hens with indifference, upon Petunia with loathing.

For weeks, guilt and shame filled his heart. He ate little and slept less. Thus his life limped along until Valentine's Day, when the Lord God Almighty Himself paid him a long-overdue second visit and relieved the Easter Bunny of his torment forever.

# Part Five

## After the Storm

Sex is nobody's business except the three people involved.

—Anonymous

Faith is under the left nipple.

—Martin Luther

The marriage supper of the Lamb is a feast at which every dish is free to every guest. . . . In a holy community, there is no more reason why sexual intercourse should be restricted by law, than why eating and drinking should be—and there is as little occasion for shame in the one case as in the other.

—John Humphrey Noyes

# Chapter Fourteen

## A Time to Mourn

The weeks which followed were the saddest ever spent at the North Pole.

When Santa streaked out of the night, his elves were out in force, their faces turned upward to catch the distant *chin-chin-chin* of sleighbells. Pacing the porch in fret over his failed watch, Fritz was the first to spy the bright light of Lucifer's antlers parting the darkness above the trees.

"Here they come!" he shouted.

Anya threw up the sash of her sewing room window and leaned out. Wendy's pale face shone above Santa's folded hands. Her husband's features seemed gaunt and drawn, his hair wild and unruly.

Those nearest the landing swarmed about, reaching to steady Santa's mount. Some helped unclaw Snowball from Santa's pocket and set her down in the snow; she scampered off with Nightwind toward the skating pond. Others lifted Santa's red-and-white bundle down from the reindeer's back and conveyed her to Anya's arms. "Easy with her," Santa snapped. "She's had a terrible shock."

Wondering murmurs arose at this, and again when Santa whispered in Lucifer's ear, reached down to uncinch his saddle, and slapped his lead reindeer briskly on the rump, sending him bounding skyward again. Santa's shout rose up like a stern whipsmack: "And God help you if you're a day late in returning!"

Then Santa elbowed aside elf after elf, disappearing into the cottage with Anya and Wendy. Inside, Fritz drew a hot bath and heated some broth. The others stood in the commons, feeling relief at Wendy's safe return, horror at rumors of Rachel's death, and shock at the harsh demeanor that had overtaken their master. When Fritz reappeared on the porch, his features were drawn, his manner distracted. Choking back tears, he confirmed the rumors, saying only that the Tooth Fairy had killed Rachel and turned her to gold. "Wendy will live," he said, "but her condition is uncertain. She focuses on no one, says not a word, hears nothing, takes food sparingly. Santa and Mrs. Claus ask that we pray for her, and for her mother."

And so, with long faces and leaden hearts, Santa's helpers returned to their quarters. There they knelt by their beds, hands clasped, eyelids shut tight, lips moving in their beards. And when they had poured out to God all the love and concern they felt for Wendy and commended Rachel's soul to His keeping, they added a special prayer for the restoration of Santa's spirits and crawled beneath the covers, seeking in vain the solace that sleep brings.

Santa leaned against the jamb of the bathroom door, arms folded, watching Anya bathe Wendy. The child's eyes stared straight ahead. Her arms and shoulders shivered as they had done throughout the return trip, though she was immersed, her head only excepted, in steaming bathwater. "So how long's the little—?" Stopping himself, Santa softened, let his arms unfold. "I mean, will she be all right?"

"We're going to be just fine," said Anya, a tinge of anxiety in her voice, "aren't we, Wendy?"

Wendy remained silent.

"Of course we are."

"Don't patronize her, Anya. Wendy's a strong girl, strong enough to deal with her own grief, surely."

With a wrung washcloth, Anya gently daubed away the streaks of blood around the little girl's mouth. When she asked if she might use her tongue on Wendy's wounded gums, the girl made no reply. But when Anya lifted her fingers to her chin to ease open her mouth, Wendy screamed and lashed out at her with such frenzy that Santa was forced to rush into the chaotic slosh and outfling of bathwater to help his wife soothe the girl.

Anya dried her and wrapped her in a warm robe. Santa carried her to the bed in the guest room and watched while Anya stood over her and kissed her and caressed her brow and wished her a good night. Then it was time to close Wendy's door, return to their bedroom, confront the blood-spattered walls and the huge gold coin lying atilt on the hardwood floor.

Since Santa's departure, Anya had avoided the bedroom. She wept anew in her husband's arms when she saw the pained engraving of Rachel's face howling up through the moonlight, her golden hands tensed to fend off death. "Oh Claus," she sobbed, "her pain hurts to look at." The object's obscene clarity rattled her, the shoulders and breasts and belly thrust into prominence, yet receding at the same time into the coin's artificial depths.

"I'll turn it away."

Santa righted it to vertical on its thick milled edge and slowly rotated the offending sight about; caught the obscenity of the obverse side; quickly turned it back to heads and rolled it like a warped cymbal against the wall, where he tossed Anya's blue knit shawl over it. But the cruel depiction of Rachel's lower body—the wrinkled soles of her feet, the splayed legs, the taut buttocks, and the wide golden gape of her vulva—burned into Anya's brain and caused her to weep the night away.

Santa alternately wept and scowled, confused by the oceanic struggle within. He did his best to soothe his wife *(the simpering bitch!)* beneath the covers, turning to stare for long stretches at the shrouded shape propped against the wall.

Strange ideas percolated in his head.

* * *

Lacking Rachel's body, they buried the coin.

"It may help Wendy," Santa confided to Fritz the next morning. A large ledger lay open on the rolltop desk's ink-stained blotter. Santa's quill pen rested slantwise across one page. He had been making notes in an odd hand—not his usual florid script but one that looked runic, ancient, unwholesome. "It might help focus her grief if we hold a funeral, all of us gathered in the Chapel." Santa's voice had a rasp to it. "Along with that wretched coin, we can bury a good deal of Wendy's pain. It might snap her out of it sooner. What do you think?"

"Sounds like a good idea," said Fritz. He disliked the hard glare Santa sometimes fixed him with, as though he found him—found all of them—utterly despicable. Worse, he disliked the preoccupation that often claimed his master, his massive thumbs massaging erratic circles into the skin of his clasped hands, the corners of his mouth struggling against a smirk. Fritz noticed patches of coarse hair sprouting on the backs of Santa's hands.

"Fine!" Santa hunched over in his swivel chair and ticked off funeral preparations, drawing Fritz into what felt like a dark plot.

Fritz went at once to the workshop, where the elves sat glumly at empty workbenches, awaiting Santa's traditional opening speech to inaugurate another year of toymaking. He walked to the podium from which Santa usually spoke. In his piping voice, he gave them Santa's orders concerning the funeral.

Then, while a team of woodworkers bent to the manufacture of a pine coffin lined with red velvet, four feet and a tad more square, and the others queued up for armbands snipped from bolts of black-dyed muslin, four of the burliest elves—Knecht Rupert, Johann, Gustav, and flaxen-haired Franz the watchmaker—followed Fritz to the toolshed by the stable and broke out pickaxes and shovels. Silently through the snow they trudged, tools slung over their shoulders.

At the Chapel, Fritz paused and picked out a smooth patch of ground near the Altar. It was dappled now in sun and shade, but Fritz calculated it would be bathed in sunlight two hours hence. "We'll dig here," he said.

Johann and Gustav measured out the plot. Then Fritz watched his four friends swing their pickaxes through the air and break open the earth.

Anya shrouded herself in magic time. For a time, she allowed nothing to exist but moving vistas of black cloth, her own nimble fingers, and the mind-numbing *mmmmmmmm* and *shutch-shutch-shutch* of her sewing machine. No thoughts or memories. Just the easy reliable thrust and withdrawal of a sharp silver needle. With the embracing slowness of eternal solitude, two black dresses and one black Santa suit furred in funereal gray took shape under her hands.

When they were completed, lying across her lap like three boneless bodies, she allowed normal time to surge back into her life. She put on one of the dresses and carried the other garments to Wendy's room, where Santa sat gazing at the sleeping girl.

Despite the depth of Wendy's slumber, she woke easily at Anya's touch. No discernible improvement. Anya helped her use the potty, washed her face, and brushed her hair, speaking softly to her all the while. While Nightwind and Snowball watched wide-eyed from the blankets, she removed Wendy's nightgown and buttoned her into the black dress. Then she told her that they would have a light breakfast before burying her mother in the woods near the Chapel.

Anya held spoonfuls of porridge to Wendy's mouth, cupping her other hand beneath the spoon to catch drips but being careful not to touch Wendy's chin. Wendy took apple juice in small sips the same way, and Anya lightly patted her lips with a napkin.

At a knock on the front door, Santa rose to let Fritz in. Since his return, there was a roll to her husband's walk, a hint of swagger. He had changed. He looked less chubby in the face, smiled rarely, spoke less often and sounded earthy and rough when he did. But then he wasn't alone, she thought. They had all changed. Odd how grief wore one down.

Low whispers sounded in the hallway. Fritz and a number of elves carried something angular and white, the coffin, past the archway and beyond. Some minutes later, they returned, slower now and struggling with the plain brass handles, the bells they wore on their caps and slippers sounding heavier as they paced.

Santa glanced in. "It's time," he said, and Anya, rising, helped Wendy to her feet.

It was peaceful in the Chapel, thought Fritz; silent and lovely and full of woe. Now that the dreadful deadmarch of thousands of elfin bells on thousands of elfin slippers had died away, the only sounds were the forlorn dripping of leaves in the trees and Santa's solemn voice raised in prayer.

"We commend to You the soul of Your servant Rachel," he intoned, standing at the head of the lowered coffin in his black suit. Anya, head bowed, stood at Santa's right with one arm draped round Wendy's shoulder. "Take her to Your bosom, Lord, and grant her eternal rest.

"Rachel Townsend was a good girl as she grew, and a kind and goodhearted woman when grown. To Frank McGinnis she was a faithful and loving wife; to her daughter Wendy, a mother full of love, and caring, and compassion without stint. Those who knew her, those who called her 'friend,' were blest indeed.

"In her last year of life, Rachel brought new light to our community. That light dims at her passing; never again shall it burn as bright.

"My helpers took her to their hearts at once, and as they loved her, so she loved them, every one. Anya, my wife and helpmate, whom I cherish and adore beyond the telling, ever patient, longsuffering in the face of her husband's blundering ways, came in the last days to prize Rachel as I did and as I do yet: I loved

Rachel and I will always love her. She . . ."

Here Santa faltered. His eyelids closed and Fritz saw a tear tremble down his cheek. When he opened them again, his eyes darted about, seeking something or someone. He tugged at his beard. His lips quivered. Fritz pictured his master in the study, the ledger lying open on his desk, the thick angular calligraphy, fibrous hair on the backs of his hands.

All around, the forest dripped.

In harsh tones, heavy with woe: *"She was my second wife. Yes, she was! She served me! She serviced me well, she did!"* Santa seemed to catch himself, shook his head to clear it. "Rachel McGinnis was bright, buoyant, quick with cheerful thoughts, and words, and deeds, a stranger to all things mean and ugly.

"Failing her mortal remains, we bury now a distorted image of her, wrought out of gold and jealousy by her fairy enemy." He paused, seemed to bunch together at the shoulders. *"Her enemy and ours, yes, a sleek, sexy, simpering—!"* Again the catch, the release. "But no quantity of—" Fritz noted with alarm the strain in his master's voice. Then, calmer: "No quantity of gold, my friends, can ever match Rachel's precious love. And no hatred, however vast and dreadful, shall ever tarnish our sacred memory of her, which will live forever in our hearts.

"Ashes to ashes, dust to dust. If indeed our Rachel must remain dead, may she find peace in the cradle of Your arms."

* * *

In the days that followed, Wendy showed little improvement. Her care had fallen to Anya and Fritz, though all the elves pitched in. They sledded their bright red bundle to and fro across the commons, Snowball and Nightwind perched upon her lap. Some tried to joke with her, pretending that she joked right back at them. Others peered in at the kitchen window awaiting a chance to help feed her, to spoon up blendered food and hold it under her nose and watch her slotted mouth open to take it in. It was a difficult time.

What made it rougher was Santa's absence.

Not that he had left the North Pole.

But he might as well have.

They saw him at meals, wearing his black Santa suit long after the others had put off their mourning, toying with his food, tucking it into his mouth like so much fodder, responding only when a question was repeated. They watched him slink through shadows in obscure corners of the workshop, claiming stray scraps of something or other and carrying them back to his locked workroom, a strange hobble to his walk.

Anya awoke each morning aware that sometime between midnight and dawn her husband had slipped away. From all appearances, he was losing weight, taking on muscle, growing hairier about the thighs and shanks. He left a peculiar odor on the sheets, not exactly unpleasant, not unpleasant at all, but not the most civilized of smells either.

Fritz made bold once to lay aside his tools, climb down from his wooden stool, walk like Oliver Twist along a corridor of craned necks, and knock on the workroom door.

No response.

Again his knuckles fell.

No response.

Yet a third time, louder, longer, more insistent. All heads turned his way and elves from every part of the workshop stood in curious clusters a cautious distance behind.

Impatient footsteps, the snap of a deadbolt thrown back, the large ornate knob turning. A crack opened in the door and Santa's eye peered out, bloodshot, slightly crazed. Fritz took in the punishing gleam of worklights behind, wild unkempt hair, half a slit of mouth, and the master's yellowed fingernails where his hand gripped the door. "What is it?"

Fritz faltered. "Some of us, sir—"

"I'm busy, Fritz, very busy."

"We're worried that you—"

"Surely this can wait." The fingers vanished. The eye pulled away.

"But Santa—"

"I have no time for this foolishness. Now get back"—(the door closed)—"to work!" The bolt slammed home and Santa's footsteps retreated.

"Please!" Fritz shouted. He raised his fist but opened it and let his hand drop to his side. The walk back to his workbench—amidst murmurs of "Nice try" and "We're with you, Fritz"—was the longest walk the brave little elf had ever taken.

* * *

The third of February, just shy of midnight, she was complete. Santa snaked his hands behind her earlobes and toggled her on, pressing his fingertips firmly up toward the brain, above where the jawbone hinged. She blinked, fixed her hazel eyes on him, and spoke.

"Santa," she whispered.

And Santa nearly crumbled.

*(Perfect. She's perfect. Get a lot of mileage out of this toy, yes indeedy.)*

*You're mad, Pan. Totally out of your mind.*

*(Dare to dream, Santa baby. Dream big. This is gonna work like gangbusters.)*

For a few hours, he put her through her paces. She performed beautifully. She bantered easily, laughed at his jokes, did all the things that pleased him in bed.

He grew to despise her.

Her skin was Rachel-soft. Her long blond hair felt utterly convincing. Every curve and angle evoked anew the feelings that had first brought them into being. But she brought out other feelings too, now that Pan took charge more often. She made him feel filthy inside, like snowbanks black with soot.

With a shudder of disgust, he switched her off and withdrew his flaccidity from the manufactured warmth of her lips. His long black fly he buttoned up. Then he closed her mouth, laid her across the makeshift bed, and pondered his next move.

It occurred to him that perhaps he was too close to this thing. Perhaps, because he knew the mechanics of her so well, it spoiled the effect. Things might go smoother if the pleasure she offered weren't a hidden one. If he could somehow integrate her into the community, convincing Anya and the others that she had returned, he might come to love her as he had the real Rachel.

Delusion billowed in his brain. Ten minutes later he swept her inert form up into his arms, left his workroom, and carried her across the commons to the cottage.

Anya was snoring lightly. Santa set his creation down in an old armchair and stripped. He caught a glimpse of himself in the full-length mirror by the bathroom and paused to admire the growing definition of his deltoids, his biceps, his pectorals, the rough tufts of hair upon his chest. The days of roly-poly appeared to be on the wane. Hard inside, hard outside.

*(Getting to be quite a hunk, Santa old buddy.)*

*Yes, but at what price?*

*(Always one Gloomy Gus in the crowd. What price? Try free, my friend. Free and easy and unfettered and unrestrained. Let's get to it, shall we?)*

Peeling back the bedclothes, he maneuvered her beneath them, climbed in beside her, and pulled the blankets up around them. With trembling hands he activated her, heard her take breath, watched her head shift this way and that as one suddenly waking in the night. She gave a soft *mmmmm* and draped a loving hand across his chest. Her left leg moved against his thigh, bending so that her toes flexed at his knee and a delicate crush of curls brushed his hip.

"Rachel?" he spoke softly.

"Ummm?" the thing replied, feigning sleepiness.

His breath caught. Then: "Make love to Anya."

"But she's sleeping." The false note of concern struck him as obscene.

"She loves being wakened that way."

"All right, Santa. If you'll promise to join in." Playfully she kissed his cheek, then shifted off him and turned to snuggle up against Anya.

Anya's sleep was dreamless. Slowly she rose out of it, luxuriating in the lips at her nipple and the fingers working between her thighs. When she opened her eyes, everything she saw told her the impossible. She blinked a question at her husband, but he said nothing. Anya touched Rachel's blond locks, felt Rachel's lips swirl in sensuous circles at her chest. "But how—?"

The golden hair twirled aside and Rachel's beautiful face beamed up at her. Anya gasped in delight. There was an aura of beatitude about her revived lover that nearly undid the horrors of Christmas night. "Not now," Rachel whispered. "Lie back and let me pleasure you."

And Anya obeyed her, running one hand along Rachel's back and taking into the other the hanging fullness of her right breast. The nipple stiffened under her thumb. Then Rachel cast off the covers and kissed her downward. She dipped between Anya's parted thighs, her hands snaking up under Anya's splayed legs to take between thumb and forefinger the hard nubs atop her breasts and worry them toward ecstasy.

Anya grew aware, through the dizzying haze of her bliss, that Santa now towered up behind Rachel, a dark fat shade whose large hands curved and turned in the moonlight to define Rachel's naked hips. His head was bent like a bull goat poised to charge. From the rising tones of Rachel's *mmmmm* and the gaspaceous accelerando of her tongue-flick and the shud and judder rhythming through her body, Anya guessed that Santa had sunk his erection deep inside their beloved and was thrilling her clitoris with his skilled fingers.

The splash of moonlight across Anya's belly, Rachel's writhing body, Santa's clamped hand at her hip, Rachel's merciless tonguetip, the rising sounds of Rachel readying to explode, the guttural moans of their musky, humping husband—all these swam deliciously before Anya as she reached down through Rachel's hair and moved her fingers firmly along the flare of her ears, down past the lobes, caressing inward as her orgasm began.

And Rachel died.

Her tongue lay still against Anya's womanhood. Her fingers became as the fingers of a corpse, cold and hard, at Anya's nipples. Her moans abruptly cut off.

Orgasm and terror seized Anya.

As she climaxed, Anya wriggled out from under her lover, casting the dead woman off in horror and hugging the warmth of her blankets about her. The pleasure that still coursed through her turned her stomach. She felt violated.

"Anya," said Santa, moving to her side of the bed. His erection parted the moonlight.

"What in the name of heaven is that . . . that thing?"

"An experiment. I wanted to—"

She spat in his face. "What sort of filth have you turned into?" she said. "Take that disgusting thing out of here and get rid of it."

"But Anya—"

"Now!" She pulled the blankets around her and buried her face in her pillow. She heard Santa throw on his clothes, muttering darkly. Then the weight lifted off the foot of the bed and he was out the door and down the hall, the front door slamming behind him like the short sharp blast of Gabriel's horn.

What woke Wendy were the muffled duet of sounds Santa and Mommy made being sad together, the sounds Mommy had told her were part of grown-up love.

Wendy loved the night. Being alone in her bed with Snowball and Nightwind curled against her brought her cautiously back into her body.

Darkness helped. Silence did too.

When others were around, she observed as through a telescope the elves' antics, the loving face of Mrs. Claus as she bathed her, the automatic workings of her mouth and throat and innards as someone spooned egg custard or cream of tomato soup into her. But the black comfort of night backed them all off and gave her space to breathe.

Now the sounds of her mother's love drew her further out. She blinked awake and turned her head on the pillow to listen. Different walls, a greater distance: but the pitch and rhythm thrilled her. Then her mother's high-pitched noises vanished and Santa's low moans choked off. A new voice, Mrs. Claus angry, stabbed through the walls like a mouthless woman shouting.

When the front door slammed, Wendy arose. Peering out the sewing room window, she watched Santa's bent form trudge toward the stable. Something heavy was slung over his shoulder, something wrapped in a floppy blanket. By the time Wendy had dressed, he was halfway across the commons, a shovel propped on his other shoulder. His boots left deep black pits in the snow.

Wendy eased out of her room, tiptoed through the darkness to the front door, and slipped into the night. She was afraid that the squeak of her boots against the snow-packed porch would turn Santa's head or bring on all the lights. But the buildings remained dark and Santa, now a tiny dot near the skating pond, kept on across the moonlit snow. Wendy lost him in the sliver of moon and the evergreens. But his bootprints, large teardrops in the snow, guided her up into the hills.

Santa's path skirted the drip and trickle of a creek to cut abruptly through towering pines and outcroppings of rock. Wendy pressed on. At times, she stopped to listen. When at last she heard not the silence of the forest but what sounded like the short sharp huff and chug of a train surging to life every few seconds, she took more careful steps, slow and silent.

Wendy set a hand against the bark of a thick ash. She made out a dark hut through the trees, and Santa bent to his digging. The flat patch of earth he had chosen was slapped with a blaze of moonlight. Propping the shovel against the hut's outer wall, he dropped the blanketed shape into a shallow hole. Looking more serious than Wendy had ever seen him, he took up the shovel again and began covering his burden.

Then Santa stopped and stood up, peering about. He turned his back to her and his pants loosened and fell about his boots. His legs were muscled and hairy. When he peeled back the dirt-clotted blanket, it seemed to Wendy that the woman he unwrapped, whoever she was, was dead. But then Santa touched her neck and she came at once to life, kissing him and wrapping her legs about his waist, and Wendy had at last a clear view of her mother's face—*her mother's face!*—her lips pressed to Santa's, her long blond hair spilling across the blanket.

Santa knew his mind was diseased. That it had been so at least since the incident in the graveyard when Pan had taken over. And that things had steadily deteriorated since then.

While slogging out to bury the doll, he had cursed Anya many times over. But she was right. This contrivance slung over his shoulder was an outrage, a madman's fantasy. He must have been insane to imagine for one moment its successful incorporation into the community.

By the time he broke open the earth, Santa thought he had regained control.

But the shape of the doll, the remembered heft of it, its womanliness, its vulnerability to violation, brought the intruder rushing to the fore. Horrified, he fell upon her. He plunged into her, groped for her lobes, felt her surge into a ghastly parody of love beneath him.

*No*, he thought, *this is wrong, this is vile, I can't be doing this.*

*(That's right, pal, disassociate. It's not you, after all. It's me. A convenient fiction, this split between us. I get to wallow like pigs in shit, you get to be as appalled as a priest pulling his pud, and your star hitter slides into home plate.)*

The doll writhed under him. *Must gain control, must put you under.*

*(Fine, fine. Just let me fuck in peace, okay? Go off somewhere and count daisies, why don't you.)*

Then the doll moaned at his mouth and whispered depravities in his ear.

Revulsion seized him. He rebelled. He saw Rachel mocked by his hands, the memory of Rachel dishonored by his selfish acts. It was enough to make the virtue well up in him and topple the intruder.

*(Now hold on here—)*

*Enough*! Santa swiped at him with all the goodness in his heart. And in a flush of anger, with more ease than Santa thought possible, the goat-god was gone.

* * *

Santa gave a cry of rage and horror, a cry that cut into Wendy's heart. Leaping off her mother, he pulled up his pants, took up the shovel, and began throwing clods of dirt on her.

She tried to rise, looking hurt and confused, saying "What's wrong?" and "Where are we?" and "Stop that!" but Santa brought his shovel down hard upon her head and she fell forward. Then Santa shouted "Die, damn you, die!" and his shovel whipped through the air again and again until she lay still.

The chug of the train began anew, picking up steam, and Wendy's eyes watched a weeping Santa bury her mother under a deep mound of earth. But Wendy herself climbed aboard the warm embracing train and let it take her, one painful puff after another, farther and farther from the hut.

She didn't notice Santa walk away, head bowed, when he was done.

Nor the falling snow that flaked and clumped against her cheeks.

Nor winter's icy fingers moving in to touch her skin, to press upon her skin, to sink beneath her skin.

Not until seven the next morning, when Anya brought in porridge, was Wendy's absence discovered. The cats glared up at her from an empty bed. Ten minutes later, Santa, dressed at last in something other than black, stormed into the elves' quarters. Quickly they were out in force, combing the countryside.

Santa cast a wide net of magic time about his lands

and took to the air in his sleigh, tightly spiraling out into the woodlands, skimming as close to the treetops as he dared. Two hours into the search, a dreadful thought seized him and he flew at once toward the hut. On the first pass, he caught the bright red of Wendy's down jacket. She was standing, dear God, in a copse of ash trees not a hundred feet from where he had buried the Rachel doll.

When the elves in that sector of Santa's domain saw his sleigh zoom overhead on its way to the commons, they guessed the reason and raced for home. Others heard the rumor shouted through the trees but kept on until the lifting of magic time confirmed it. Then they too broke off the search.

Santa's sleigh stood empty outside the cottage, the reindeer restless and neglected in their traces. Growing clusters of elves crowded about the porch, waiting.

Inside, Anya feverishly tongued Wendy's frostbitten fingers and toes while Santa knelt beside the little girl, chafing her hands and pleading with her not to die. But Wendy opened her eyes just once and made a soughing sound low in her throat. She raised a hand to him. And then, as all mortals do in time, little Wendy slipped down the rabbithole of death and was gone.

Santa wept. He crushed the dead girl to his chest.

Anya stroked her forehead, then turned away, wanting to dole out her grief bit by bit. With two small safety pins, she fastened a black armband around Santa's arm. Then she draped a shawl of black knit about her shoulders.

"It's time we told the others," Anya said, touching her husband's head. He rose and sobbed upon her shoulder. Then he released her and nodded. Turning back to the bed, he lifted Wendy's lifeless body into his arms.

Someone saw movement in the cottage and someone else caught a glimpse of Wendy being carried by Santa. Wasn't certain, he said, but it looked as though she was beaming up at him. Mrs. Claus appeared at the door and rumors of full recovery flew backward through the crowd.

Santa stepped out onto the porch.

And the rumors fell to the snow.

"Our beloved Wendy," he announced, "is dead." He stood there for the longest time and displayed the bald fact of it. No one spoke. No one moved.

Then Anya touched her husband's elbow. He gazed at her, confused. Nodding like one bumped awake in travel, he looked over the crowd toward the gingerbread house to his right. Like a green sea they parted to let him pass. Those in back glimpsed only Santa's bare head moving and Mrs. Claus's white bun bobbing at his far side. But the front ranks saw it all: Wendy, skin white as porcelain, her long auburn hair waving unbraided as they walked, her patent-leather shoes giving a ghastly carefree bounce; Mrs. Claus with one hand at her husband's arm, the other clutching an embroidered handkerchief to her lips; and Santa, face drawn, the color drained from his cheeks.

Wilhelm and Fritz helped bring Wendy's bed away

from the far wall of her bedroom and prop it up by her picture window. Then they joined the others outside. The crowd watched Santa lay Wendy down and bend a slow kiss to her forehead. Mrs. Claus knelt beside her, cradling the dead girl's face in one hand and smoothing her hair against the pillow with the other. She folded Wendy's hands across her waist, fussing with her clothing until Santa stepped in and raised his wife.

Then began a parade of elves past Wendy's corpse, a parade that stretched across three days and nights. The line hugged the perimeter of the commons, running the length of the workshop and veering at the stable, then going past Santa's cottage and making a wide bulge out, which twisted back to the elves' quarters, curved round the skating pond, and hugged the hills almost to the gingerbread house again.

Those who, cap in hand, had said one farewell to Wendy wanted to say another. They rejoined the line. Soon the far bulge flattened out, the end of the line met its beginning, and the visitation became continuous.

Midafternoon of the first day, Englebert and Josef retrieved the black armbands from the recycling bins in the workshop and passed them out. Over their protests, they were thrust forward to the front of the line.

At sunrise on the second day, Knecht Rupert disappeared into the woods and returned with an armload of snow crocus. Until Anya called a halt to it, there was a brief incursion into the hills and hordes of elves returned with the purple and yellow flowers clutched to their chests. Soon a blanket of soft petals covered Wendy from chin to ankles, filling her bedroom with fragrance.

And on the following night, Heinrich, heartsick at the happy sound his half-dozen bells made dangling from his half-dozen caps, not to mention the bells jangling at the tips of his dozen slippers—Heinrich closed his fists around the cold silver X-cut spheres, wrenched them with a muffled *clk-clk-clk* off his clothing, and placed them, shiny with candlelight, above Wendy's folded hands on the crocus blossoms. Those that followed saw. And seeing, did likewise. Anya's sewing scissors were passed round the circle of mourners until, to an elf, they held their bells clutched tight in their hands and moved solemnly through the silent night, contributing, when it was their turn, to the shimmering coat of moonlight that silvered and grew about Wendy's corpse.

Such were the rituals that developed in the course of their three-day vigil. But none so simple nor so moving as the ritual approach to the body, the kneeling, the gaze upon Wendy's face, the kiss upon her brow, the reluctant rise, the slow nod to Santa and his wife, and the stoop-shouldered departure.

Mrs. Claus held together well.

But Santa looked worse at each pass.

The first day, he avoided their eyes. He stood there without a word, looking down at Wendy and letting her death assault him full in the face.

The second day, he stared at them as though they

were unearthly beings that angered and appalled him. Late afternoon, he seemed like a fat old man with no home, no food, no one to love.

By the third day, the strangeness he had shown of late began to dominate. Above his forehead, twin bulges rose at the hairline as if inch-thick brass rings pressed his flesh outward in torment. And his grief grew, all that day and into the night and on into the dawn that followed.

The odd thing about their visits to Wendy's side was that no one expected them to last more than a few hours, a day at most. They thought their shared grief would peak, that the flow of elves across the threshold would cease and Santa would lead them back to the Chapel to bury Wendy beside her mother. But even as the cloud cover grew darker and more oppressive during those three days, just so did Santa's sorrow feed the communal woe, wrapping them in ever more unbearable layers of grief. Death coaxed them hour by hour—none more so than Santa—toward some awful orgastic brink. But, like a cruel lover, he withheld release, letting the torment build and build in them.

When Santa could stand it no more, he broke from the house with a roar of agony, sending Friedrich and Helmut tumbling into the snow. Anya followed, her mouth red and wet, her tears streaming free. Clouds churned above him like blankets of pitch. Trembling before the weeping elves, Santa ran his fingers through his beard in a gesture of supplication. Then the buttons from chin to belt popped like cherries into the snow and his red suit peeled open under his hands.

"Help me Lord!" he supplicated, in a voice that tried their hearts. Then abruptly, full of gall and grapeshot: *"Show yourself, you god of scum and shit!"* Santa shouted this aloft, rending his garments, tearing off his boots, and hurling his belt away from him like a shiny black snake twisting through the air. Patches of red and puffballs of white filled the air about him and fell in fury to the snow. He stood there naked, his body wavering between two extremes: one was the round soft Santa they had always known; the other had horns and hoofs and hair, eyes that burned, and a shout that hurt their eardrums.

"Heal me, oh my God! *Bully pantheon tyrant, I spit in your face!* Let me vomit my soul into oblivion, let me fling away all trace of Santa, for Santa is a sack full of sin and ashes, a fraud, a fiend, and I must be rid of him or my heart will burst! *I defy you! I hurl figs at you out of my arse! May you choke on them, you slayer of the innocent!"*

And his wife wept and tore her dress and let her hair tumble down, as she knelt naked in the snow beside her husband and opened her hands to the heavens. When he was penitent, she was the sweet-faced old woman they knew; but when Santa raged and shook his fist, she swayed toward him and her body appeared to tuck and smooth and firm and tighten, fir-green tresses flowing down her back, her eyes reflecting—as the moon, the sun—her mate's outrage.

Santa's alternating rage and self-loathing washed against the rapt circle of elves. And though they were mightily confused, they too stripped and knelt, joining hands, holding them high. They keened into the clouds, weeping and swaying with the buffet of Santa's words, but giving vent to a delicious defiance when Santa veered that way.

"Dear God," implored Saint Nicholas, "hollow me out, scoop me clean of presumption and lust." But Pan surged forth and bellowed, *"Forget what the wimp says! Physician heal thyself!"*

The split raged in him, first one side of him holding high ground, then the other. "Mercy I pray. Give me, if such be Thy will, the gift of nullity. *Go ahead, blast me! You scared to? Do it! Annihilate the fuck out of me!* The immortal blood pounds in my skull. Naught passes before my eyes but cascades of boys and girls falling, endlessly, into the grave. They die. We live. Dear Lord, the burden crushes. *Get the fuck down here! Get the fuck down here right now! We got things to duke out, you and me, and I'm raring to take you on!"*

Then it happened.

Those in front of Santa saw the shaft of light fall upon him and strip away the rage and pain, salving his visage with soothing. They saw the body come back full and Clausean, the droll little mouth, the twinkling eyes, the rosy cheeks, the bowlful of jelly—all there in the wink of an eye. Gone the horned bellicosity. Gone the defiant fist, the goat-god's savage glare.

The elves gazed along the bright chute of light, up into the firmament, and their deepest pain fell from them like a mere mood, as the hand of God swept aside a thick batting of cloud: Pure love beamed down upon them from the beatitude that was the Creator's face.

# *Chapter Fifteen*

## *A Time to Rejoice*

And God carried on many conversations in that hour, as many as there were creatures to hear and be heard. Every deer and elf He took aside, off from the others, addressing his inmost hopes and fears and refreshing his parched soul with the waters of divinity.

And each of them felt singled out and loved for his unique qualities.

And so it was.

But Santa and his wife, kneeling naked in foot-deep snow, He held in thrall. For He wanted all to witness the wonders in store for them.

And when the elves had been newly dressed, inside and out, God unbound the beloved pair and spake thus to them: "Santa, Anya, do you not know how precious to Me is the least mote of your being? Can you not feel within you the pulse of My continuous creation? Does your faith falter so, is your charity turned so inward, are your hopes so blighted by misfortune, that you have grown insensible to truth?"

Santa took Anya's hand in his. "Forgive us, Lord, our unfaith," said he. "Though immortal by Your grace, we share with all humanity feelings of love and loss, the—"

With a flick of His fingernail, God silenced him. Then, though it was barely dawn, He suffered the sun to top the sky, moving like a mole behind the clouds. When it reached its zenith, a precise circle of cumulus irised open. Golden light coned down around Santa and his wife, so that the snow cover melted away in a wide radius about them. Beneath their knees thick grass sprouted. Around them the earth turned verdant. Soft breezes warmed their bodies. Beyond that radius, all remained ice and snow and rapt elves, and a fresh descent of snowflakes, large and clumped and fragile as puffs of dandelion.

Now there rose up four saplings, reaching toward the heavens and thickening as they reached, resolving at last into palm trees stretched thin as Chinese handcuffs and arching out, broad-leafed, thirty feet overhead. Beneath the unclothed couple the earth rumbled and warped. Like bread rising in a rectangular tin, it plumped up and out. And the grass upon this uplifted bed, with its bedposts of palm, split and twisted into moss, luxuriant and spongy to the touch.

Then God stretched forth His hand and beckoned past the gingerbread house into the woods. A faint snap was heard by all. Then they saw the coin, thick and clean and solid gold, rolling through the trees. Out of the hills it came, leaving a deep milled track of snow in its wake. Heinrich split apart to let it pass, and it rolled through him as feathers of snow fell and melted upon it. Onto the bed of moss it rolled, coming to rest against the palm tree at Santa's left. Rachel's face agonized out of sun-gleamed gold.

And God said, "Though you hate the means by which it was made, love the coin. Only love the coin and all will be well."

And He began to withdraw behind the cloud cover.

"But Lord," Santa said, "what will become of the Tooth Fairy?"

Anya chimed in, "And the Easter Bunny?"

Their hearts thrilled to see God smile. And He said unto them, "Leave those two to Me."

"But our dear Wendy—" Santa said.

And God's smile turned enigmatic and He repeated, as He faded, His injunction: "Only love the coin." But they could scarcely hear His last word, and then He was gone.

Fritz was struck heart-sore at God's disappearance. To judge from the groans that rose from his brethren, he was not alone. But the Father, as He had done at their first creation, inlaid His healing hand and toyed with their emotions, turning wretchedness to regret and, by degrees, to blessedness.

God's departure drew all eyes to Santa's bower, where divine love infused the brilliant cone of light, the bed of moss it fell upon, the gleaming coin upon that bed, and the immortal pair who now laid hands upon that coin.

Santa rolled the golden disc between them and set his hands at ten and two o'clock. Below him were Rachel's nether parts, down to the sculpted soles of her feet. "Only love the coin," he said.

Anya placed her hands between his. "Oh, Claus, she seems in such agony." Rachel's face howled, twisted rivulets of hair streaming past her ears, her neck bent sharply back, her nipples thrust forward. The arms, mere suggestion, resolved into hands taut with vain rebuff.

"Close your eyes, Anya," Santa suggested, doing likewise. "Close your eyes and explore her features with your fingers." His right hand moved to Rachel's rump, tracing the familiar curves of her buttocks. Touching this mockery brought back at once the self-loathing he had felt making love to the doll he had created. But those feelings he now put by, bringing to the fore all his love for the mortal woman. As he caressed her hindquarters—the golden buttocks and the gaping labia of gold between them—their year together flashed before him and he almost fancied that the cold metal warmed beneath his touch.

"It's astonishing," Anya said, "how something made in such an awful way could capture so precisely the softness of Rachel's cheek."

Santa felt Anya's right hand beside his left, still clutching the striated edge of the coin. "Use both hands, Anya. I've got it." Anya's fingers slipped away.

"The breasts are simply breathtaking."

"Are your eyes closed?" he asked.

"Yes."

"Touch your face to hers," Santa said. "Make her suffering your own." He ran his index and middle fingers past the gold nub of her clitoris to the inverted V of private hair, fine and curly, etched in gold. Then, defying the coin's abrupt angle there, Santa strove to push further.

"Yes, I can feel it. Oh, Claus, she's so cold. And her mouth is stretched so wide."

"Press your mouth to hers, Anya. Lick about her lips. Breathe into her. I think I'm starting to sense some give back here."

"Yes. Her nipples seem to be softening. I can feel the tension leaving her hands."

"Her mouth, Anya. Look to her mouth." The coin edge beneath his left hand no longer curved hard about. When he opened his eyes, he saw that the edges all round were pulling inward little by little. His fingers inched along Rachel's right buttock as though he were a sculptor working tough clay. He felt resistance at his fingernails but pushed on until he rounded her hip. "It's yielding, Anya!"

"Mmmmm."

Now Santa brought his other hand down and pushed his way through gold until he had her other hip, bone-hard at its turn but covered now with something less than metal and more than skin. His belly pressed against her buttocks as he reached around her and, fighting the stubborn metal, felt his fingers meet at her navel. He ran his hands down the flat of her tummy and found a stiff yield of hair and the start of her thighs.

Her toes flexed against his legs.

And something of Santa's flexed too.

He was turned on by joy. His blood pulsed and he laughed as his growing member throbbed with love for the reviving Rachel. Into the golden gape of her vulva he eased, feeling her flesh yield and grow warm at his entry. Closing his eyes again, he leaned forcefully into the upper reaches of the coin, willing his powerful chest down along her back, willing with all his heart that his lips would not crush against flat hard metal but come to rest upon Rachel's soft neck, his beard pressed playfully into endless billows of blond hair.

Anya's eyes were shut. Over her head, palm leaves rustled. Tropic breezes caressed her skin. Astonished murmurs came to her from some far-off dream world.

What was reality? Hands pilloried in gold, now flexing, now responding to her hands. Rigid ropes of hair that had begun as faint suggestion, passed into a cabled mass, and now frayed and separated under Anya's touch into fibrous strands. Stiff jaw relaxing shut. A tongue losing its metallic taste, softening at the lick of Anya's tongue. The flutter of golden eyelashes against her cheek.

Anya cried for joy. Into the moving taffy of the coin

she sank her eager hands, finding there the dead woman's arms, straight down to the elbows. Her fingers explored the length of the softening torso, the ribs and midriff. Kissing her crimped lips, she sobbed along one gilt cheek.

When Anya opened her eyes, Rachel was kneeling upon the moss, but a Rachel gilded and trembling, twisting her neck like a wild mare. Santa had her by the flanks and was moving within her. "Claus, she's not breathing!"

"Keep loving her," he gasped, eyes on fire. "She's almost free."

Anya lay on her back and brought her lips to Rachel's left nipple. The right one she tormented with thumb and forefinger. Bringing her free hand to Rachel's sex, she found there the glistening gold nub of flesh and danced her fingertips over it.

Rachel arched up and stiffened.

"Anya, we've lost her!"

Rage.

Bound across bedroom.

A sharp intake of breath.

Then pain everywhere, swift and slashing, a pain like the swift chill of a winter's dive.

She had dropped out at once, preferring the peace of the void. Now something coaxed her back. Hands of love pulled her toward pain.

Suddenly she had returned. The hands, though they adored her, coaxed her into cruelty and raw hurt. Yet she craved their touch. She knew them. Through the agony, she struggled to put faces to them, caught them, lost them, saw a little girl, *her* little girl. Wendy!

There came suddenly a remembrance of stretch and pressure below: Wendy emerging, coated with vernix, milking her, sleeping, raising her head, turning over, crawling, toddling, struggling with words, waving forlornly from a pre-school window, learning to read and being read to, writing notes to Mommy and Daddy and Santa Claus, playing with elves in snow, standing with her mouth ravaged and the Tooth Fairy's arms grappled about her.

Rachel's body throbbed. Though her eyelids raised and lowered, she saw nothing. She needed to exhale, but her lungs burned at the impossible task.

Then the pain zoomed upward and peaked. Riding her scream, it paid out bit by bit until a divine point of inflection twisted it up into pure pleasure. And death tumbled away empty-fisted. A gush of immortality shot through her and held at her center.

Through her howls, she heard sobs upon her throat. Anya's sobs. Rachel's vision cleared and there was Anya's radiant face, and upon her shoulders Santa's kisses, and in her quim Santa's cock. And Anya was sobbing, "You've come back to us, you've come back" over and over again. Rachel hugged the dear soul and kissed her, the memories flooding into her now.

Then Santa, disengaging, fell to the moss and clipped and cuddled her like a man starved for love.

A surge of green, shrieking with delight, descended

upon them and a sweep of tiny hands lifted them into the air.

Pandemonium broke out in the commons.

Fritz dove in with the others to touch the trio of lovers, to hoist them high and fling from his throat the joy that had built up as he watched God's miracle unfold. Green caps, skyrocketed above, were caught in midfall and catapulted back into the sky.

Then someone dashed into Santa's cottage and brought out three robes, red for Santa, green for Anya, and blue for Rachel. They put them on and stood beneath the palm trees, trading hug after hug with the elves until they felt their spines would never again straighten for stooping.

But the sun burrowed back down to the horizon and the clouds sealed up again. Moss became grass. The palm trees shrank into the earth. Fritz expected snow to reflocculate in the circle but that didn't happen. Even so, the ground seemed hungry for snowfall.

Then Fritz saw Rachel, radiant in immortality, turn toward the gingerbread house. In the midst of recinching her robe, her fingers froze. Fritz, tugging at Gregor's sleeve, nodded discreetly in her direction.

The crowd fell silent.

Rachel sat on the edge of Wendy's bed, resting a hand upon her daughter's folded hands.

"How did it happen?" she asked.

Santa told her. She was spared the gruesome details

of her late husband's resurrection. Santa felt it prudent as well to omit any mention of the Rachel doll, lest acts he had committed out of desperation be misconstrued.

As he spoke, her eyes remained fixed on Wendy. Santa and Anya glanced from mother and daughter to the drawn faces outside the picture window. New snow fell like somnolent feathers. It looked like midnight outside.

Rachel bent to her daughter and kissed her cheeks.

They were cold.

Bloodless as marble.

She pressed her lips to Wendy's lips. Held them there, remembering. Sobbed without breaking the seal, keening softly into Wendy's mouth. Her tears fell warm upon the little girl's face.

A jinglebell clattered to the carpet. Then another, and another.

Anya gasped.

Wendy's right hand fell to her side, sending a cascade of bells jangling to the floor.

Rachel, disbelieving, brought a hand to her mouth. Wendy's cheeks flushed out, turning from waxy white to carnation pink and at last to full fleshtones. She yawned and stretched, setting off splashes of tintinnabulation.

She blinked. "Mommy, why's it so noisy in here?" she asked.

Then Rachel hugged her fiercely and kissed her over and over, despite Wendy's protest. So tight were mother and daughter intertwined that Santa and Anya embraced them as a unit, kissing ear or cheek or wave of hair.

Wendy was smothered in bodies. Three pairs of feet waltzed her about the bedroom, skating gingerly over a floorful of jinglebells. Snowball and Nightwind, perched on the sill of the picture window, looked absolutely appalled.

In the commons, ecstatic elves leaped and pranced and hugged one another silly. Fritz shouted, "Look, she's got her teeth back!" but only Gregor, hugging him and breaking into an atypical grin, heard what he said.

The snowfall stopped and the black clouds turned pure white and dispersed and the fat round godlike flaring sun burst apart over all eternity, scattering rays of joy and sunshine everywhere.

Santa, in close consultation with his Maker, proposed to wed his wives in the Chapel on Valentine's Day, God presiding. Anya and Rachel willingly accepted and Wendy clapped her hands.

The week leading up to the ceremony saw everyone in a frenzy of activity. With Wendy's help, Rachel pieced together two beautiful white-lace wedding gowns and a powder-blue bridesmaid's dress. Anya gave the dollhouse contingent a crash course in clothing construction. Under her direction, they turned their skilled hands to the manufacture of tuxedos: a Pavarotti-sized red one for the groom and hundreds and hundreds of tiny green ones for the guests. To Fritz fell the preparations for the wedding feast, and none could recall in sheer cornucopial splendor any meal to match it. Knecht Rupert, with Johann and Gustav taking turns at the bellows, practiced the pump organ way off in the woods and when the happy day arrived, he swung to and fro upon his bench beside the Altar, note-perfect and in harmony with the world.

"Are we really immortal now, Mommy?" asked Wendy, stroking Nightwind as Rachel fastened a lace collar to Anya's dress.

"Yes, dear. No one can ever harm us again."

"And we'll never die again?"

"That's right, honey." She pulled Wendy close and kissed her forehead. "Do me a favor and bring me my sewing basket. Right behind you on the bookshelf. We have lots to do before tomorrow."

And tomorrow dawned pure and brilliant. The Chapel was flooded with winter sunlight. Two towering oak trees bent in toward one another, and from them a natural aisle led outward. Down that aisle the wedding party (which is to say everyone) marched, belting out a wedding song that Fritz and Gregor had cobbled together while preparing garnishes in Anya's kitchen. It was long on enthusiasm, their song, if short on merit, and its first verse went thus:

*Here come the brides,*
*A day past the ides;*
*Here comes their hubby,*

*All jolly and chubby.*
*To nature's bowers*
*'Midst hearts and flowers*
*We march and dance and sing;*
*We'll see them wedded*
*And stripped and bedded.*
*We wish them everything.*

When at last they attained the Chapel, the Perfect Light of God hovered and gleamed before the great oaks at the end of the aisle, just in front of the long flat rock of the Altar. Anya and Rachel paced hand in hand between blocks of bearded ecstatic elves, Wendy following after, clutching a nosegay and beaming with pride. Behind them came Santa, looking serenely debonair and stifling a belly laugh; and Fritz, his best man.

Fritz stood to Santa's left. To Santa's right stood Anya, then Rachel, and Wendy breaking into a full-toothed grin beside her mother. Someone tapped Knecht Rupert on the shoulder, and he came out of an inspired improvisation on the march theme and brought it to a sweeping finish on the tonic, tearing his hands away at last so that the final chord's thrilling affirmation echoed through the trees.

Now the Light transformed. And God the Father stood revealed before them, white of robe, white of beard, twice Santa's height and holding an open book in His hands.

"Dearly beloved," He said, "we are gathered together

in this beautiful setting to join three blessed souls in wedlock.

"Some souls might wonder at this, saying one wife to one husband is God's way. But I say unto you (and who better should know), let threesomes and more flourish upon this planet. Let men and women seek for love where they may, and let them unloose the grasping hand of jealousy, rejoicing instead in the righteous unfolding of a spouse's holy lust. For lust built upon love and caring is divine lust; and wedlock, like all useful locks, must at times be unlocked to welcome in beloved friends.

"My servant Martin Luther, though guilt-ridden to a fault, glimpsed something of the truth when he approved the bigamy of Philip, Landgrave of Hesse. But he closed himself off.

"My servants John Humphrey Noyes and Brigham Young reached beyond monogamy for a time. But they too closed themselves off—the Oneidan, by fishing in the murky waters of stirpiculture and copulation by committee; the Mormon, by prizing procreation over pleasure, by denying women their natural urges toward multiplicity, and by rousing the nosy-parker anxieties of an America in the throes of a Victorian intolerance from which it has yet to recover.

"Adam himself, at the beginning of time, could have enjoyed Lilith as well as Eve. But he imposed a duality upon them, projecting his own poor judgment onto Me and casting aside the 'wicked' wife in favor of the 'good.' Foolish one! He chose exclusion in a universe

I created expressly to favor inclusion. Adam, the first man, closed himself off.

"But My dearly sainted Nicholas and his dear saintly wife Anya now open themselves to embrace and clasp to their hearts My beloved Rachel. She is to serve as their helpmate and they as hers and one another's. I say that it is good, good beyond exceeding good. Henceforth, let the word go forth and let it be known and celebrated through all the world that humankind was shaped for polyfidelity, that elves and mortals and all creatures great and small are polymorphously perverse, and that from this time polygamous and polyandrous urges shall be heeded and revered. No more shall husband or wife skulk in shame to the bed of a second beloved, but wife or husband shall with open arms embrace the new and worthy lover, even as Anya now embraces Santa's Rachel. For just as your God is a triune God, so shall trinitarian love flourish on this planet."

Anya stole a glance across Santa's belly at Fritz. He had never looked happier, and it did Anya's heart good to see him so. Then she turned the other way and cast an admiring eye upon her new bride. It felt funny—and wonderful—to be taking a wife, to be taking this wife. She thrilled to see Rachel standing there, whole and lovely, her hand resting on Wendy's shoulder.

God turned to Fritz. "You bear the rings?"

Fritz nodded serenely. He fetched an oblong jewelry box from his coat pocket and opened it to reveal six gold bands, holding them up proudly for all to see.

Hermann the goldsmith, standing tall and thin-faced in the third row, blushed furiously and ran a giddy hand in circles over his face.

Then God led them through the exchange of rings and vows. Santa kissed Rachel, and Rachel kissed Anya, and Anya kissed Santa. God laid His hand upon each of them in turn, blessing them. Then He did likewise to Wendy—who gasped at the sheer ecstasy of it—and said, "Blessed be Wendy, type of all good children everywhere. She shall brighten the hearts of all who know her and be a light henceforth unto the children of the world."

He raised His eyes out over the crowd, back toward the distant commons. And all knew, without knowing what, that another miracle awaited them at home, something that involved Wendy.

But Wendy, God's hand resting upon her head, saw clearly the new life He had brought into being. She knew also what her mission was to be, and how God's gift fit into it. And, hearing His words issue from His mouth in every human tongue, Wendy was instantly fluent in them all, knowing that she would eventually need each of them.

Then God stretched His arms over the crowd and spoke the benediction. "Go now all ye who are here assembled. Love thyself; love one another; love this world and those who dwell therein. Live well, make toys, and be at peace, now and forevermore. Amen."

God vanished back into Everything, where He had always been, and universal hugging and kissing filled the Chapel. A figure in red and two in white were swirled and spun through a roiling mass of green, while over the elftops, buoyed by crafty hands, rode a giggling, grinning, happy-as-could-be Wendy, shouting out "Happy Valentine's Day!" in all the languages of the world.

If, during the festivities that followed in and about the commons, a few elves here and there went missing, neither Santa nor his wives took any notice of it. So their surprise was indeed genuine when, as things wound down, the elves raised them up and ran with them into the woods.

If Santa felt any misgiving about the direction they took, he was too drunk with happiness to reveal it. When they reached the hut which had once concealed his trysts with the Tooth Fairy, he relaxed into delight and joined his brides in admiration for what he saw.

For the elves had completely made the place over. Karlheinz and Max had laid toothsome little Thea to rest beside Santa's buried Rachel doll; her bed had been broken up and burned. The ashwood four-poster was gone too, as was every scrap of quilting and fur, all the blankets and bedding, every remembrance of that sorry time of grasping lust.

New skylights peeled back the darkness. A fire blazed upon the hearth and stacks of fresh-cut pinewood climbed halfway up the stone wall. A kitchen nook and a bath had been added, and a large bed spoke boldly from one wall. It had room to spare for marital gymnastics, but it also felt perfect for napping or lazing upon.

After a flurry of thanks and good wishes, the elves discreetly withdrew. And here the three newlyweds spent untold months of magic time—more than two days of normal time—in honeymoon retreat.

Upon their return, Rachel resettled herself and her daughter in Santa's cottage, and she and Anya moved their sewing and craftwork into the gingerbread house. She helped Anya manage the domestic side of things at the North Pole. She introduced the more technically minded elves to the joys of computing and helped design tasteful toys that took advantage of electronic smarts. She delighted too in teaching Santa's helpers, most of whom were stone-cold illiterate, to read. Many were the times that an excited student would rush up to her, bursting to share some choice passage he had found in the book he held open before her.

And what of Wendy? Of the acts she had witnessed at the hut, Santa was relieved to find she had no memory; but he spoke to her, just in case, of having missed her mother so much that he had done many foolish and much regretted deeds. During the week of her parents' honeymoon, Wendy spent most of her time at the stable. For when they had returned from the Chapel, God's new gift poked its head over the half-door and watched wide-eyed their return.

As a Shetland is to an Arabian, so was this reindeer to the least of Santa's team. She had a delicate filigree of antlers atop her head and a nose that glowed green as a traffic light through night fog. Her fur was milk-white and fine, her eyes an engaging shade of gray. At first Wendy called her Ivory, but later, when Santa read to her out of Ovid, Ivory became Galatea. "Galatea means white as milk in Greek, Daddy," she explained to a bemused Santa. "Besides, I think Galatea the green-nosed reindeer sounds better than Ivory the green-nosed reindeer, don't you?"

Santa laughed and said he did.

When Wendy shared her mission with Gregor, he fashioned a miniature sleigh for her, modeled on her stepfather's. Every Christmas Eve thereafter, she hitched up Galatea and followed Santa into the sky. Then, splitting off from him, she went one by one to the homes of children on her list. For Santa had taught her how to turn her gaze to the world, watching boys and girls carve out their lives, second by second, from the limitless possibilities before them. And each year, she chose a hundred who were very well behaved (but not of course in a priggish sort of way) or who tended toward kindheartedness but needed one small miracle to tip the scales. These she kissed awake and led by the hand to her sleigh. Through the night sky they sailed, sharing the wonders of the world which passed below.

The children she so honored woke on Christmas morning with the certainty that something wonderful (but what it was they could not say) had happened to them, that they had been blest beyond measure. It gave thereafter a focus to their lives; they developed low-voiced but persistent obsessions, one in music, another in medicine, this one in public service, that one in private enterprise. And each excelled and carried an aura about him or her, an aura of hope and goodwill that inspired everyone they touched and, when at last their lives ended, brought masses of grief-stricken mourners to their graves.

Wendy reserved a special time for Mrs. Fredericks, whom she visited each year until the old woman died, sitting on her lap and telling her teary-eyed listener of the wonders of living at the North Pole. After her death, Wendy placed a snow crocus upon her grave each Christmas Eve, missing her to tears.

The rest of the year, she helped inspire the elves. She served as a focus-group-of-one for new toy ideas and tested every prototype. Praise came quickly to her lips, and she learned to soften her criticisms with suggestions for improvement. She came to know all the workers, their quirks and foibles, their strengths at the workbench and their weaknesses, the secret gifts she could spring on them to brighten their faces. And she took it upon herself to learn what she could about every aspect of Santa's operation: she dabbled in wood and clay and metals, in fabrics and typography and printed circuitry, in dolls and board games and stuffed animals; she learned the ways of wrenches and hammers, looms and presses, lathes and sanders and bandsaws; and for a time she disappeared into the incestuous circle of clockmakers, emerging weeks later with a new cuckoo clock of her own design.

But the time Wendy loved best was night time. For Santa Claus would lift her onto his generous lap in the big armchair, and she would watch her mommies rock and knit by the fire and listen to her daddy's booming voice give life to the story he held before them.

Santa loved those times too.

The coming of Rachel and Wendy had turned him into a family man. He swore off long nights at the workshop, excepting only the December crunch; but even that he did his best to minimize by using the tools Rachel introduced him to: Gantt charts and PERTs and Hoshins, top-down design and prototyping, focus groups and usability testing and post mortems, TQC and QFD and FLURPS, along with huge doses of TLC, her own addition to the acronymic broth of best business practices.

He took Wendy and his wives for long walks in the woods, sometimes together, sometimes one at a time. He pitched in with the cooking and cleaning. He stretched out on the rug before the fire and played card games with Wendy or wrestled playfully with Snowball and Nightwind. As close as he had been to the children before, he felt umpteenfold closer having Wendy to watch and talk with and love. His Christmas deliveries became more precious to him, and he thanked God every day for bringing her into his life.

His elves became as sons and brothers to him. He gave them more free time and often joined them when they pulled Wendy on her sled. He even laced up ice-skates (something he hadn't done for centuries) and joined in the post-Christmas ice-a-thon on the skating pond. It soon became a tradition, at that event's climax, to link arms, speed-skate round and round faster and faster, and whip Santa off—his loud booming whoops of jollity filling the snow-flecked air—into the commons, where he would roll and tumble and come up halfway to the cottage, staggering like a drunken snowman.

But Santa's favorite moments were those he shared with Anya and Rachel in the intimate heartspace of the marriage bed. He loved his wives, especially when the three of them came together like a swirl of wind and fire under the down comforter.

Even now, as you read these words, the jolly old elf lies delirious beneath them, enjoying the give and take of their favorite triadic practice, 969. The bedclothes have been flung to the floor and moonlight spills boldly across their sheets. Anya and Rachel murmur words of love to Santa and to one another. From the waist down, his body lies in normal time, his thighs spread wide to welcome the kisses of his wives, his sex tight and hard and veined in silver beneath their fingers. Above, he moves through magic time, the better to serve and observe them.

Part of the time, Santa's head rests pillowed between two sets of feet. Rachel's right leg warms the heartside of his torso, Anya's left the other. He contemplates with holy rapture the curves and folds of their loins. His fingers work their flesh like a friar telling his beads. When his head flutters in and out of magic time, their bodies seem to strobe in the steady light of the moon. He feels as if he's flying through the night. Their flanks rock to the rhythm of his hands like the soft white haunches of Donner and Blitzen twitching under the gentle slap of leather across their backs. Their long beautiful bodies move like his team in harness, supple, articulate. Down below, where Lucifer's gleam might light up the night sky, the glistening blood-purple tip of his penis emerges from the mouth of this wife or that. Rachel favors tight lips and the suck and swirl of salivation. Anya, going wider and deeper, brings her tongue into it. Together, they give him heaven.

And when his head is not pillowed and marveling, he does his best to return the favor. Bifurcating at the waist, he arcs beneath them, giving each wife in turn his full attention. He hums as he licks, something they've told him excites them immensely.

Moving in and out of magic time, Santa's brain plays strange games. He sees Superman standing behind a seated Clark Kent in his Daily Planet office, fooling Lois Lane by changing clothes so fast she can't detect the flicker. Santa watches him repeat the trick with his new now-savvy bride at the Fortress of Solitude, splitting into two, then four, then as many ardent supermen as he can sustain without distracting himself, crowding around his wide-eyed Lois and loving her with the multiplicity of his manhood.

Had Santa a hand free, he would slap his forehead for not having the idea sooner. Time enough for that, he tells himself; and time enough for Anya and Rachel, if they like, to please him in the same way. He imagines them riding him everywhere in blurred overlap, opening to him like blooms in time-lapse photography the infinite variety of their love. Just picturing it makes Santa's pillowed head burst apart at the beard and split the night with a rousing *ho-ho-ho*. His delight spills into the hum of his cunnilingus. That familiar feeling starts to rise in him like the unspeakable wonder of life itself, and he readies himself to give his beloved women the whitest Christmas they have ever enjoyed.

God bless us, comes his last coherent thought before sweet oblivion claims him. God bless us every one!

# *Epilogue*

## *Tooth and Claw*

Fear not the flesh nor love it.
If you fear it, it will gain mastery over you.
If you love it, it will swallow and paralyze you.

—*The Gospel of Philip*

Subduction leads inevitably to orogeny.
And the earth moves.

—*Anonymous*

# *Epilogue*

## *Tooth and Claw*

Underground. Valentine's Day. For weeks, anxiety unrelenting had shattered the Easter Bunny's nerves. He had hopped about his room, sniffing aimlessly at the dirt, staring for hours at a bent piece of straw. Once he had peeked in at Petunia, only to pull back in disgust. He hadn't dared venture into the rest of his domain.

Upon waking that morning, however, anxiety had given way to calm. It was a calm as deep as sadness. He left his room at last but kept to the confines of the burrow. Everything, down to his hens and the blush-colored eggs they laid, seemed glazed with a patina of resignation and regret. He knew what was coming and welcomed it.

When God's footsteps first shook the earth, he went to his room, found its precise centerpoint, and hunkered down with as much humility as he could muster. Trees toppled. God's approaching tread matched the steady dead-march of his heart.

The Easter Bunny glanced up at the domed roof. A dark crack opened along the arc of the outer wall. Then the roof lifted from the burrow like an earthen shield. He blinked away a thin trickle of dirt that fell as the roof rose and daylight flooded in. Shafts of sun streaked through settling dust. But what captured his eye was the towering figure of God the Father, Who propped the giant disc of earth against an oak tree and, turning His gaze on him, sadly shook His head. "What, Mister Ophion, am I to do with you?"

"I beg your—?"

"This I believe is yours." God gestured north and the Easter Bunny could see dried egg remains lift from a distant mirror, defy space and time, and come together at God's fingertips like a jelly-bean. God stooped and laid it at the Easter Bunny's feet. "To voyeurism, which I shut My eyes to, you have added rape, an act intolerable in mortal men, let alone in an immortal entrusted with spreading happiness on the anniversary of My Son's resurrection."

"But I can expl—"

"Further, you have seen fit to lend aid and comfort to the Tooth Fairy. Sinning by omission, you have helped her mutilate and torment a child, devour that child's mother before her eyes, and dishonor her father's corpse."

"It was her fault. The Tooth Fairy. She forced me into it."

The tip of God's index finger stopped his lips. It stung like iodine on a cut. "No more lies, Mister

Ophion, Mister Boreas, Mister North Wind. Pause a moment. Pause and think about your misdeeds. Then you may confess your sins and beg, if you will, for mercy."

His lips were free again.

God sat upon the lip of earth, His feet resting inside the burrow near where Santa Claus had burst in. The Easter Bunny began to ask Him why He had called him such peculiar names, but the stern look in the Father's eyes stopped him.

He paused. He pondered. One by one, he named his sins and humbly begged God's pardon for them. Then he raised his head. "But it's just not fair. Really it isn't."

"What's not fair, My beloved?"

The sweetness in God's voice broke his heart, but he went on. "When You created me, Lord, You chose to make me a rabbit. If You'd only kept to scale—please forgive my presumption—I might have mated with mortal rabbits and been content. Instead, You made me an order of magnitude larger than normal. Even that wouldn't be a problem if I had a mate, a real Petunia just my size to love and honor and fill with seed. Instead I roam the world alone. And, dear Lord, as You well know, my sex drive, like everything else about me, is ten times that of a normal rabbit's. Lately, I fear, it has overwhelmed my better judgment."

"Go on."

"And also, well," he looked away, embarrassed, "this may sound funny, but I've had the feeling lately that

You may have made me forget things about myself, that there's more to my past than You've let on, that maybe I—dear God forgive me, it seems so absurd now that You're here—that maybe *I* was the true creator of the world way back when and somehow You snatched that position from me."

"Interesting. Very interesting."

"Of course it's all nonsense. I see that now. You needn't say a word about it. But this mate thing, oh dear Father, it's that that drives me buggy."

God reached down and lifted the Easter Bunny into His lap. The folds of His robe felt like a soft patch of pure heaven against his underbelly. The hand that stroked him made tears of joy start in his eyes. "I understand," said God. "And I see how to make things right."

Yes! thought the Easter Bunny. God's going to bring my Petunia to life, just like Pinocchio. Or He'll scrap her and fashion from His infinite love a fresh new mate, white and soft and fluffy, always eager for me to top her. Or maybe He'll fill the burrow with dozens of does. Hell, I can handle scores of the twitchy-tailed beauties. Nay, hundreds, thousands. Bring them on. Let legions of lovers smother me in kissyfur.

But God's hand covered his eyes and at once he saw straight back to the dawn of creation. "All begins in Chaos," said God. "But soon the goddess Eurynome rises out of it like naked love, full-thighed, full-breasted, her hair tumbling in wanton ringlets about her shoulders. She tries to rest her feet but finds nothing save herself and Chaos. Look there, her long lithe hands part sky and sea. She dances lonely upon the waves."

The Easter Bunny thumped against God's palm, snared by the image's fleshy perfection. "And there you are, the north wind she stirs up as she moves. She wheels about and snatches you up in her hands, rubbing you thick and tight until, behold, you become the serpent Ophion. See, she holds you close, dancing, ever dancing. Coiling about her limbs, you copulate with her."

He saw it all and remembered, even as God spoke it. He saw Eurynome, goddess of all things, turn herself into a dove, brood upon the waves, lay the universal egg. He saw himself coil sevenfold about the egg and hatch it and stare in amazement as all of creation, all the stars and planets, everything upon the earth and under the sea and in the firmament, leapt forth and took its place, pushing Chaos all atumble into oblivion. He saw too how it had gone bad: his boast that he alone had created all things, the heel she planted upon his head, the loss of his fangs, and his banishment to the dark places beneath the earth.

Now God brought the vision forward to the point of his rebirth as the Easter Bunny. The distant brooding of innumerable hens. The sound of his Creator's voice instructing him, his leaps into the air—all of it as he had always remembered it. But then there befell a memory splice: God paused in the past, as He had never done before, and looked about the burrow, His eyes full of prescience. He stretched out His hand, set a finger between the Easter Bunny's back legs, and—like a cartoonist erasing a smudge—massaged away the genitals, leaving only one small hole to pee with. Then the splice was over, and it wasn't a splice at all but the Easter Bunny's sole memory of his creation.

God lifted His hand from His creature's eyes and set him down in the burrow. "Does that clear up our little problem?"

"Yes," he said, confused. He couldn't begin to guess what problem the Father was talking about.

"Good," said God. "By the way, you've been doing a wonderful job with your Easter deliveries and a wonderful job managing things here. Keep up the good work."

Exhilaration filled his heart. "I do it all," he said, "to please You and to make the children happy."

"Bless you, My beloved," said God, and blest he felt. "Now be at peace. It's time I paid a visit to another of My servants, one not so contrite and cooperative, I fear, as you have been."

The Easter Bunny knew He was talking about the Tooth Fairy, though he had no idea how he knew. But he beamed up at the Lord and watched the roof close out the sunshine and the crack reseal itself, wondering what on earth the thing made of pellets over wire mesh was doing in the room next to his. When he had hauled it outside, crushed it with heavy stones, and skritched dirt over it, he headed back to the laying house to see how things were going with the hens.

Easter was little more than a month away and he was determined it would be the best Easter ever.

Rain pelted the Tooth Fairy's face.

The storm, at its height, billowed out of control. Lucifer lay exhausted on the beach. His antlers blushed pale pink from the abuse he had suffered since Christmas. Gripping his penis, she waited for signs of renewal.

As the wind whipped up her hair, the teeth of her necklace rattled upon her breasts. She forced her eyelids not to blink. Sheets of rain beat against the whites of her eyes and washed across her irises, flowing like sorrow down her cheeks. Squatting beside the blasted cedar, she awaited with relish the final showdown.

Where wails of typhoon fury had filled her ears, there now abruptly sounded the *Sanctus Dominus!* of angel choirs. The roiling sky turned blue and filled with billows. Angel faces beamed upon them, psalms of heavenly praise blasting in triumph from their throats.

Then God parted the clouds, sitting in state upon His golden throne, and glowered down at her. Lucifer's feeble head rose from the sand to stare in wonder. Letting go of his limp lovehandle, she stood defiant before the Lord.

"Call off your minions!" she shouted. "You're not about to overwhelm *me* with your heavenly bullshit!"

A flick of God's hand and the angels vanished. Pointing at Lucifer, He gestured north. Instantly, the reindeer sprang into the air and flew off, his antlers as bright, his gait as sure, as ever.

"Santa and I had a bargain—!" she protested.

"Do you want to continue to be the Tooth Fairy?" He asked quietly, resting His hands upon His throne and fixing her with His worst glower.

"Listen, just cut the—"

"Do you want to continue to be the Tooth Fairy?" If anything, the question came at her lower and more simply inflected than before. It chilled her to the marrow.

"Fuck you, all right? All right? You and the other shitheads of this world want to call me the Tooth Fairy, that's your lookout. My real name, as you well know, is Adrasteia. If I harvest molars and bicuspids and canines, it's because I damn well choose to."

"It's the position I gave you."

"Sure, okay sure, I pretended to kowtow to you back then. But I never lost myself. I never forgot who I was. An ash nymph I was from the beginning—proud sister to the Furies, born from the blood spilled when Kronos castrated Ouranos—and an ash nymph I remain. That gives me an integrity that Santa Claus and the Easter Bunny and you, you big blowhard, lost long ago."

"Let's not stray from the point. You've engaged in practices which—"

"And what makes you so high and mighty? Where do you get off sitting in judgment? You trying to come on like some *deus ex machina* and bring me to heel, you holier-than-thou son of a bitch?"

"I warn you. Don't provoke Me."

Something flared about His head. The sharp sting of ozone filled her nostrils. "You remember who you used to be, don't you?" she taunted. "When your mother Rhea gave birth to you and spirited you away from your child-eating father, your care fell to me and my sister Io and the goat-nymph Amaltheia, whose milk you shared with baby Pan and from whose horn you fashioned Cornucopia, the horn of plenty. Don't you recall how I pressed your infant lips to these nipples and let the maddening suck of your gums moisten me below?"

"You will cease this idle—"

"How I toyed with your baby penis, how I licked you down there and made you break out in a smile provoked by something other than gas? And when you matured beyond boyhood, how all three of us taught you lust? Look here, little fellow, long before you violated your mother and went on your libidinous rampage through the likes of Leda and Io and Europa, I was your first lover as well as the nurse of your babyhood. But when the old ways died and the Christers came in, you caved in with the rest of them, took on the Grand Persona they demanded of you, and forgot your true godhood, your triumph over Kronos, forgot, by God, that you were none other than almighty Zeus!"

"Enough!" He said. His fingers fastened upon her throat, though He remained where He was. "If Zeus you crave, foolish nymph, then Zeus you shall have!"

As He rose to His feet, the Tooth Fairy felt His other

hand pin her to the gritty sand and splay her legs wide. The placidity of God's visage split apart and out peered the face of old: Zeus's face, with its full salt-and-pepper beard, its wild corona of curly hair, and its ruddy-cheeked rage.

His white robe he tore asunder. Beneath it lay the old armor it thrilled her to see. His body was muscled and hairy where it emerged from his chiton. Medallions and weapons hung about him everywhere.

Without looking away from her, Zeus shot a hand into the heavens and filled his fist with fire. Heavy bolts of burning light into the swollen wound of her womanhood he hurled. Thirteen times the fire struck. Thirteen times it singed her flesh, burrowing deep inside her womb.

"You shall leave Santa Claus and Anya and Rachel and Wendy and those they love forever in peace. From this day forth, the North Pole is off limits to you.

"You shall avoid the Easter Bunny at all costs. He has been reformed.

"Never again shall you dare to harm one hair on a child's head. The mere thought of doing so I disallow.

"These my words you shall heed, or I swear by the God I have become, I will return and annihilate you. Slowly. The pain I have visited upon you now shall be, I promise you, as the tenth part of a fleabite when set against the torments I shall mete out on that day!"

Then he vanished from the sky. The sizzle of her flesh filled her nostrils. Her belly was one flaring pit of pain. Healing, when it came, was horrendous and slow. Still, she thought, she would survive it. She would endure the expulsion of mortal hurts and let immortality make her whole again.

A smile, despite her agony, appeared on her lips.

But then something caught inside her, a thing of claws and scales. Her smile rounded into a howl. Her screams split the sky. Through pain immense, she watched her belly stretch and swell like some demon had flexed his thorned fist deep inside her womb. Then, when her flayed insides hung in ribbons and the ribbons frayed to crimson fuzz, he began to pull his invisible arm out of her, the claws delving deep red furrows in the blistered flesh of her birth canal.

But what emerged from the bubbling froth was far worse than a demon's hand. It was squat and fat, her infant, and when its girth stuck halfway and her straining labia refused to stretch further, it blinked its bloody eyes at her. "Muzzer," it buzzed with murderous hate. Then it twisted about, teeth flashing like razors, and episiotomized her perineum all the way to her anus and beyond. The fat thing tumbled out, dragged its bloody afterbirth down to where the breakers thudded in, and battened on it.

Thank God that's over, she thought, lying spent and sweaty on the beach. But then, as one who having vomited feels an instant of well-being but is immediately seized by renewed wrack, she suffered the thrust of the giant's fist again into the bleeding wreckage of her womb. Her belly ballooned up, as did her agony, redoubling the torment that had gone before.

There on the beach beneath a slate-gray sky, the Tooth Fairy gave birth to thirteen impossible imps, each fatter and uglier than the one before. Thirteen times her belly ballooned. Thirteen times her vulva blurted out a brat. Each dropped goblin took longer than the one before, stretching torment beyond itself. Many times she screamed for death to take her.

Deaf ears.

When the last one spilled out, the universe was one solid throb. Clotted sand stretched from her sex to the sea. From belly to thighs, she was nothing but bruise and blood. Her lungs hurt from howling.

Then they attacked her breasts. One fat whelp waddled up, sniffed at her torso, and, having found his prize, put two three-fingered hands around her right breast and opened his head about her nipple. His suck staggered her. A second one dragged himself up from the waves and, seeing what his brother was about, took a pull at her left teat. One by one, the others crowded around and reached their heads in, snuffling at the blue-veined bulges that held the stores of milk they craved. "Wait your turn," she said, and three heads lifted as one and glared.

Then the first one bit her. She whacked him on his large flat head and said, "No!" His eyes rolled toward her. He growled over his meal and bit into her so hard that rivulets of milky blood trickled down the sides of her breast. A tongue came out of the crowd and licked up the spill. Its owner, baring his teeth, sank them into her, seeking milk ducts in the most direct way he could.

Then thirteen heads tore into her and made mincemeat of her chest, finding the lactation they demanded in the bloody ruins of her breasts.

Her hands tore helplessly at their hunched backs as they fed. But eventually she gave it up, embracing the pain as her lot. For her baker's dozen bastards she even felt a mother's love. No question they were wicked and selfish and nearly impossible to control. But they were hers. Even through the agony of birth and first feeding, part of her understood what wonders she could work with them.

And that's what she did.

Her nights she spent as usual going from bed to bed collecting teeth and leaving coins; and despite her every intent, her thoughts turned benign in those bedrooms and left her furious afterward. But the rest of the time she spent with her brood, suffering anew their feeding frenzies and then, as her bloody chest healed, sitting them down on the shore and filling their eager hearts with hatred.

Hatred of God.

Hatred of Santa Claus and his kiss-ass crowd of sycophants.

Hatred of mortals of every stripe, especially children.

She mapped out a mission for them and for ten months drilled every detail into their heads. She made little Santa suits for them, taught them world geography, gave them lessons in flight and magic time, showed them how to scan the earth for likely victims.

They learned fast, her brood, demonstrating a marked precocity for all things vengeful. When Christmas was but two weeks away, she sent them out, one each day. Her firstborn went first, Gronk of the piercing eye and the tight fist. He slouched and slavered down to the sea, then lifted off and bumblebee'd eastward away from his brothers' envious taunts. They turned then and savaged her for milk. But she only grimaced, looking ahead to Christmas Day when they'd be gone for twenty-four hours, wreaking havoc on the world and leaving her in peace.

And so it was. Her imps went forth and made the holiday season less joyous. Food and water they randomly polluted with their undetectable urine and feces, bringing on cramps and stitches, dizziness and fainting spells, nightmares that induced deep despair. They smothered family pets in their sleep, withered the branches of Christmas trees, and stole benevolent thoughts from sleepy heads. But their favorite task was to roam the streets on those nights leading up to Christmas, hunting for bad boys and girls to feed upon. Their screams they drank with glee, gobbling down their sinful little bodies to augment their own stores of wickedness.

Thus was a new tradition established. And the Tooth Fairy saw that it was good.

But her boys had one more tradition they'd long been scheming to institute. For they were precocious in more ways than one.

When, on the day after Christmas, they came swarming back to the island, they fell, full of spunk and vinegar, upon their mother. The vinegar of their misdeeds they waited until evening to recount. But the spunk homed in at their groins and made them stiff, with which stiffness they penetrated mommy dearest, unleashing upon her the unholy force of their desires.

And the Tooth Fairy laughed and saw that this too was good.

And when they were spent at last and she lay drenched in imp spunk, she hugged her loathsome brood to her and said unto them: "Thus shall you go forth into the world every Christmas hence, my boys, spreading evil cheer. And thus shall you return to your mother's arms.

"God damn us, my blasted little boys. God damn us every one!"

# *Afterword*

## *Making Light of Santa Claus*

**Robert Devereaux**

Montaigne once said, "There is no man so good, who, were he to submit all his thoughts and actions to the laws, would not deserve hanging ten times in his life." Saint Jerome warned, "A fat paunch never breeds fine thoughts." More to the point, Goethe had this to say: "The ideal goat is one that eats hay and shits diamonds."

Born in 1947, I was brought up in a modest three-bedroom home on Long Island. Here's what I remember about Santa Claus. I remember being too excited to fall asleep right away on Christmas Eve. More than likely, I keened my ears into the stillness, knowing it was too early for Santa's visit but caring not in the least. In the crisp morning, I woke to the astounding realization that Santa Claus had been by. My three-years-younger sister Margie and I raced down the hall, skidding on our pajamaed knees before a rain-festooned tree topped by a lighted star and anchored with a green striated bulb we called the Toilet Plunger for its resemblance to a float ball. "Presents!" we exclaimed, re-racing and re-exclaiming until we tired of the game. No gifts were ever unwrapped in our house before breakfast, and our parents were unbearably slow in waking on Christmas morning. Still, the bracing aroma of pine needles pervaded the air amid the certainty that we had indeed been visited by the jolly old elf.

I wasn't much of a visual child. Not even before my mind's eye did I spin notions about where Santa stood and what he looked like as he bent to our tree. Neither did I much wonder how he gained access to our chimneyless house. My images of him were culled from magazine ads, black-and-white TV, Christmas songs, and a ViewMaster disc that told Rudolph's story in dioramas I can summon forty years later with near-total recall.

As for the Easter Bunny and the Tooth Fairy, I had no images of them at all. Yet their unquestioned visits made our house feel and smell special indeed.

I wrote the initial version of *Santa Steps Out* in 1988 and 1989. Why did I do that?

First, I had after long gestation brought to light my initial attempt at a novel, *Oedipus Aroused* (a clever botch never published, though it landed me a mediocre New York agent). That book had taken two years of research into 13th century B.C. Delphi, Corinth, and Thebes, into Minoan and Mycenaean quirks, customs, clothing, weaponry, roadwork, abortifacients, bull-leaping, the vast network of oracles of which Delphi was only the most famous, and so forth, and nearly another two years to weave all of it into a novel. I promised myself that my next effort would require as close to zero research as possible (true except for bunny behaviors, which are drawn from Marshal Merton's *A Complete Introduction to Rabbits* and especially from R. M. Lockley's delightful *The Private Life of the Rabbit*).

Second was the emergence of the basic imaginative material.

Precisely how that happened is lost to memory, but here's the gist: Suppose the all-giving Santa Claus had once been the all-grasping Pan? Suppose further that the creatures of our common childhood fancy—that magical triumvirate we accepted without question, who slipped into our homes to leave us money and candy and gifts—shared a forgotten, forbidden, pagan past? And that a crossing of paths which never ought to have happened did, by dint of heavenly bumble, happen?

Greek mythology had been an enduring love of mine since, at age nine, I played Zeus in a dramatization of *The Iliad*, twice performed in the school auditorium at Newbridge Road School—with a different Hera each time, I note with delight and curiosity. Here was a way to bring into renewed existence the chaos, the daring, the sheer exuberance of that treasure trove of myth, to celebrate the vastness and majesty of our Dionysian impulses while having great heaps of fun.

We never really lose our younger selves. Rather, we accrete new selves about them. The spellbound child at our core remains, I believe, as emotionally attached to these three beloved nocturnal visitors as it always was. (For a study of precisely this topic from the perspective of a child psychologist, see Cindy Dell Clark's *Flights of Fancy, Leaps of Faith*, University of Chicago Press, 1995).

Moreover, all three, unlike say Batman or Superman, are in the public domain. This, I'm sorry to say, is not true of Rudolph the Red-Nosed Reindeer, nor was I able to persuade the holders of Rudolph's copyright to license him to my use, which is why Santa Claus has a different lead reindeer in this novel.

What cinched it for me, though, was realizing where the Tooth Fairy's coins came from. Goethe's goat.

*Santa Steps Out* has had a tangled time finding its way into print.

In 1989, David Hartwell at William Morrow & Company held the manuscript for many months, eventually sending me a brief rejection. Meanwhile, I had squeaked my way into the Clarion West Writers Workshop for 1990. My primary reason for wanting to attend was David's presence on the roster of instructors. When upon his arrival one Sunday in July I introduced myself, he carried on about *Santa* in a way that astonished and delighted me, going so far as to buy me dinner at a Mongolian restaurant a short walk from our dorm and generally acting as if the work of a pretty-much-unpublished writer mattered.

At the end of that week, during which David had given me, in private conference, a detailed criticism of *Santa Steps Out* (six months after his last glimpse of it, the man a natural-born editor), he took me aside. "Now that I've seen the range of your short fiction," he said, "I want you to revise *Santa* along the lines we talked about and submit it again."

I did so. After another period of deliberation, yet another rejection came in. David, it seems, was ready to buy the book this time, but no one at Morrow would support him.

I had since signed with a second agent on the basis of her love for *Santa*. Alas, that love could not be translated into a sale. She did however sell *Deadweight*, my first published novel, to Jeanne Cavelos for the Dell Abyss line of horror novels. Jeanne had seen and rejected *Santa* a year earlier. She too wanted eventually to publish it, "after your readership has grown," she said. Jeanne, bless her twisted little heart, left publishing to pursue teaching and her own writing career. In any case, it's unlikely that Dell would have gone along with her, any more than Morrow had with David Hartwell, unless my career had skyrocketed into the realms of bestsellerdom.

For years, my favorite brainchild lay dormant. Then at the 1996 Pikes Peak Writers Conference, I had the good fortune to meet Pay LoBrutto. Years before, when I had been sending my *Santa* synopsis to agents and editors, Pat had been working for Meredith Bernstein. He urged her, in vain, to request the manuscript. Said Pat at Pikes Peak over a microbrew: "You mean nobody's bought it yet? Send me a copy!"

I did. Pat loved it, vowing to do what he could to usher it into print, saying indeed that he wanted to be able to tell his grandchildren that he was the one who had edited my odd little Santa novel.

Pat brought it to TOR Books, where, as it happened (did I think the gods were smiling on me, you bet I did), David Hartwell was senior editor. For the longest time, it seemed as if a TOR *Santa* would fly. The manuscript had the advantage of Pat LoBrutto's editing expertise, David stood foursquare behind the purchase, and the head of the company had bought in as well. *Santa Steps Out* came as close as a book can come to a yes without quite getting there. Then the marketing weenies, from what I gather, killed it. In his rejection letter, David assured my agent that if he ever returned to small press publishing, he would publish the book himself. There's a bit more, and in all fairness writers are rarely privy to what really goes on inside a publishing house, but that will suffice.

So what's the problem here? Why do so many benighted souls run screaming from *Santa Steps Out*? And why is it that others, saints and angels every one of them, embrace my jolly old elf with such enthusiasm?

Turning down my request for a blurb, Peter Straub,

in all good humor and based solely on the synopsis, wrote me as follows:

> My work load is so impossible at the moment that I have to pass on reading the extraordinary tale outlined in the pages you sent me. If good old Dark Highway is looking for the hideous, the blasphemous, and the prurient, Jason Bovberg ought to show up at your house every day to shine your shoes, make breakfast, and wash your dishes. Clearly, we all missed a great many educational experiences by sleeping through the Tooth Fairy's visits to our bedrooms, and we underestimated Santa tremendously. Me, I always had my doubts about the Easter Bunny, and it's nice to see them confirmed.
>
> Well—wow! Of course, anything so deliberately provocative depends completely on the writing—on the second-by-second delivery of its effects. That you came so close to getting what would be ordinarily unpublishable accepted by trade houses in New York must mean that you have found a way to give weight to your transgressions.
>
> Even though I have no time to provide a blurb, I do want to see the finished book—and I'm not begging for a free copy here, I mean only that I'll look for a way to order the book—but even more, I want to see the reviews. After all, you're not just

throwing down the gauntlet, you're using it to slap them in the face.

I quote Peter at length because (1) I like him, (2) it's prose from a master's pen after all, (3) I promised him an inscribed copy in exchange for permission to quote him and I like to get value for money, and (4) his words hint, tongue in cheek to be sure, at outrage and offense, at transgression and blasphemy.

But again I ask, where is the outrage in this novel? My three protagonists aren't, after all, religious icons. One might, to stretch a point, claim that status for Saint Nicholas, but surely not since the transformations wrought upon him by Thomas Nast, Clement Moore, and the ad men at The Coca-Cola Company.

God? He's treated with the utmost respect, he swears only in incomprehensible foreign tongues, he plays a cameo role (Marlon Brando, if you please, to Jack Nicholson's Santa Claus). In any event, he turns out to be Zeus, so his appearance should hardly count as a slap in the face of true believers.

In fact, the most twisted offshoots of Christianity would, I believe, be thoroughly in my camp. Just as some fundie lunatics want to ban Halloween, others lobby to be rid of Santa Claus. During my near-zero research, I came across a pamphlet by Sheldon Emry entitled "Is Christmas Christian?" (Lord's Covenant Church, 1976).

Here are three brief passages:

> [S]ecret Baal worshipers have foisted upon us their "Santa," their counterfeit "God," who appears to do "good," even as God, and they have presented him to us with white hair and beard, sparkling eyes, and a deep, low laugh. . . . Do you need still more proof that "Christmas" has its origins in Baal worship? Read on. We will "take apart" more of this strange "festival."
>
> [M]ost of Christendom, even professing Christians, have been deceived by the forces of darkness into acting out the rituals of Baal worship which are an abomination to our God.
>
> [Most men in Church pulpits] ignore or ridicule such information as you have read in these last pages. Could the reason be that many are not followers of Jesus Christ, but instead are secret priests of the false messiah of Babylon and they only profess to be Christians so they can get in Church pulpits and lead God's sheep into the "ways of Baal worship?"

As a longstanding Baal worshiper, I am astounded at how uncannily, though his head be full of muddle, Pastor Emry has set his wagging finger so squarely on the truth. Brothers and sisters, we must complexify our efforts at obfuscation. The Freemasons, the Illuminati, and those sly purveyors of the lone-gunman theory must surely heap scorn upon us for our ineptitude.

But I digress. . . .

In pondering the question of *Santa's* reception by the affronted, I have come to the tentative conclusion that it won't be the loonies who regard *Santa Steps Out* as blasphemous (body-haters that they are, they'll slam as usual my explicit sexual descriptions, but the religious content shouldn't faze them)—no, it will outrage, if it outrages anyone at all, the mainstream believer with an imperfect understanding of storytelling.

How dare I cast dirt upon the image of their beloved Santa Claus, the gentle Tooth Fairy, the generous Easter Bunny? That's what I hear them asking. For in many ways, these three secular creatures touch the hearts of children far earlier, far deeper, and far more effectively than God or Jesus or Mary ever could. It is they who carry the weight that more traditional religious icons may once have carried for the average American youngster.

A dear friend of mine, a psychotherapist who has not yet read the book, suggests another reason. Santa Claus, she notes, is a grandfather figure, a friend to children. Eroticize him and he becomes disquieting, a figure of potential incest and child abuse. I think at once of Jean Hersholt from the Shirley Temple *Heidi* film, no more perfect a grandfather than he. Were he to be sexualized, would he appear as a threat to Heidi? I don't think so, as long as he manifests no sexual interest in children (which is decidedly the case with my characters). Yet I find this theory intriguing and I'll be curious to see if it figures at all in reader response to the book.

Why then do I judge this work to be not offensive in the least?

Because it's a vivid and heartfelt dream. Only nuts of the medievally monkish sort whip, hairshirt, castrate, or otherwise do injury to themselves over the contents of a dream. In dreams, anything goes; they follow their own logic, wending where Psyche's whim takes them.

Because it tells the truth, it does so joyously, and it is no more outrageous in its way than *Salome* or *Titus Andronicus* or *The Bacchae*, three classic literary works which dabble expertly in excess.

Because the multiform emotion known as passion is a godsend. By no means are all of its forms pretty. Some have the capacity to kill or cripple relationships. But the erotic form of passion is as divine as all the rest, the stuff souls are made of.

Because sacred cows often deserve a vigorous milking, a swift kick to their fly-encircled rumps, a one-way trip down the chutes of the slaughterhouse, a fall beneath the butcher's knife. Besides, it's always useful to discover that gods and goddesses have feet of clay, that they too suffer temptation and a measure of imperfection; it eases the burden of being human.

Offense, I have found, is far more often taken than given in this world. Each venture into a new narrative opens up new avenues into yourself. If you are reading these words after having taken your way through *Santa Steps Out*, I trust that the journey both enriched and entertained you. If beforehand (one of my vices, I must confess), may your upcoming trip be a safe and pleasant one, a turn-on and a treat.

And if my good-hearted reader finds aught in these pages tart to the taste, or bitter:

Think but this, and all is marked—
That you have but slumber'd here
While these visions did appear.
And this weak and idle theme,
No more yielding but a dream,
Gentles, do not reprehend.
If you pardon, we will mend.

*—Fort Collins, October 1997*

# *About the Author*
# *Robert Devereaux*

Robert Devereaux is the author of two earlier novels, *Deadweight* and *Walking Wounded.* His short fiction, published in many places, has also appeared on the World Fantasy Award's final ballot. Robert lives in northern Colorado with his beloved Victoria, no TV, and too many books and CDs. In his spare time, he likes to act and sing, take long hikes in the Rockies, soak in hot tubs, and help Vicki prepare a murg masalam so flavorful that the cooks delight in leaving and re-entering the house just to be greeted anew by its seductive aroma.